PRAISE FOR DONNA GRANT'S
BEST-SELLING ROMANCE NOVELS

"Grant's ability to quickly convey complicated
backstory makes this jam-packed love story accessible
even to new or periodic readers."
–Publishers' Weekly

"Donna Grant has given the paranormal genre
a burst of fresh air..."
–San Francisco Book Review

"The premise is dramatic and heartbreaking;
the characters are colorful and engaging;
the romance is spirited and seductive."
–The Reading Cafe

"The central romance, fueled by a hostage drama, plays
out in glorious detail against a backdrop of multiple ongoing
issues in the "Dark Kings" books. This seemingly penultimate
installment creates a nice segue to a climactic end."
–Library Journal

"...intense romance amid the growing war between
the Dragons and the Dark Fae is scorching hot."
–Booklist

SKYE DRUIDS SERIES

Iron Ember ~ Shoulder the Skye ~ Heart of Glass
Endless Skye ~ Still of the Night ~ Blood Skye

DARK KINGS SERIES

Dark Heat ~ Darkest Flame ~ Fire Rising
Burning Desire ~ Hot Blooded ~ Night's Blaze
Soul Scorched ~ Dragon King ~ Passion Ignites
Smoldering Hunger ~ Smoke and Fire
Dragon Fever ~ Firestorm ~ Blaze ~ Dragon Burn
Constantine: A History, Parts 1-3 ~ Heat ~ Torched
Dragon Night ~ Dragonfire ~ Dragon Claimed
Ignite ~ Fever ~ Dragon Lost ~ Flame ~ Inferno
A Dragon's Tale (Whisky and Wishes: *A Holiday Novella*,
Heart of Gold: *A Valentine's Novella*, & Of Fire and Flame)
My Fiery Valentine ~ The Dragon King Coloring Book
Dragon King Special Edition Character Coloring Book: Rhi

DARK WARRIORS SERIES

Midnight's Master ~ Midnight's Lover
Midnight's Seduction ~ Midnight's Warrior
Midnight's Kiss ~ Midnight's Captive
Midnight's Temptation ~ Midnight's Promise
Midnight's Surrender ~ A Warrior for Christmas

CHIASSON SERIES

Wild Fever ~ Wild Dream ~ Wild Need
Wild Flame ~ Wild Rapture

LARUE SERIES

Moon Kissed ~ Moon Thrall

Moon Struck ~ Moon Bound

WICKED TREASURES

Seized by Passion ~ Enticed by Ecstasy

Captured by Desire

Books 1-3: Wicked Treasures Box Set

✦ . ✛ . ✦ . ✛ . ✦

✦ HISTORICAL PARANORMAL ✦

THE KINDRED SERIES

Everkin ~ Eversong ~ Everwylde

Everbound ~ Evernight ~ Everspell

KINDRED: THE FATED SERIES

Rage ~ Ruin ~ Reign

DARK SWORD SERIES

Dangerous Highlander ~ Forbidden Highlander

Wicked Highlander ~ Untamed Highlander

Shadow Highlander ~ Darkest Highlander

ROGUES OF SCOTLAND SERIES

The Craving ~ The Hunger

The Tempted ~ The Seduced

Books 1-4: Rogues of Scotland Box Set

THE SHIELDS SERIES

A Dark Guardian ~ A Kind of Magic

A Dark Seduction ~ A Forbidden Temptation

A Warrior's Heart

Mystic Trinity (a series connecting novel)

DRUIDS GLEN SERIES

Highland Mist ~ Highland Nights ~ Highland Dawn

Highland Fires ~ Highland Magic

Mystic Trinity (a series connecting novel)

SISTERS OF MAGIC TRILOGY

Shadow Magic ~ Echoes of Magic ~ Dangerous Magic

Books 1-3: Sisters of Magic Box Set

THE ROYAL CHRONICLES NOVELLA SERIES

Prince of Desire ~ Prince of Seduction

Prince of Love ~ Prince of Passion

Books 1-4: The Royal Chronicles Box Set

Mystic Trinity (a series connecting novel)

DARK BEGINNINGS: A FIRST IN SERIES BOXSET

Chiasson Series, Book 1: Wild Fever

LaRue Series, Book 1: Moon Kissed

The Royal Chronicles Series, Book 1: Prince of Desire

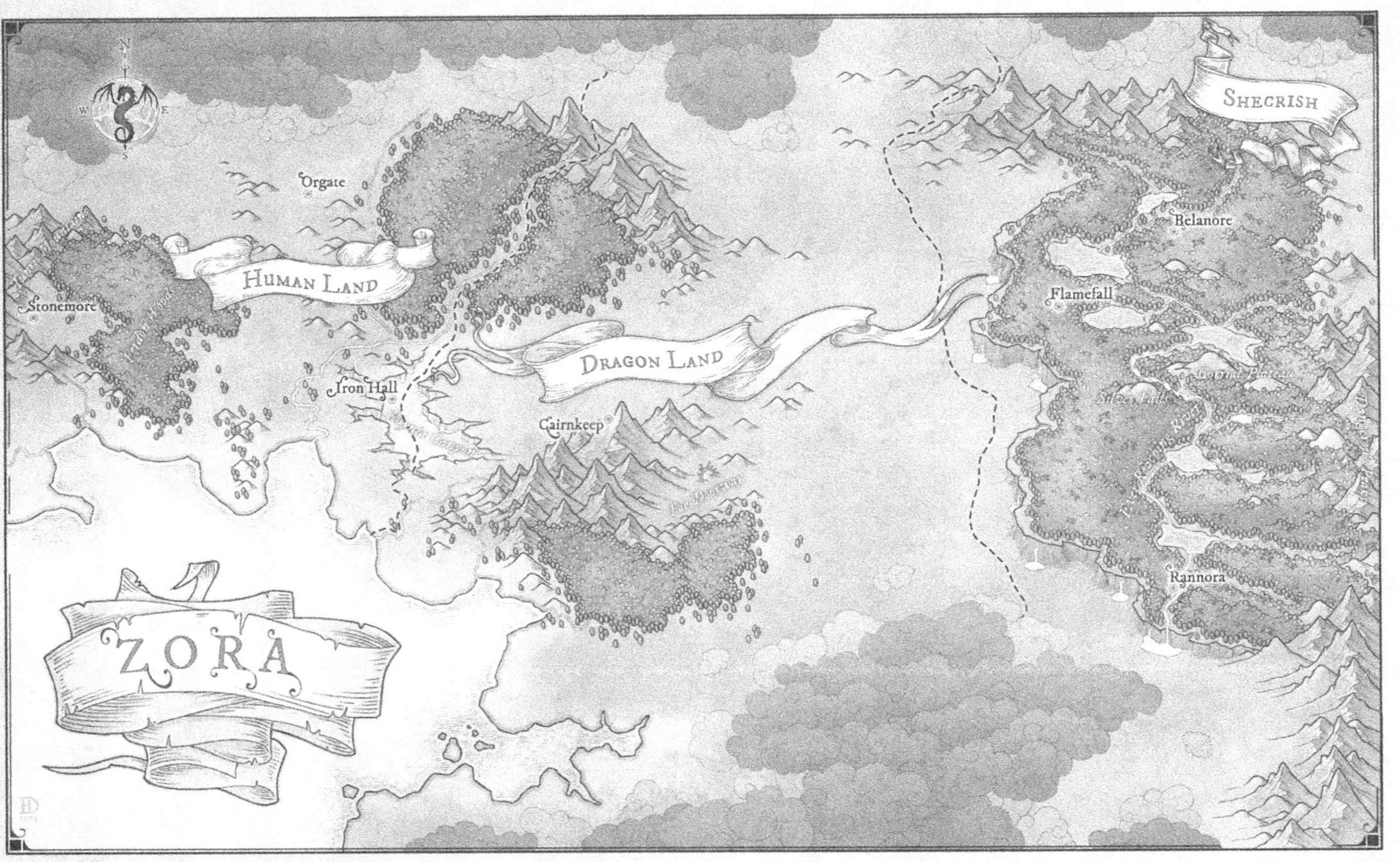
N
W
E
S
SHECRISH
Orgate
Belanore
Flamefall
Stonemore
HUMAN LAND
DRAGON LAND
Iron Hall
Cairnkeep
Rannora
ZORA

THE UNCROWNED KING

THE BASTARD DUOLOGY

NEW YORK TIMES & USA TODAY BESTSELLING AUTHOR

DONNA GRANT

CHAPTER 1

Derek was gone. Vanished.

As if he never was.

Kora stared at the table where he had lain seconds before, screaming her name. Emotion swelled in her chest, pressing against it before rising to her throat, where it lodged awkwardly. The rest of her body was numb. Painfully so. She stepped forward, her hand reaching for him as if he were still there. As if she would be able to touch him.

Her knees buckled. Strong arms grabbed her before she hit the ground and propped her against the wall for support. Dimly, the sound of bickering voices reached her, but she was lost in thoughts of Derek. The alarming wounds on his chest, his fear for her in his pale olive eyes that soon turned to horror for himself.

Unbidden, Miena's voice broke into Kora's mind.

"Does she know, Derek?" Miena asked.

Kora found her gaze locked on him. A secret hung there, waiting to be revealed. Did she want to know? Whatever it was, it would only hurt her.

"Does Kora know you love her?" Miena asked, a smug smile curving her lips.

Kora looked from Miena to Derek. She saw the truth in his eyes. She was right. It was meant to hurt.

He loved her. And now, he was gone. Miena had taken him. She would wipe Derek's memory of Kora and everything else. For all Kora knew, Derek might have already forgotten her.

She swallowed in an attempt to wet her dry mouth. Sweat dripped from her brow near her temple. She wiped it away with her shoulder and caught sight of the black marks on the wall caused by dragon fire. It had been a blaze meant to kill her. If Merrill hadn't grabbed her when he did, she would be dead.

The haze of dismay began to clear. The voices she had ignored sharpened. And the stench of evil permeated the area, reminding her why she came to Stonemore. She turned to find Merrill and Villette quarreling. Villette had been Kora's intended target, the one responsible for the unyielding fist of evil that controlled Stonemore and the surrounding areas. The Star Person who traveled the universe, meddling and corrupting as she went.

The one only hellhounds could kill.

Flames erupted over Kora with a thought. They covered her body and flickered at the ends of her hair while consuming her clothes. She stalked forward, her gaze locked on the right side of Villette's face and neck, scarred from a previous encounter—likely with a hellhound. Miena might have gotten away, but Kora could still end Villette once and for all.

Villette's blue eyes grew round with fear at the sight of Kora. She raised a hand. "Let's talk about this," she begged frantically.

"I'm done talking." Kora had released Miena. She had believed

Miena when she said she would kill Villette. How could Kora have been so naïve? So trusting? She knew what Miena was.

Villette backed up quickly, her long, blond hair whipping about as she glanced behind her. "You need me!"

Merrill stepped between them, his tall form blocking her. Dark blue eyes met Kora's. A lock of dirty blond hair fell across his forehead. He was the reason she was alive. Did dragon fire hurt dragons? She didn't see any marks on him. Maybe he healed quickly.

"I'd like nothing better than to see the end of Villette." The Dragon King sighed, his lips twisting ruefully. "But she's right. We need her."

"Nay." Kora had known when she came to Stonemore that she would have to face the powerful Villette on her own. Her family had been killed before they could slay the Star Person, and then Kora had run in an attempt to forget all she had lost. And in that time, thousands of innocents had died. No more. "She dies today."

Merrill didn't stop her when she started to walk around him. Instead, he said, "If you want Derek back, we need her alive."

Villette stood stiffly, her gaze moving from Merrill to Kora, injuries from a recent encounter with others still healing, her flesh pink and raised. "I know Miena better than anyone. I can find her," Villette pleaded.

"You had your chance to attack when she stood here with us and did nothing," Kora stated. The flames around her leaped higher with her anger, eager to devour the evil.

Villette's blue eyes narrowed. "My sister is more powerful than me. You have no idea what it took to capture her the first time."

"Exactly. You're useless."

Merrill turned and focused on Villette as he crossed his arms over his muscular chest, but his words were directed at Kora. "Perhaps she is when it comes to battle. But she has other uses."

"I don't like your tone," Villette replied acerbically.

Merrill ignored her and turned his head to Kora. "Trust me."

A week ago, Kora would've laughed at the very thought of putting her faith in a dragon. They were responsible for annihilating the hellhounds on Zora. Granted, it had been done on orders from Villette, but that didn't make the loss of Kora's family and friends any easier. And being the last of her kind had been unbearable.

Dragons were the enemy.

At least, they used to be.

When Kora met Derek, she'd had no idea what he was. It had never dawned on her that dragons could change forms to look human. If she had known, she never would've shared her body or her deepest confidences with him. She certainly wouldn't have fallen for him. But by the time she learned the secrets he so closely guarded, her heart had belonged to him.

Her throat constricted, and a deep, bottomless ache began in the center of her chest. She felt hollow, empty. Barren. As if a part of her had been stolen before she even knew it was there. The agony and excruciating anguish robbed her of breath. How would she go on? She couldn't stop thinking about Derek.

He could've taken her life the moment he discovered she was a hellhound. He could have informed Villette. But he had done neither. Instead, he had saved her from another dragon—and nearly got himself killed because of it.

Kora had barely accepted what Derek was when she learned that Merrill was also a dragon. Her world had spun out of control, and all she'd been able to do was try to stay upright and put one foot in front of the other. Suddenly, the lines dividing her from her enemies weren't as clear as they once were.

Merrill had asked for trust. She couldn't rely on her judgment since she had gotten it so wrong with Miena, but Derek had earned her trust time and again. And he believed Merrill. Which meant she should, as well.

"All right," she murmured to Merrill.

Villette snorted. "Do you honestly think any of your friends will come after you've ignored their calls for so long?"

Merrill slowly swiveled his head to Villette and gave her a hate-filled glare.

She threw up her hands. "Just wanted to put that out there."

The moment Villette turned as if to walk away, Kora threw out her hands. Balls of fire shot from them and landed on the floor, encircling Villette.

The Star Person drew up short, her head whipping around to pin Kora with a dark look.

"What is this for?"

Kora shrugged. "Insurance."

"I want to stop my sister," Villette said. "I could've left already, and you couldn't have done anything about it."

Merrill dropped his arms to his sides. "Perhaps. But you willna be going anywhere now."

"If we're going to work together, we need to trust each other," Villette argued.

Kora rolled her eyes. She had been betrayed by a Star Person for the last time. Villette couldn't do or say anything that would make her trust her. *Ever.*

She extinguished the flames on her body but then remembered her clothes were gone. She had gotten used to Derek using his magic to clothe her after she called her fire. Until she found new attire, she'd be walking around naked. Which meant she needed to find some immediately.

"I can give you clothes," Villette said. "With a wave of my hand. But you must lower the flames."

Merrill made a sound in the back of his throat. In the next instant, clothing covered Kora once more.

"So can I," Merrill stated.

Kora had expected Villette to be able to wield such power, but Merrill? She'd assumed Derek's magic came from the cuff Villette had given him. Had she been wrong? She knew next to nothing about dragons, other than that they'd killed her people. Maybe it was time she found out more.

If they were to be...friends.

Before she could come up with a question, Merrill said, "Rhi."

Kora frowned and looked from him to Villette. Neither gave anything away. "What is Rhi?"

"No' what. *Who*," Merrill replied. "She's a Fae."

"What's a Fae?"

Villette laughed and looked down at her nails.

"We're fucking magnificent," said a female voice behind Kora.

She turned at the odd accent to find a woman of incredible beauty sitting on the table, one long leg crossed over the other. Midnight locks fell past the newcomer's shoulders in soft waves. She wore all black from head to toe, and it didn't appear as if anyone would be able to stand on the high, slender heels of her boots. Silver eyes studied Kora before her gaze slid to Merrill.

"About bloody time," she said before flashing a bright smile.

If Kora had thought the woman was beautiful before, the smile lit up her face, transforming her into something ethereal. She couldn't stop staring.

"It's good to see you, Rhi," Merrill said, his lips softening.

Rhi lifted a slim shoulder. "It's always good to be seen." She looked at Villette before focusing on Kora. "Want to introduce me?"

"Rhi, this is Kora. Kora, Rhi." Merrill then motioned behind him with his thumb. "That's Villette."

The air crackled with tension as Rhi pushed off the table with her hands and landed nimbly on the impossibly high heels. Her gaze never left Villette. "And the fire?"

"That's all Kora. She's a hellhound," Merrill explained.

One of Rhi's brows rose as she looked at Kora with a grin. "Impressive."

"It seems hellhounds can kill Star People," Merrill added.

Rhi folded her arms across her chest as she and Villette stared at each other. "Then why is this one alive?"

"It's why I called for you."

There was an undercurrent of anger and resentment in the room that Kora didn't understand. She felt as if she were on the outside looking in, and it was an uncomfortable position to be in. However, she found it peculiar that Villette had decided to refrain from speaking. There was definitely something between them.

"Someone needs to get to Earth immediately and warn everyone at Dreagan that an attack is coming from another King. Tell them no' to kill him. Just incapacitate him," Merrill explained.

"Attack?" Rhi asked.

"Rhi," Merrill urged.

She was there one moment, and the next, she wasn't.

Kora stared at the empty space. With nothing but silence,

Kora's thoughts returned to Derek. She hoped he wasn't in pain. She squeezed her eyes closed, trying not to think about what Miena might be doing to him. When Kora opened her eyes again, Rhi was there.

The Fae turned her back to Villette and let her unease show. She walked closer to Kora and motioned Merrill over. When she spoke, her voice was barely above a whisper. "Done. Now it's time to tell me what's going on."

Merrill exchanged a look with Kora. "A lot."

"Then you'd better start talking."

Kora glanced at the table, remembering how Derek had stared at her, his gaze pleading. "Derek is a dragon. They made him. And took him."

Silence met her statement. Rhi blew out a breath. "Shite." She briefly pressed her lips together. "We need to get to the others."

"We can no' leave Villette unattended," Merrill said. "She's our link to Miena."

Rhi shot him a flat look. "She's not coming with us. And you can't really think she'll help."

"We need her to find Derek."

Kora wished Merrill was wrong, but she knew he wasn't. "As much as it pains me to say it, we need her."

"All right," Rhi said. "Who's Miena?"

Merrill's lips twisted. "Villette's sister."

"I was afraid you were going to say something like that," Rhi muttered.

Kora longed for water to coat her throat and wet her mouth. "You two go. I'll watch Villette."

Merrill shook his head. "There are parts of the story only you can tell. And the others need to hear it."

"Others?" she asked, though she was afraid she already knew what he'd meant.

"Dragon Kings."

It was one thing to accept that not all dragons were evil, but to cross the border to their land and be surrounded by them? Kora wasn't sure she could do it. But then she thought about Derek and all he had done for her. She wanted him back. She wanted to rewind time and leave Miena locked away. She wanted to be in his arms once more.

She couldn't go into this fight alone. She needed Merrill and the dragons. She even needed Villette. Derek had risked his life for her. She owed him the same.

"I'll return after I take you two," Rhi said. "And I'll be sure to veil myself so no one can see me. If she tries anything, I'll stop her."

Kora shook her head, confused. "What is *veiling* yourself?"

"Veiling means that I'm invisible to others," Rhi explained. "I was veiled before I showed myself to you. It is something the Fae can do. Fae are magic, like you and the dragons. And we have some added benefits, like being able to teleport. If someone says my name, calling for me as Merrill did, I know where they are."

"Derek can teleport, but he uses a cuff."

"Ah. I see. It is rare to have such a piece. Let me take you to my mate, Con."

"So, he is real?" Kora wondered how different things would be now if Derek had gone to see Con.

Rhi nodded. "Aye, he is. And if any dragon is in trouble, nothing will stop him—or any of the Kings—from finding them."

"She's right. We willna," Merrill confirmed.

Rhi held out her hand. "Come. I'll take you both to Con."

CHAPTER 2

Kora barely had time to register that she was going to the land of the dragons before light replaced the shadowy cavern. So many voices... She stiffened, expecting to see dragons towering over her.

But she didn't see different-colored scales. She saw people. Even children running, their laughter floating between numerous conversations.

Everyone fell silent as they noticed their arrival.

Kora realized her arm was still extended from having grabbed Rhi's hand, but the Fae was no longer there. She lowered her arm to her side and scanned the faces of the men, women, and children. They looked normal. Like anyone else. But she knew they weren't. How many were dragons? All?

"Breathe," Merrill whispered from beside her. "You're safe here."

Safe? With dragons? That simply didn't compute. Not after decades of running and hiding, hearing the screams of her family in her nightmares. She inhaled, waiting to smell the stench of evil. But there was none. Not even Villette's lingering stench.

A man with blond hair pushed through the crowd, his face breaking into a wide smile as he approached Merrill. His long strides ate up the distance. Then he enveloped Merrill in a tight embrace. Kora sidled away to give them room, but she noticed that Merrill was slow to return the hug. Almost as if he wasn't sure he should.

"You have been sorely missed, brother." The man leaned back, his deep brown eyes raking over Merrill. His grin faded, replaced by concern. "We've been worried."

Merrill gave him a fleeting smile. "I know."

Another man stepped forward, controlled and commanding. His blond hair was trimmed short on the sides with longer waves on top. His eyes were as dark as a midnight sky. The other male stepped away in obvious deference.

Merrill lifted his chin as the black-eyed man approached. Kora braced as the tension ratcheted up a notch. She put more space between them. Though she wasn't without magic, facing off against a dragon meant certain death for hellhounds.

"It hasna been the same without you."

They all had the same strange accent as Merrill did. Proof, she supposed, that she was standing among dragons. Had her family known they could change shape? She didn't think they did. At least she had never heard them speak about such a thing.

Merrill looked away briefly. "I had to stay away."

"I understand." Then the man took a deep breath and turned to her. "Forgive us. We've been searching for Merrill for weeks. We feared Villette had harmed him, and we're overjoyed to see him once more. I'm Con."

Con. *The* Con. The one Merrill had urged Derek to seek out. The one who could have changed the entire trajectory if only Derek had spoken to him.

"This is Kora," Merrill said. "She's a hellhound."

Surprise widened Con's eyes for a fraction of a second. He bowed his head to her. "It's nice to meet you."

"Our kind destroyed her family," Merrill stated.

Kora hadn't thought the tension could get any worse, but with those five words, it did. She tried not to fidget under the intense stares of those around her. And there were many more than she had first thought. Con's surprise shifted to alarm, and, dare she say it? Distress.

"Do we know which dragons crossed the border and committed such a crime?" Con asked.

Kora dragged in huge mouthfuls of air, but she couldn't seem to loosen her lungs enough to take any in. Everything she had thought she knew and understood about her enemy had been violently ripped away and turned upside down. Her nemeses were no longer villains. Facts were being realigned. Derek was gone, and a dragon had said her family's murder was a crime.

Her eyes burned with tears. She spun around, looking for a way out. She was shocked to discover the room was even larger than the cavern. There were stairs and doors everywhere. Which one would lead her out? She needed time to think, to adjust. To breathe.

Time Derek didn't have.

"Follow me," a woman said as she moved into Kora's line of sight. "I can take you outside."

Kora knew she shouldn't trust anyone, but she trailed after the petite brunette anyway. No one stopped her. Kora didn't look at anything as she hurried up the steep steps to a door. She burst past the woman to get outside and gulped in the fresh air.

She bent over, bracing her hands on her knees to gain control of her emotions that were steadily spinning out of control. Only when she was sure she wouldn't break down did she straighten. Kora found herself standing at the narrow point of a fertile canyon with steep walls of lush green rising up on either side and extending into the distance as it widened.

"Raynia Canyon. It is something to behold, isn't it?"

Kora looked over her shoulder to find the brunette leaning against an enormous, exposed root protruding from a crack in the canyon wall. Behind the spiderweb of roots, she saw arched double doors.

"I'm Sian." The woman gave her a warm smile.

"Kora."

Sian pushed away from the root. "I don't know what you've been through, but I've been around the Dragon Kings long enough to tell you that you are safe with them. Though, sometimes, I don't think they understand how their numbers can intimidate."

Kora swallowed and nodded, wrapping her arms around her middle. "You trust them, then?"

"Completely. For a long time, just three of us called Iron Hall home. Me, Jenefer, and Tamlyn. Tamlyn is a Banshee. The murders of the magical children at Stonemore drew her here. Jenefer is an Amazon, and I'm an Alchemist. We did what we could to help Tamlyn, but she ran into trouble one day. Cullen, a Dragon King, saved her and the child that night, and he has been with us ever since. He's not just her mate. He's also my friend. All the Kings are."

Kora knew that none of the dragons here had slain her family, but after fearing dragons for so long, it wasn't easy to put that aside and trust them.

What about Derek?

He was different. She hadn't known that he was one of those responsible for the hellhounds' deaths until after she had gotten to know him. Until after she had fallen for him. He might have taken lives, but he had done it after being manipulated and lied to. In her mind, Villette was to blame.

Thinking of her brought to mind Miena and everything yet to come. Kora looked once more at the canyon's green slopes and then turned to the door. "I'm ready to return."

Sian led her back inside. This time, Kora took in everything. The vestibule was large enough for four men to stand side by side without touching. The steps were smooth and perfectly rectangular, with a glow to them. She couldn't decide if it came from within or was part of the stone itself.

As she descended the stairs, Kora counted seven different stairways and over a dozen doors on either side of the incredibly large room. Light drew her attention to its source several hundred feet above. Her steps slowed as she saw the complex, intersecting root system, allowing both light and water from the outside to filter in. Liquid dripped from the roots into a large pool beneath the tree in the center of the room.

She scanned the chamber again and found four giant heads carved from the rock. One faced north, the others were turned south, east, and west. East and west had their eyes closed and slight grins while north and south had open eyes.

Kora was entranced by the time she reached the bottom. "What is this place?"

"Iron Hall," Con said. "The underground city was abandoned

long ago. Half of it extends across the border onto our land. It has become a place of refuge for those in need, as well as our friends."

As he spoke, she realized that the room had cleared out, leaving only her, Merrill, and Con. Even Sian had disappeared.

"We gather when there's trouble," Merrill explained. "I should have warned you."

She walked to the stone edge that retained the water and looked into the dark pool. "I never thought I would be standing with dragons, much less asking them for help." She turned to face the two men. "I also never expected to fall in love with one."

"I didna get much from Rhi before she left, other than that there's trouble." Con looked between them. "Whatever happened at Stonemore, the two of you have a home here."

Merrill shook his head. "It isna me Kora speaks of. It's Derek."

"Derek?"

Only the slightest tightening of Con's features alerted Kora that he was shocked. She had a feeling he kept tight control of his emotions. Dragon Kings. That's what everyone kept calling them. What made them different? What made them Kings?

"Aye. And he's a King," Merrill said.

Con's shoulders lifted with his inhale. "I think you two had better start from the beginning."

"What is a Dragon King?" Kora asked.

Merrill walked to the pool and sat on the edge. "For us, it is when the magic of our world chooses us to rule our clans. Only Kings can shift from dragon to human and back at will."

"Magic didn't choose Derek, but he can shift. We saw him," she stated, looking directly at Merrill and daring him to lie.

Merrill's dark blue eyes held hers. Then he looked at Con.

"Villette and her sister, Miena, created Derek and Bryok. They actually crafted six eggs in total."

"*Created*?" Con asked, his voice croaking with indignation. He spun around, took two steps, then turned back and ran a hand down his face, seemingly in control once more. "You said six eggs. There are others?"

"Derek guarded them," Kora said. "One of Villette's that hatched was wrong. They killed him. And she destroyed Miena's third egg out of spite. Leaving only the other two."

Rage rolled off Con. By the concern on Merrill's face, it wasn't something they saw often.

"Who the bloody hell do they think they are?" Con demanded in a voice as soft as a whisper.

Merrill grunted. "It gets worse. We doona know how, but Villette imprisoned Miena. It was Miena who had been trying to speak to me since I arrived at the palace. I ignored her. Villette's magic, which prevented me from communicating with any of you, also dimmed Miena's voice. Once Villette had Miena locked away, she used Derek and Bryok to hunt the only other beings able to kill the Star People."

"Hellhounds," Kora said. "Derek was sent to my village. My parents died, but my uncle, cousin, and brother got me away. We hid after that, but they continued their plan to bring Villette down."

Con folded his arms across his chest. "Because you can smell evil."

She blinked. "How do you know that?"

"You are no' the first hellhound we've encountered. Xaneth is Rhi's cousin and mated to a Reaper."

Kora blinked, letting his words settle. Exhilaration and relief soared through her. She wasn't the last. There were others. But with that realization came another. She slid her gaze to Merrill.

He shrugged. "You never asked."

She had so many questions about this Xaneth, but they would have to wait. "Bryok killed my uncle, cousin, and brother not far from Stonemore. After that, I ran and hid." Kora paused. "I shoved aside my magic and abilities after that. I fought against the need to hunt evil until I no longer smelled it. Until I forgot how to *be* a hellhound. And all those decades, Villette was taking innocent lives. She sent her dragons to kill and terrorize humans."

A muscle ticked in Con's jaw. "Why?"

"Derek believed the dragons were enslaved," Merrill answered.

Kora nodded. "Villette convinced him that some Star People and humans with magic were holding the dragons."

"How does stirring up hate for dragons and magic help her cause?" Con asked.

Merrill's lips twisted. "It didn't. It was just a way for her to gain power. She told Derek various lies, and he believed her, wanting to see his kin freed."

"Blindly?" Con asked.

Anger burned through Kora. "Nay, not blindly. She repeatedly wiped his mind when he questioned her and discovered that she lied. And no one else told him differently."

"Bloody hell." Con shook his head, then looked at Kora. "Where do you come in?"

"When I decided it was time to face the past, I went after Villette, knowing one of us would die. But I was tired of running and hiding. My and Derek's paths crossed. There was an…um… attraction. He offered to take me to Stonemore and get me inside. I had planned for us to part ways once I got through the gate, but we ended up remaining together."

Merrill propped a foot on the pool's edge. "Meanwhile, Villette returned to the palace, badly burned."

"We hoped it had killed her," Con interjected.

"It nearly did. She got away before you could, but the wounds severely weakened her. It allowed Miena's voice to grow louder and reach Derek and me. She hinted at Derek's memories being taken and promised answers if he freed her."

Kora shifted uncomfortably. "I might have trusted Derek to get me to the city, but I didn't tell him I was a hellhound. He found that out after I died battling the priests. He was shocked but didn't tell Villette." Kora saw Merrill and Con exchange a look but couldn't read either of them. "I didn't want Derek to get hurt, so I went after Villette alone. It didn't go well. I was transported somewhere else, and she sent a dragon after me."

"Bryok?" Con asked.

Merrill shook his head. "An Amethyst. One who looked verra much like Alasdair."

"His brother. Gordon," Con said.

Kora stomach tightened. "That's what Villette called him. Gordon."

"How the fuck did she get Alasdair's dead brother?" Merrill demanded, his visage darkening with fury.

Con lifted one shoulder in a shrug. "Your guess is as good as ours. Alasdair has killed him twice, and he always comes back to life."

"Derek killed him once, and then I did. Then we saw him alive. Fuck," Merrill muttered.

Con nodded at Kora, so she continued. "Derek found me. He's

the reason I was able to get away. Then Bryok came. Derek gave me his cuff and sent me back to look for a woman named Katla. He said she was in Stonemore, looking for Villette. That's when I saw him change for the first time."

"Interesting," Con said. "Did you find Katla?"

"I did. After I explained who I was and asked for her help, she agreed. The priests took her before we could get to Villette, though. They plan to kill her."

Con's nostrils flared. "They'll have a harder time than they realize."

"Who is she?" Merrill asked.

"It's a long story. One to tell after we get this current situation taken care of."

Kora was curious about the story, too, but it would have to wait. She continued. "I then went to the only other person I knew who wanted Villette dead."

"Merrill," Con replied.

Kora nodded. "Aye."

"I knew Derek was in trouble," Merrill said. "I had Kora take me to him using the cuff. It was a good thing. By then, he was fighting both Bryok and Gordon. I evened the score, but he was gravely wounded in the battle. Before I could get us out of there, Villette appeared."

"That's when you reached out to me?" Con asked.

Merrill bowed his head in agreement.

Kora hadn't known any of that. She had only caught a glimpse of Derek in battle. It had been vicious. "After I left Merrill," she said, "I went to Miena. Derek had spoken to her. He didn't know whether he believed her, and I..." She paused and swallowed. "I should've known better than to release her. I knew she was evil. I smelled it. But I needed help."

"You believed her. Doona beat yourself up over it. It was a tough situation," Merrill said.

"One made even more so when Miena didn't kill Villette as promised. Instead, she took Derek and Gordon."

Merrill shot her a crooked smile. "But no' me. You saved me from that nightmare."

"How?" Con asked.

"Derek took Bryok's cuff and gave it to me. Derek didna know Miena made them and thus bound the wearer to her. She prevented me from removing it, but Kora ripped it off before Miena forced me to follow her," Merrill explained.

"Then he saved me from dragon fire." Kora shrugged. "Miena left with Derek to wipe his memories and send him to Earth to kill the dragons there and then everyone else."

Con's mouth parted in shock. "What?" he bellowed.

Merrill raised his hand. "I already sent Rhi to warn Ulrik."

"We need to get to Earth," Con said as he turned to walk away. "Lotti!"

Kora looked at Merrill, her brows raised. "If that's where Derek is, then that's where I need to be."

"If he smells you, he'll kill you."

"If he...if he loves me, then he won't hurt me." At least, she hoped he wouldn't.

Merrill stared at her for a long moment. "And if he comes after you?"

"It's a chance I'll have to take."

# CHAPTER 3

It was that quiet place between waking and dreaming, where time stood still, and possibilities were endless. A place where the past, present, and future collided.

A place only for him.

He floated there, content and relaxed. The thought of waking made him pull back. He didn't know why he had such a compulsion to stay within sleep's comforting embrace. He could attempt to figure it out, but why? There was no need. There was no need for anything at the moment.

Time was forgotten.

Ignored.

There was no pain in this place. Somehow, he knew if he shook off the sleep, there would be heaps of agony.

But for what? Who? Himself? Others?

He couldn't remember. The more he tried, the more restless he became. So, he let it go.

As he drifted, he felt a presence. A woman. The edges of her silhouette gradually took shape. He made out dark hair, but her face wouldn't come into focus. It felt as if she—or someone else—were purposely preventing him from seeing her.

He might not be able to see her face, but he knew her eyes were on him. He felt her reaching out to him. His arm lifted, and he stretched his hand to touch her. She started to disintegrate, little by little. A whisper reached him just before she faded completely.

"Derek."

His eyes snapped open. Whether he wanted it or not, he was awake. He remained still, his tail curled around him as he scanned the area with his senses. He was in a cave, deep within a mountain. Alone. He felt the frigid temperatures seeping through the many layers of rock. He lifted his head and looked around the cavern. It was tight. One of his wings had knocked down a row of stalactites and sheared off stalagmites. Outside, a blizzard howled.

He tried to stand, but a thick stalactite pressed into his back. A growl rumbled through him as he crawled to the entrance just to get to his feet. He looked back and slowly scanned the cavern. Where was he? How had he gotten there? And why couldn't he remember anything?

Derek. Was that his name? Was it someone else's?

He walked out of the cavern and upward through the lava tube. It wasn't a comfortable fit. His wings scraped the sides, and he had to keep his head ducked. The moment he spotted light, he moved faster. He couldn't wait to get out of the mountain and find some answers.

He burst through the tunnel and spread his wings as he jumped. With three beats of his great wings, he was in the sky. Yet nothing looked familiar. A knot formed in his stomach. Something was very, very wrong. He knew he was a dragon. He knew the sky, the mountains, and the snow that pelted him. But he knew nothing about himself.

He dipped his wing and turned to fly over the cave he had exited. The air was so cold, ice formed along his scales. The entrance to the tunnel was near the middle of the mountain, easily discernible. A quick look showed no other access points. Maybe that was why he had chosen it.

The wind roared like a living beast, brutally lashing him and blowing around large amounts of snow that impacted visibility— even for him. The wind tried to smash him against a mountain several times, but he steadied himself, his wings flapping mightily.

The mountain range had steep, sloping sides and sharp ridges. The summits stretched straight up as if reaching for the sky. They stood like frozen giants. The trees and ground were drenched in snow, and it was white from horizon to horizon. And his black scales stood out like a beacon.

He didn't see anyone. Not a dragon, human, or animal. He frowned at the thought. Why would he care about mortals? Then it dawned on him that the silhouette of the dark-haired woman was, in fact, a human. Who was she? Who was Derek? He had so many questions his head pounded.

He remained in the air, fighting against the blizzard, for some time. It focused his mind and body on something other than the thoughts and questions continuing to run rampant. He was so engrossed in the battle with nature that he didn't see the woman at first. Her fur-lined, blood red cloak drew his gaze as it stood out against the backdrop of pristine snow. But she was no ordinary human. He felt her magic, the power that swirled about her as vast and mighty as the wind.

She watched him from beneath her hood. He circled back and flew over her. His enhanced eyesight caught her smile. There was no fear. At least not for him.

Intrigued, he landed, perching atop one of the pointed peaks with his wings spread, looming over her. She tilted her head back, causing the hood to fall. The wind caught the dark strands of her hair and whipped them about her head in a wild dance. Was she the woman from his dreams? Her hair was dark. It was hard to tell from the voice since the one in his dream had only whispered.

She had large, bright green eyes, high cheekbones, and plump lips. She was gorgeous, and she knew it. She was a woman who used her assets to get what she wanted, and he was sure she always got it.

And by the direction of her gaze, she had set her sights on him.

"It's about time you woke."

He startled. Her voice was in his head. *"You know me?"*

"Of course, I know you."

"Who am I?"

"You, my magnificent beauty, are what others fear."

He stared at her, unsure if that was something he should be proud of.

"You don't remember, do you?" she asked.

"Nay."

"Then we should talk. Come."

"Not back to the cave. It was too tight."

She laughed, the sound like a tickle in his mind. *"It won't be once you shift."*

"Shift? To what?"

"To look like a human."

Could he do that? She certainly sounded sure of it. But before he could respond, she was gone. He didn't have to guess where she was. He sighed and leaped into the air before heading to the cave. As he neared, he slowly lowered to land on the narrow outcropping of rocks. He folded his wings against him and stared into the dark opening. The irritation of scraping them wasn't something he would go through again. But how did he shift, as the woman had suggested?

As if his thoughts had produced her, she moved out of the shadows but remained inside the cave. "You're thinking about it too hard. It's a natural gift. Just imagine yourself as a human."

The instant he did as she suggested, he changed. Snow pelted skin instead of scales. He lifted his hands and looked down at human fingers instead of talons. His gaze moved lower over a flat stomach to bare legs. He scrunched his toes in the snow and felt the ice cut into his skin. Blood flecked the whiteness, but he healed instantly.

When he looked up, the woman was gone. He forgot about inspecting this human body and followed her into the tunnel. He had expected walking to be unsteady until he got used to it, but it came easily.

Something else he had forgotten, apparently.

Just what had happened to him?

He found the woman in the same place he had woken. He halted just inside the cavern. She waved her hand over a place on the floor, and bright orange flames erupted, shooting sparks upward. He watched them for a moment then returned his gaze to her. He wanted her to be the woman he'd seen in his dream, but she held herself differently. So, what did she want with him?

"Who are you?" he asked.

"You have a voice. Use it."

He swallowed, hating the uncertainty he felt at every turn. Also the fact that she ordered him around. "Who are you?" The voice that came out was deep and roughened as if it hadn't been used in a while. Or had he been screaming?

Something about that thought made his heart skip a beat.

"My name is Miena. I am your friend."

A friend would say that. But so would an enemy—especially to someone like him, who didn't remember anything.

Her lips curved into a smile. "Your suspicious nature is what has made you so powerful. But it has also made you a target. You have every right to be wary. I was the one who brought you here to recover."

"From what?"

"A battle that nearly ended your life. Your name is Derek."

He recalled the voice from his dream as it whispered in his ear, beckoning him. *Derek.*

Miena ran her fingers through the dark fur that edged her cloak. "You fought against the Dragon Kings."

Derek forgot about the voice and focused on Miena. "Who?"

"They're dragons who have crowned themselves leaders. Your people do not want the Kings. You fought for them but were outnumbered. You sustained a blow to the head that left you incapacitated. I got you out. You healed, of course, but it seems you have amnesia."

"Will I get my memories back?"

Her lips flattened, and worry creased her face. "You should have already attained them." She smiled softly. "Give it a few days. We'll know by then if this is permanent or not."

"Did I go after my enemies alone?"

"You believed you could take them on your own. You nearly did."

"Were you there?"

She stared at him for a long moment before removing her cloak to reveal a flowing, off-the-shoulder white gown. The left edge of the neckline was red and continued down the wispy bell sleeve. Red continued along her left side to flare out into the skirt, blending with the white. It reminded him of blood mixing with snow.

It was a gown meant to draw attention. Derek may have lost some of his memories, but he recognized the provocative woman who stood before him. He studied her—and his lack of physical interest.

"Were you there?" he repeated.

She drew in a breath, a flash of annoyance crossing her beautiful features. "I saw enough."

"Does that mean you helped?"

"I got you away to heal."

Which meant she hadn't joined the battle.

"A *thank you* would be nice," Miena stated.

He bowed his head. "Thank you."

"Since you're healed, it's time to finish what you began with the Dragon Kings."

Derek moved to lean against the wall. "I didn't vanquish them on my own before. Perhaps I should wait until I have others with me."

"You don't need an army," she said with a brash smile. "You *are* the army."

"Against how many?"

"I know what you can do."

He snorted. "And yet, my first attempt nearly ended with my death." If he could believe her.

"It would be wise not to doubt me," she stated in a voice laced with warning.

He had sensed her power earlier, but it slammed into him now, pressing him against the stone wall. Jagged pieces of rock cut into his skin. He clenched his teeth, even as blood oozed from the wounds and ran down his back. Just as quickly as it had all begun, it ended. He moved away from the wall, wondering about her interest in him.

Miena drew in a deep breath and then slowly released it, smiling. "I forget that you don't remember me. Let me remind you. I am the most powerful being in the universe. I am a Star Person. We move through the stars from planet to planet. We are power and might. And nothing gets in my way. When I say you're capable of taking on the Kings on your own, I mean it. You don't need anyone. Not even me. That's why I didn't step in to fight alongside you."

There was truth in her words. The problem was figuring out which of them were factual and which weren't. Because there were lies in there, too. Derek wasn't sure how he knew but he did. And he wisely kept it to himself.

She huffed. "You still don't believe me."

"I only have your word."

"It was always good enough before."

He stared into her green eyes, trying to discern who she was. "When I had my memories."

"Then go ask someone. They'll tell you how heinous the Dragon Kings are. Then I expect an apology for doubting me."

Derek turned on his heel to leave. The sooner he learned the facts, the better. Something deep inside him drove him to dig through the layers of words and deceptions to the truth. He wouldn't be able to rest until he did.

"One more thing," Miena called.

He paused and looked back at her.

"If you run across a hellhound, kill it."

Derek shook his head. "Hellhound?"

"The only beings alive who can kill a Star Person. They have a specific scent. You'll know when you find one. You've killed enough of them." She walked closer, animosity darkening her face and twisting her visage to something ugly. "Run it to the ground. Burn it until nothing is left. Do you understand?"

He bowed his head.

She motioned him away with her hand. "Go on. Go see what you can find."

CHAPTER 4

Iron Hall

As if there hadn't been enough surprises for one day, coming face-to-face with another Star Person had nearly done Kora in. Her response was instantaneous and instinctive. She jerked to her feet as flames engulfed her.

"Oh! That is amazing," a woman with a throaty voice said. "A real hellhound. I've never gotten to see one before. Look how the flames dance along her hair."

The woman's red hair was pulled away from her face to hang in a long ponytail down her back. She wore a sleeveless, golden brown tunic with a plunging neckline that showed off thick silver armbands around each arm. The tunic hugged her full breasts and showed an inch of her toned, flat stomach before ending above the waist of the deep brown trousers that hugged her long legs and tucked into tall, leather boots. She had the walk and demeanor of a warrior.

And she walked beside a Star Person.

Merrill came up beside Kora but didn't look at her. His gaze was on the woman who spoke. There was a hint of a smile as he said, "Jeyra."

"I should kick your arse for what you've put Varek through," Jeyra stated, then grinned. "But I won't. This time."

Kora watched the warrior wrap her arms around Merrill. He was quicker to respond this time as if he was getting used to embracing others again. Kora's gaze returned to the Star Person, who had frozen at the sight of Kora's flames. Con stood with her, talking rapidly.

This Star Person looked and acted differently than Villette and Miena. Her blond waves were parted on the side and brushed her shoulders. A simple, long-sleeved, beige tunic hung softly against her curves and was tucked into black breeches that showed off her figure without conforming to it. A wide leather belt wound around her waist and matched the knee-high boots.

But the turquoise eyes took Kora aback. There was no hostility or cynicism there. Just curiosity and wariness.

"This is Jeyra," Merrill told Kora as if she hadn't just declared war on the Star Person in the room. "She's Varek's mate and a fine warrior. Jeyra, Kora."

Jeyra's smile was filled with warmth as she looked at Kora. "I hope those flames aren't for any of us. We're all friends here."

Kora looked past her to the blonde. She drew in a breath, waiting for the reek of evil. But there was none.

"Including Lotti," Jeyra added. "She's Alasdair's mate. I've stood beside her to battle Villette."

Dragons who weren't enemies, and now Star People who might be trustworthy? Kora's flames flickered out. How would she find her footing in this world that kept turning on its side? She longed for Derek to take her hand and steady her.

"Sorry," Kora mumbled, covering herself with her hands as she sat on the rim of the pool once more.

The cool stone against her bare flesh made the situation even more embarrassing. Merrill didn't bat an eye as he clothed her with magic once more.

"There's no need to apologize," Con said. "I should've prepared you."

Lotti flashed Kora a shaky smile. "I'm nothing like Villette. I want her gone, and I'm working toward that."

Kora wasn't sure how to respond, but then she didn't have to because Con filled the awkward silence. He succinctly told Lotti and Jeyra everything she and Merrill had shared earlier. Kora was happy she didn't have to repeat everything again, which gave her time to think—about all the changes happening around her. And Derek.

The not knowing where he was or if he still remembered her was tearing her in two. She wanted to give in to those feelings, but she couldn't. Not now. She had to focus on finding him and stopping Miena. She channeled her rage, fears, and every ounce of resentment there.

"We need some of the Kings to go to the Fae doorway," Con said. "I'm no' leaving Ulrik and the others to safeguard Dreagan."

Kora felt as if she had stepped into another reality. She didn't know what a Fae doorway was, but she could guess it was somehow tied to Rhi. And it seemed logical that Dreagan was a place important to the Kings. Their home on their world, perhaps?

"What if splitting up the Kings here is exactly what Miena wants you to do?" Merrill asked.

Con turned his head to him. "I thought of that. You got away from her, which means she knows you'll have told us everything so we can prepare."

"True. But she isna coming herself. She'll send Derek."

Hearing his name and imagining what Miena might tell him was another blow to Kora's battered heart. She hated feeling so… helpless. But that's what she was. She could end a Star Person's life with her flames and move faster than most, but what else did she have? Nothing. She couldn't teleport or create clothes and food out of nothing. She was only good for one thing.

"She wants us to leave the dragons defenseless here," Merrill said.

Con ran a hand down his face. "We prepare here. Rhi alerted the Kings at Dreagan, and they'll take precautions there."

Kora watched the exchange with interest, along with Jeyra and Lotti. The way Merrill and Con interacted spoke of a history of many centuries together. As well as deep-rooted trust—the kind only someone who had stood beside another in the most disastrous of situations and come out together understood.

"Ulrik and the others will be on the lookout," Merrill said.

Con put his hands on his hips, his gaze going distant. "They'll spread the word to the Reapers, who will tell the Fae if necessary. Ulrik will also alert the Skye Druids. And the Warriors."

Kora didn't have a clue what a Reaper or a Skye Druid was, but she wanted to. What other differences were there between Zora and Earth? She hoped she got the opportunity to find out.

Con lifted his gaze to Merrill. "Erith is aware of the situation with Villette."

There was a moment of silence before Merrill's eyes widened, and he grinned. Kora had to bite her tongue not to ask questions.

If they wanted her to know, they would have spoken the words. It stung to be left out, but she *was* the outsider here, and she had to remember that.

"Where is Rhi?" Con asked.

Merrill said, "She's guarding Villette, who is surrounded by Kora's fire. But I didna feel right leaving her alone."

Con's lips pinched, and Kora wasn't the only one who noticed.

"What is it?" Merrill asked.

It was Jeyra who answered. "She's pregnant."

Kora didn't think she'd heard that right. The only ones on Zora who could give birth were the animals. Then again, Rhi was from another realm. One where their bellies would swell with a child. The prospect of it seemed as unattainable as touching the moons.

The smile that crossed Merrill's face was one of true joy. "That's fantastic news. Congratulations."

But the revelation made Kora acutely aware of the position they had put Rhi in. It didn't take long for Merrill to reach the same conclusion.

"I'll trade places with her," Lotti said.

Kora jumped to her feet. "Take me with you. Please. I should remain to watch Villette."

"We can no' be in two places at once." Con sighed. "But I willna bring Villette here. She doesna know about the city's existence, and it's going to stay that way."

Merrill shrugged one shoulder. "Then we go to Stonemore."

"That's where we were?" Kora asked.

He nodded as he turned his blue eyes on her. "It's not in the same mountain, but it's in the same range."

"How do you know?" Jeyra asked.

Con sliced his hand through the air. "We can sort that out later. I need to get to my mate."

"Kora and I will go now." Lotti motioned Kora over.

The moment Kora reached her, Lotti touched her, and they were suddenly back in the cavern. The stink of evil hit Kora. She knew without looking that Villette was there. Rhi sat on a table, swinging her legs as she leaned back on her hands. Her face split into a grin at the sight of them.

Lotti hurried to her, and they exchanged quiet words. Kora turned to Villette, whose entire demeanor changed at the sight of Lotti. The look went beyond disgust and loathing. It was hatred on a level Kora only thought *she* knew until that moment.

Villette's gaze swung to Kora. "One bad choice after another. You would think you would've righted things long ago, but you keep making mistakes."

"No one wants to hear what you have to say," Rhi said as she and Lotti came up beside Kora.

Villette chuckled softly. "Kora knows it's the truth. If she doesn't change her tactics, she'll lose Derek. Or she'll lose her life at his hand rather."

"That's enough," Lotti stated, her turquoise eyes flashing angrily.

Villette laughed and crossed her arms over her chest smugly. She had gotten her point across just as she'd intended. The problem was that Kora had already been worried about the very things Villette spoke of. Hearing them aloud only confirmed her concerns.

Rhi turned Kora away and gently nudged her to follow. Kora hated the cavern because it was where she had last seen Derek.

But she wanted to be there *because* it was the last place Derek had been. She slowly followed Rhi as Lotti trailed behind her.

The Fae stopped at the other end of the cavern and faced them. "I probably don't need to tell you not to listen to anything that vile bitch has to say, but don't listen to anything that vile bitch has to say. She's trying to get under your skin."

"Too late," Kora replied.

Lotti shot an angry look over her shoulder. "I hate that I'm even associated with someone who is so...so..."

"Revolting?" Rhi offered. "Wicked?"

Kora grinned. "Despicable."

"Ohhh. Good one," Rhi said with a smile.

Lotti wrinkled her nose. "All of that and more."

"I don't want her help," Kora said. "It seems wrong."

Rhi nodded. "It is, but sometimes you have to work with the enemy to bring down another adversary. You aren't in this alone. You have us."

"You don't know me."

Lotti shrugged. "They didn't know me either, yet they all supported and helped me when I needed it. We'll do the same for you."

"And find Derek," Rhi added.

No one spoke about returning his memories. It wasn't as if anyone could snap their fingers and do it. Well, perhaps Miena could, but she wouldn't. She'd die before allowing Kora and Derek to be together. He would only get free of Miena's hold if Kora could get him to remember her.

And fall in love with her again.

"Hey," Rhi said to get her attention. "You have the strength of the Dragon Kings, as well as the Fae, Star People, Warriors,

Banshees, and so many others. We don't want a war. Con and the others have done everything they could to prevent it, but we've all known it would lead to one."

War. Was that what this was coming to? This wouldn't be just hostility between the dragons and Villette. This would be everyone against everyone. The very thing Villette had been building toward.

The Kings didn't know Derek. They said they would find him, but they hadn't said they would save him. If it came down to protecting their own or him, who would they choose? The answer was obvious to her.

Derek was in the enemy's hands with his memory wiped. When he woke, it would be Miena who shaped his world, thoughts, and actions. It had taken him hundreds of years to unravel Villette's lies. Miena wouldn't give him that chance. She had promised to get deep into his mind and scrub it. There was a good chance that when Kora encountered Derek again, there would be nothing there she recognized.

"Keep clear of Villette," Rhi said. "I'll be back."

Kora stared at the empty spot where the Fae had stood. She rubbed her hands up and down her arms, chilled, then glanced at Lotti. If she could learn to accept dragons as friends, she needed to make the same effort with Lotti. "I'm sorry for...before."

"It's fine." Lotti's lips curved into a quick smile. "Really."

"It isn't. If I had smelled you before reacting, I would've known you weren't evil."

Lotti tucked a strand of wavy blond hair behind her ear. "After dealing with Villette and Miena, I don't blame you."

"I made the situation worse. There are two of them to deal with now."

"There was always two of them. Even if you hadn't released Miena, we would've had to handle her once we dealt with Villette."

Kora faced the Star Person. "You sound certain that we'll defeat both."

"Because we will." Lotti sank onto a rock and patted the one next to her. "Tell me about Derek."

Kora sat as her mind drifted through thoughts of Derek. Just thinking about him brought a smile to her face. "I thought it was his pale olive eyes that drew me when I first met him. They certainly capture your attention. But it didn't take me long to learn it was so much more than that." Her smile widened. "His hair is almost as long as mine and black as the midnight sky. He's protective and gentle. Powerful and imposing."

"Sounds just like a Dragon King," Lotti said.

Kora's smile faltered. "He stood against Villette for me. The knowledge that they had created him cut him deeper than any weapon could. It crushed me. But not nearly as much as learning that he loved me."

Lotti reached across the space between them and covered Kora's hand with hers. "You love him."

"Aye. None of that matters if he doesn't remember me, though."

"Trust me, it does. A dragon mates for life. I promise you this: He'll know you no matter how many memories they take from him."

Kora needed to hear that. She took those words and held them close, settling them next to the single thread of hope that remained inside her.

CHAPTER 5

The wind caressed his scales as Derek soared beneath the glow of the two moons, its touch as light as a lover's, the *whoosh* of his wings soft. There was little human movement in the dead of night, but a daring few snuck out to commit foul deeds.

But the night belonged to a world mortals would never appreciate. Nocturnal animals that blended into the shadows to hunt for their prey. Flowers that bloomed solely beneath the glimmer of the indulgent moonbeams. Plants that favored moonlight to the harsh, relentless sun. A symphony of sounds only heard when the double moons reigned in the inky sky.

Derek soared over the top of the forest. He had traveled southeast, far from the snowy mountains. The trees were turning the vibrant shades of autumn as a crisp nip entered the air, warning of the winter to come. He found a clearing and dove toward it, tucking his wings as he picked up speed. As he reached the treetops, he shifted forms, tucking and rolling before landing with one knee on the ground.

He rose as smaller animals scurried to safety. Changing forms had become easier after the first time. Maybe it had always been easy. He wished he could remember, but found nothing but a void each time he searched for something from the past. It terrified him. He didn't know who he had been, what he thought...

Or who he knew.

Derek glanced at his nakedness. Miena had warned him before he left that he couldn't walk among the humans while naked. He hadn't wanted to ask her what human males wore. Instead, he had studied them in the first village he came across. From then on, he had only to think about the tunic, breeches, and boots for them to appear on his body. Derek chose all black. As he rolled up his sleeves to his elbows, he tried not to think whether the color choice had been something he would've worn before the injury to his head. That was how life would be now.

Before and after.

And he hated every moment of it. No amount of despising his situation would change it. Only knowledge could.

Derek took his time walking through the forest, enjoying the sights and sounds. Miena hadn't appeared to him again, but he didn't doubt she would pop up when she wanted. So far, all the mortals in the two villages and one city he had visited had relayed the same thing: Dragons were to be feared.

But with that came a deep-rooted terror of anything—and any*one*—with magic.

None of it sat well with him. How could it when he was a dragon, and magic was a part of who he was? It wasn't like a second skin he could shed and forget. It was in his flesh and muscle, in his bones, his very essence.

Derek didn't have to wonder what humans would think if they discovered the truth. They would attack without thought or reason. When that kind of fear drove someone, that was all they could focus on. There wasn't room for consideration or rationale. There was only the need to kill what frightened them.

The tales he heard about the dragons striking without rhyme or reason were disturbing on many levels. The humans didn't pose a threat. But he was told the dragons would land in the middle of villages and engulf structures in dragon fire. The worst, however, were the stories of the dragons eating mortals.

Why? He kept asking himself that over and over, but he had yet to come up with a reason. He was missing something, some piece that would surely cause everything to make sense.

And all the while, in the back of his mind, Derek wondered if the humans spoke about him. He couldn't shake the thought that he could have—*might* have—attacked mortals. It troubled him, and the more he contemplated it, the more agitated he became. He could ask Miena, but would she tell him the truth? He just didn't know.

And that was the rub. The uncertainty. The constant, mind-numbing doubt.

Derek wanted to accept whatever she told him, if for no other reason than to have someone to fill in the blanks. She expected him to believe every word that fell from her lips—the power emanating from her was proof of that. But he didn't.

A few things felt right. His name, for one. He'd also sensed there had been a battle but couldn't discern where or with whom.

Shifting, obviously. He also suspected that everything Miena said about herself was true. There had been arrogance in her words, and a superiority only someone who wielded such tremendous power could have.

Why him, though? Why had she chosen to aid *him*? If she had helped at all. He didn't like the conflicting thoughts, especially when it involved someone who held all the answers. It would be easier if he believed everything she said.

He stopped at a tree and sat between two large roots that cradled him perfectly. Derek leaned his head against the trunk and stared at the blanket of stars through the tangle of branches. He had soared high, aching to touch the stars, expecting breathing to become difficult. But it didn't. He had finally stopped when he could see the thin layer of atmosphere that separated him from space. He hadn't crossed it.

Derek wondered what it was like to move about the stars like Miena and the other Star People. How many other worlds were out there? How many dragons? Were there others who were alone, like him?

A sigh escaped. He wasn't lonely. Far from it, in fact. It made him think that he had been on his own before. It was just a deep sense within him. The same kind of acknowledgment that he'd gotten about his name. If only it was so easy to discern other truths.

He closed his eyes and let the night music of the forest fill him. Sleep wasn't a necessity, but he found it cathartic to shut his eyes and rest. It helped to calm his chaotic thoughts.

As he settled deeper into the tree, a cool wind brushed against him, ruffling his hair. He reached up, and like the many times since he'd woken in the cave, he expected to find long hair.

Instead, it barely brushed the back of his neck. He dropped his hand to his lap and tried to settle again. It was more difficult this time. Simply closing his eyes wouldn't be enough. So, he let himself be pulled under as sleep claimed him.

"Derek."

The voice came from nowhere and everywhere. It moved through him, around him. Derek looked about, finding everything blurry. Only the dull colors of the dream were there. He squinted, but it was of little help. He turned in a circle, searching for whoever it was.

"Hello? Who are you?"

"Derek."

The voice was the softest of whispers. A sigh upon his skin.

He reached out, hoping to touch something and bring it into focus, but everything remained out of reach. The blurred colors shifted slightly as if taking him to a different place, but he couldn't decipher anything more than before. They altered again. Then again, and again.

"Derek."

"I'm here! Right fucking here!" he shouted in frustration.

He knew it was useless to lose his temper, but he was on edge. And the dream wasn't helping.

"Derek."

The voice was behind him, loud enough that he recognized it was a woman. He spun around, finding a figure standing before him as distorted as everything else. The only thing he saw with any clarity was the long waves of her dark hair. He moved to her, and she lifted her face to his, but there was nothing there. It was blank.

Derek startled awake. He realized he was gripping the roots

and released them as he took in a shuddering breath. He shook his head to dispel the dream, but there was no forgetting the empty face. No nose, eyes, or lips. Derek pushed to his feet and rolled his shoulders. He heard the distinctive sounds of a village waking and realized dawn had arrived.

He waited another hour, watching the movement of people before making his way to the small town. Most of those who lived there farmed the land or had livestock. They welcomed him with smiles, and he soon learned why. While the population was small, the residents grew exceptional crops where nearby villages came to purchase and trade. The market was set up on the far side of the village.

Derek wandered through the market, noting the many different offerings. He paused beside a table set up with freshly baked bread. Alongside it was a red scarf, and upon it rested long slivers of obsidian.

"You won't find any better."

Derek looked up to find a skinny lad of about thirteen. His sandy blond hair was too long, his clothes a little large on his gangly frame, but he was clean and articulate, with a glint in his brown eyes that warned Derek he rarely had a customer leave without a purchase. "The bread or the black glass?"

"Both," the boy stated proudly. "Me dad is the baker. I'll take over one day. Until then, I find, cut, and polish the black glass."

Derek found himself grinning. "I have no doubt."

"You don't look like you need the glass. I figure you could fight the beasts yourself."

A sinking feeling filled Derek's stomach. "Beasts?"

"The dragons, of course."

"Do they come often?"

The lad shrugged. "Me dad was my age the last time a beast was seen. But you can't be too careful."

"Indeed. What does the obsidian do?"

The boy frowned in disbelief. "It penetrates their scales and kills them."

"Are you sure?"

"Would we be selling them if it didn't?"

Derek had offended him. "Apologies. I've never heard of such a weapon."

"It's all right," the boy said with a shrug, his smile back. "But how is it possible that you've not heard of it?"

"I've traveled a great distance."

"You don't have dragons where you're from?"

Derek shook his head. "None that I've seen."

"Well, if you're traveling around here, you're tempting fate without a weapon. Even someone like you."

"Someone like me?"

"You're a warrior, aren't you? You have that look. We don't get many of you 'round here."

Derek crafted a coin with magic and flipped it at the lad. "I'll take your best loaf."

The boy's eyes lit up when he caught the coin and looked at it. "This will buy you everything we have."

"I just need one."

The lad barely paid him any attention as he handed over the bread. Derek walked away as he pondered the information he had obtained. He tore off the end of the loaf and bit into it as he continued wandering. Three other stalls were also selling obsidian.

He almost told them the black glass wouldn't kill a dragon, but he knew they wouldn't listen. And if they did, they would want to know how he knew.

Derek didn't remain in the village. He had learned all he could, and none of it was good. He didn't return to the forest. Instead, he headed down the road that would continue his journey south. Once he was out of town, there was nothing but rolling hills covered by crops, separated by low stone fences. He set his hand on the rock and jumped over a fence to strike out across the field.

The grass brushed his knees as he walked through it. For a split second, a memory began to form, but it vanished almost immediately. He was frustrated at having thoughts begin only to be yanked away before he could discern anything about them. It was why he didn't see the man in the middle of the field, leaning his hands atop his shovel at first.

Derek almost continued walking, but something about the way the stranger stared at him made Derek deviate toward him. The man didn't alter his stance as Derek approached. He was on the shorter side, his white hair long and wild as if it hadn't seen a comb in weeks. Despite that, he was clean-shaven. His skin was tanned from hours spent in the sun, wrinkles forming at the corners of his gray eyes and across his forehead. It was as if he furrowed his brow often. He wore a shirt the color of dried grass, and trousers in a deep brown like the rich soil he had been digging in. There were calluses on his fingers, and dirt clumped on his boots.

"Morning," Derek called in greeting as he stopped a few feet away.

The man inclined his head. "I was hoping you would walk my way."

Derek frowned in confusion. "Me?"

"Aye. I saw you land this morning. I've always wondered if some of you could change shape."

Surprise shot through Derek, followed by suspicion. "And what do you think I am?"

The man chuckled and dropped one of his arms to his side as his other hand slid down the handle of the shovel. "You want me to say it, do you? Alrighty, then. A dragon."

Derek studied the old man, noticing there was no fear in his visage or voice. It was the opposite of what Derek had encountered in the places he had visited since waking from his injuries.

"I'm Ashmadu, but everyone calls me Ash."

"Derek. Why aren't you afraid like all the others?"

Ash's brow creased as he looked at Derek dubiously. "I may not have spoken to a dragon before, but I assumed your kind knew about us."

"Enlighten me," Derek pressed. He was really tiring of not knowing things, though this one may have nothing to do with the blow to his head.

"I'm a tomte." When Derek didn't respond, Ash sighed. "Only those with magic can see us. We are inexplicably drawn to crops."

Derek ran a hand over his jaw, the rasp of whiskers scraping his palm. "You're invisible to humans?"

"To every being who doesn't contain magic, aye."

"That means you move freely about the realm."

Ash nodded once. "We do."

"What do you know about a recent battle the dragons had?"

"If it happens within the border your people created, we know nothing. Not even we dare to cross that boundary."

Impatience flared within Derek. "Surely, you must have heard that some dragons crowned themselves Kings and took over."

Ash released a long breath. "The only strife we're aware of is the one where humans are banishing or killing those of us with abilities. From what little I've heard, the dragons are fighting against that."

"Tell me more. I need to know everything."

CHAPTER 6

"This isn't necessary," Villette stated. "I've offered my assistance."

Kora swiveled her head toward Villette. "Right. Just like you stopped Miena when you had the chance."

"I already told you. She's more powerful."

"But had you done *something*, I could've helped." Kora snorted. "Instead, you did nothing. You showed your true colors."

Villette's blue eyes turned glacial. "You're going to eat those words when I find not only my sister but also Derek."

"How exactly are you going to do that?" Lotti asked.

Villette waved her hands at the flames. "I can't do anything locked away as I am."

"Tell me what you plan, then," Lotti said. "I'll find them."

A look of insolence colored Villette's face. "And make myself worthless? No, thank you. Besides, you don't have a connection to Miena like I do. You might be one of us, but you aren't part of our family."

"If the others are like you and Miena, I don't want to be," Lotti retorted.

Kora observed the interaction with curiosity. Lotti had shunned the other Star People in favor of being with the dragons. Well, not just any dragons—the Kings. Specifically, her mate. The word wasn't unknown to Kora. Her people had called their significant others by that term. It was the knowledge that dragons coupled for life that she clung to. None of the female mates she had met were dragons, which meant there really might be a chance that she was Derek's mate.

She hadn't planned to befriend a dragon, and never imagined she would give her heart to one. But here she was, working with them. It seemed so normal. Derek should be here, meeting everyone and learning where he fit in. He might not have been born like the others, but he was alive. That counted for something.

"The more time I'm stuck behind these flames, the more time Miena has to implement her plan," Villette stated.

Kora strode toward the woman who had taken so much from her. Every fiber of her being—and the ghosts of her ancestors lining up behind her—demanded that Kora end her right now. Villette might actually aid in locating Derek, but she would betray them eventually. It was who she was. The centuries of her rule in Stonemore and the surrounding areas proved that. Her reach was long. Her command immense.

"I won't stop you," Lotti whispered from behind her, as if reading her thoughts. "Villette has committed inconceivable atrocities and needs to pay for it."

She'd certainly been behind unspeakable brutalities. Kora thought about the red-robed priests in armor who had struck her down while trying to get to a child they believed had magic. That was all Villette.

"But," Lotti said in a low voice, "what if she can find Derek?"

Villette shot Lotti a withering glare. "I can. And I *will*. As soon as the flames are gone."

For the first time, Kora understood the difficult position Derek had been in. Now, it was her turn. Did she set aside her need to avenge her family and all the other hellhounds to find the man she loved?

Derek had chosen her.

And it had cost him dearly.

Lotti walked to stand in front of Kora. She kept her voice at a whisper. "Utilize her now. When her usefulness is up, do what you need."

It was a solid plan—one that would require Kora to be at the top of her game. Villette had lived millions of lives to her one. That meant Villette had more wisdom and was well-educated in manipulation and deception. Kora had spent several hundred years shutting out the world and her abilities. She would have to learn. And fast.

But she wouldn't be alone.

Kora nodded in silent agreement. Lotti squeezed her hand and moved to the side as they faced Villette.

"I'm not jesting. The flames can hold us for a reason. I can't do anything until you lower them," Villette said.

Kora still hesitated. Was she ready for this? She would have to consider Villette's every word and action. She would have to antic-ipate ten moves ahead of her nemesis. The thought terrified Kora. Because all of this was about more than getting Derek back. He was just the first step.

Once they located him, the long process of helping him remember who he was would begin. If things went their way, he wouldn't fight them. But everyone realized that he most likely would. Battling him and Miena at the same time would be problematic. And that didn't even take Villette into consideration.

What if it all blew up in her face? What if trusting Villette cost everyone their lives? She had already created a mess by releasing Miena. Did one man's life mean more than the countless others that could follow?

Her very essence screamed, "*Aye!*"

But her mind was another story. It listed every wrong decision and bad choice she had made throughout her life. And the list was long.

Who was she to decide such important things? She was nobody. The last hellhound on Zora, and one who had ignored her gifts until recently. She was the last person who should be making decisions.

Kora felt a presence behind her. For a heartbeat, she thought it was Derek and imagined him wrapping his arms around her before pressing his hard chest against her back to steady her. She could almost feel his warm breath as it grazed her neck, and his mouth lowered to her ear, ready to deliver words of wisdom.

But it wasn't Derek. And no amount of yearning would return him. Kora looked over to find Merrill with Con and Rhi. With them was another man with auburn hair, who walked straight to Lotti. That must be her mate, Alasdair. The look the two exchanged was so full of love that it felt like a punch to the gut.

Kora physically ached for Derek. She hadn't known the depth of her feelings until it was too late, and she hadn't grasped his until he was being taken away. How could she have been so blind? Perhaps because she'd had nothing for so long.

Then she'd had it all.

For only a brief moment in time.

"Is this where you threaten me?" Villette asked as she looked at each of the men. "There is nothing any of you can do that will harm me."

Con shrugged. "By the burns still healing on your body, I disagree."

"Only two people in this room could kill me," Villette continued, as if he hadn't spoken. "And Lotti doesn't have the power yet."

"Oh, I'm getting there," Lotti countered.

Villette grinned expectantly. "We'll see." Her blue gaze shifted to Kora, and she lifted a blond brow in question.

Everyone waited for Kora's decision. What would Derek do? What would her brother do? Kora had to take the emotion out of it. She needed to look at the facts. Derek had been taken against his will, had his memories altered, and was likely being manipulated to carry out Miena's sick plan—not unlike what Villette had done to him. Derek deserved to be free of their hold and told the truth. She hoped someone would do the same for her if she were in his place.

Then there was Miena. She was Kora's mess to clean up. If going after Villette had taught her anything, it was that Miena would be harder to bring down. She would be expecting an attack. But would she anticipate her sister helping them?

Kora had to think ten steps ahead.

"I'll lower the flames," Kora finally said.

Villette grinned. "Excellent."

"On one condition."

The Star Person rolled her eyes. "How many times do I have to agree to help?"

"You've agreed to locate Derek, aye. I want more." Kora knew she was pushing. There was a fine line between getting Villette's agreement and putting her enemy's back against the wall, where she would agree to anything to stay alive.

Villette didn't break eye contact. "Well? Are you going to state what that might be, or shall I guess?"

"You'll not only help locate Derek, but you'll also aid in getting him away from your sister," Kora stated.

"That was implied."

A sound like a growl rumbled from Merrill, who stood on Kora's left. If Villette heard, she ignored him. Others might be witnessing this conversation, but it was just between the two of them. That meant there was room for Kora to botch something.

She tried to imagine what her brother would do, or even her uncle, but her memories of them were too faded to bring up anything useful. So, she turned to the only other person she could: Derek. He had been wary of Miena. No matter what she had offered, he had suspected there was more to it. On the flip side, he hadn't believed Merrill either.

One could argue that Derek had been too skeptical, and his doubt had kept him from deciding. Whereas she hadn't taken any time to consider things beyond ending Villette when she freed Miena. And to think, only that small flower had held the chains so tightly that not even a Star Person could get free.

A plan began to form, and Kora twisted her lips. "Nothing is implied. It will be stated and agreed upon."

"Go on," Villette said tightly.

"After we've rescued Derek from Miena, you will join us in removing your sister once and for all."

"Do you have any idea how hard it is to kill one of us?" Villette asked. She glanced at Lotti. "For the first two hundred and fifty years, we're susceptible to a great many things. After that? It takes quite a bit to snuff out our lives. Why do you think Miena was imprisoned? If I could've killed her, I would have."

Merrill grunted. "I doona believe that for a minute."

Neither did Kora. "I'm sure you've thought up ways, though."

"Maybe," Villette replied, shrugging one shoulder.

"I didn't say you would kill Miena. I said you would join us. I will be the one to take her life."

Villette said nothing as she stared at Kora.

"Either you agree to the terms, or you remain within the fire." Kora looked at the red-orange flames licking the air as high as her shoulder. "Your choice."

Villette rolled her eyes in disgust. "Of course, I agree to your stupid demands."

"Bind your vow with magic," Alasdair said.

Villette slid her blue gaze to him. "Haven't taken enough from me already, Alasdair?"

"I'm the one who told him about it," Lotti said.

Kora hadn't known a vow could be bound with magic. If she had, she had lost that memory. She was glad Alasdair had spoken up. It would go nicely with her plan.

Villette cleared her throat. "I'll bind the vow. Does that make everyone happy? Miena is my enemy, too, remember?"

Kora stepped forward, but Merrill's hand on her arm made her pause. He looked at her, concern in his eyes. She turned on her heel and walked away from Villette, waiting for the others to join them.

"Are you sure about this?" Merrill asked.

Kora shook her head. "But you're the one who pointed out that we need her."

"Behind the flames, aye. I'm no' sure letting her out is the answer."

"Need I remind everyone that time is wasting," Villette urged, her impatience clear.

Lotti caught Kora's eyes. "This binding vow will ensure that neither of you harm the other. Whatever she doles out to you will return to her times ten. And vice versa. You should also be aware that your life forces are combined."

"Meaning?" Kora asked.

Lotti swallowed. "Meaning, the two of you will keep each other alive."

"There's always a loophole somewhere," Rhi said.

Lotti shook her head. "Not this time. Villette won't be able to leave until she fulfills the vow. Also, Villette won't be able to harm Kora. In effect, they'll do everything to keep the other alive. It's either the binding vow, kill her, or leave her here."

"And we need her," Kora said with a sigh. She met Lotti's turquoise eyes. "Are you sure about the vow?"

"Absolutely. You need to be specific in the wording. She will have to agree to everything, but she will also have a chance to state her wishes. You'll have to agree to them. Then the magic will bind you."

Kora had come to end Villette. Now, she would be bound to her. Nothing had turned out like it was supposed to, but she was glad. Because had it, she never would've met Derek.

"It sounds like the only way," Con said.

Kora looked at each of them. They all nodded. It looked like she was doing this. She took a deep breath and turned to face Villette.

CHAPTER 7

Derek waited expectantly for Ash to speak. He was the one being who might give him an unbiased recounting of things—things humans wouldn't know. He wanted to shake Ash to get him to start speaking immediately. It was all Derek could do to keep his hands to himself.

The tomte stared at him for a long moment before he thumped the shovel against the side of his boot to knock off the dirt. "You'd best come with me. It won't be good for mortals to walk past and see you talking to air."

Derek had forgotten that Ash was invisible to some. He followed the diminutive man over three rolling fields before Ash walked to a copse of trees. Derek expected to see a hut of some kind. Instead, Ash headed toward a tree and ducked into the hollow opening. When Derek didn't immediately follow, Ash stuck his head out and motioned him forward.

There was no way he would fit into the opening, but Derek

went anyway. He was surprised to find that once he stuck his leg into the hollow section, the entrance expanded to accommodate him. Magic traveled up his leg and pulled him in before spitting him out on the other side.

Derek stumbled forward, barely catching himself before he ended up in a sprawl on his face. When he straightened, he found Ash moving a kettle over a fire. Derek looked around in stunned silence. A vase of flowers sat on a dining table with two chairs, and past that was the hearth with an arched facing. There was a stove on one side with a sink and shelves with dishes. Pans hung on hooks along the wall.

He walked around the table and saw that the room containing the hearth had an armchair, a stool, and four sets of bookshelves overflowing with tomes. An arched doorway led to another room —likely the bedroom.

"I hope you like tea," Ash said as he walked to the kitchen.

Derek nodded without thinking. Apparently, he instinctively knew some things. "Are we inside the tree?"

Ash chuckled. "In a manner. Sit, sit." He motioned to the armchair.

Derek paused at the sight of the chair that was too small and looked around for another seat. "I don't want to take your chair."

Ash chuckled and dragged a chair from the table, angling it toward Derek before he sat. Then he stared at Derek, waiting.

Derek hesitantly lowered himself into the armchair, hoping it would expand as the entrance had. But it didn't. There was a slight groan when Derek settled his full weight, yet it held.

"Hmm. Where to begin." Ash laced his fingers over his gently rounded stomach.

"From the beginning."

Ash's gray eyes darted to him. "That far, huh?"

"I need to know everything."

"If you don't mind me asking, how is it you don't know this information?"

Derek could lie, and he almost did. But the thought of it soured his stomach. "I had a head injury. I'm trying to catch up on things."

"Head wounds can be tricky, even for us magical beings. Alrighty." Ash stretched out his legs and crossed them at the ankles. "I've never heard how old Zora is. Someone out there probably has the answer, but it isn't me. It has long been whispered that it was meant only for you dragons."

"Then how did others get here?"

"Good question. Infants arrive, but no one knows how or who brings them. Many have tried to find out, but no one I know has discovered the answer. It's how I was brought here. It's how everyone I know came." Ash scratched his cheek. "I suppose the babies make up for the fact that only animals can reproduce."

It was like being sucker punched. "No one else?"

"No human or otherwise. Just the creatures."

"What about the dragons?"

Ash shrugged, his lips turning down. "I suspect so since they are animals. Like I said, we don't cross the border to find out."

Someone must have that information. Derek didn't know why it was suddenly so important to know about the dragons and their young, but the question was seared into his brain now.

"There are more humans than any other," Ash continued. "Maybe even dragons. Stories passed down through my people said that two mighty dragons, a male and a female, erected the border using magic that would alert them if someone crossed into their territory. It was meant to keep the humans out. From that moment on, it seems the fear mortals have about anything with magic spread like a plague, erasing all rational thought."

Nothing sounded familiar to Derek so far, but whether that was because those memories had been affected or he'd never known any of it remained to be seen.

"The humans know the threat of death if they step onto dragon land. However, dragons are supposed to remain on their side of the border, as well. But that doesn't mean they always do." Ash gave him a pointed look.

Derek shifted uncomfortably in his chair.

The kettle began to whistle, so Ash rose and moved it out of the flames using a towel. He tottered back to the kitchen, mumbling something about forgetting things before returning with the tea bags and cups. He dropped them into another kettle to steep before pouring steaming water over them.

"The tomte live for close to three thousand years," he said as he poured some tea into the cups. He handed one to Derek before taking his to his chair. "It's odd. If a baby looks human, the mortals will take it into their villages and find it a home. For those who are different, like the tomte, we tend to find our way to others like us. Unlike some, we keep in contact with each other. We might live hundreds of miles apart, but no one passes information like us," he stated with a grin before sipping the tea.

Derek took a small drink, somewhat surprised at how good it was. "How do you pass communications?"

Ash waved away his question as if it didn't matter. "We talk. And I know there have been dragon sightings for a very long time. Two particular dragons—a blue one and a gold." His gaze became pointed. "As well as a black dragon with scales edged in silver."

Derek stiffened because Ash had just described him. "When you say a long time...?"

"A very, very, *very* long time."

"There must be other dragons with my coloring." If there weren't, then that meant Derek was extremely old. And if he were as old as he feared, then that meant he had lost centuries of memories.

Ash took another drink. "Those two dragons mostly targeted human villages."

"Mostly?" The moment the word was out of his mouth, Derek wished he could take it back. But he wanted answers, and knowledge was power. However, that didn't mean the truth wouldn't hurt.

"They also had a taste for hellhounds."

Derek recalled Miena's words about the scent of a hellhound. He rested the cup on the arm of the chair as he held the rim.

Ash's eyebrows flicked upward. "From what I hear, the hellhounds have been wiped from Zora. Also, the attacks on the humans tapered off somewhat. Oddly enough, more dragons have been seen lately. Particularly around Stonemore. Does that city ring a bell?"

"None." Derek wished it did, but nothing sounded familiar yet.

"Hmm. It's not far from the dragons' western border. Anyone with magic who goes to the city ends up dead. They target children, if you can believe it. Word is, a Banshee was spotted rescuing the kids about to die. Then, a dragon joined in. After that, dragons were seen around the mountain city."

Derek didn't like the sound of any of that. "How many people have the dragons killed?"

"Not a single one."

Derek's brows snapped together. "You said two dragons targeted the human villages. How is it that more arrived and have left the mortals alone?"

"They're after the ruler of the city. That little tidbit has spread widely among the magicals. Everyone is watching Stonemore to see what happens. Some say a war is brewing. The humans certainly want it."

"And the...magicals?" Derek asked.

Ash grinned. "Some say the tomte are lucky because the mortals can't see us, which means they can't hunt us or run us out. Many others fled their homes and went to Highvale."

Something about that name sounded familiar.

"You know it?" Ash asked.

Derek shook his head. "Maybe."

"It's a city only for those with magic. It's hidden, and the only way to find it is with magic. Many magicals have lost everything and want to rise up against the humans."

Derek wrinkled his nose. "The mortals would be slaughtered. They don't stand a chance against those with magic. Surely, they know that."

"They believe they will win. After all, they've killed a few of us, and an untold number of children. They've even run enough of us off to make them believe they're capable of anything."

Derek sipped the tea as he stared into the fire's flames. "But you don't know anything about Dragon Kings."

"Now, I have heard that term."

Derek slid his gaze to Ash, every muscle tensed in expectation. "What did you hear?"

"That a Dragon King attacked Stonemore." Ash finished the last of his tea and rose to pour himself another cup. He lifted the kettle to Derek, who shook his head. "From the accounts I've heard—and understand they were passed through several retellings—the dragons aren't fighting each other. Wait. I take that back. There *was* one occasion recently."

"Where?" This was it. This was what Derek had come to find out. He waited with bated breath to learn if Miena had lied.

Ash returned to his chair, his face lined in thought. "If I'm not mistaken, it was north of Stonemore. Aye. That's it. My cousin saw the entire thing. It involved two amethyst-colored dragons and one with lichen scales. But it was the two amethyst ones going at it. She said they were trying to kill each other."

"Do you know what they were fighting over?"

Ash shook his head. "'Fraid not."

"How dependable are the stories passed through your people?"

"If we tell it, ninety-seven percent. We depend on accuracy to stay informed. We do not embellish. However, if the story passes to us from others?" He shrugged. "Who can say?"

Derek finished his now-lukewarm tea. "Do you know anyone named Miena?"

"Can't say I do. Who is she?"

"A Star Person."

Ash's face drained of color. "We do not interact with them. They are more powerful than you can imagine. It is speculated that they create the realms and bring the infants here, stolen from other worlds. We are playthings to them."

"How many are there?"

"I don't know, and I don't want to know," Ash said tightly. Then his eyes narrowed. "How do you know this Miena?"

"She said she found me hurt after my battle with the Dragon Kings. She took me somewhere to heal." Derek paused and then told Ash the rest. "She said I should attack again. That I was the only one who could free the dragons from the Kings."

Ash sat forward in his chair and nibbled his lower lip for a moment. "Let me reach out to the other tomte and see if anyone has heard about any other recent dragon battles."

The offer startled Derek. "Why would you help me?"

Ash grunted as he rose to his feet and grinned. "Because you look like someone in need of it. Besides, I don't see anyone else offering."

Derek found himself smiling for the first time since he'd awakened.

CHAPTER 8

It had to work. Kora swallowed. It felt as if she had failed at every turn. She had to get this right. For Derek and the safety of all on Zora.

"You look like you're about to be sick," Villette said.

Kora ignored the words and walked to her archenemy. She began to chant, *it'll work,* in her head. As if by thinking the words she could put her plan into action.

Villette's lips quirked haughtily. "Maybe because you're conspiring against me when I'm aligning myself with you?"

"Only to save your own skin," Merrill said.

Villette cut her blue eyes to him. "The enemy of my enemy and all that."

Kora stopped before her, staring across the flames into the face she equated with evil. Old burn scars on the right side of Villette's face and neck mixed with healed pink skin, presumably from dragon fire wounds. There was only one thing that could scar

Villette in such a way—hellhound fire. It's why she didn't try to budge once Kora encircled her with it.

Villette's gaze returned to her. The smug expression vanished. There was no smile, no superiority. Villette projected honesty as she said, "I mean it. You need me, but I also need you. I can't fight Miena on my own."

Kora wanted to believe her for the simple reason that it would make her decisions easier. But she had learned through heartache and pain that nothing in life was easy. She had come to Stonemore to face Villette on her own, knowing it would likely mean her death. It had been worth it to attempt to take her down.

She had wobbled when Derek became involved. Now, many, many others were entangled in this fiasco, including children who escaped death within the city. Kora had foolishly believed that this had been about her at the beginning. She had been wrong, but she didn't see the error until it was too late. Now, she needed to consider others with every decision and action.

Kora put her right arm through the fire. It devoured the sleeve of her tunic, but nothing more. Her gaze held Villette's, waiting to see if the Star Person would proceed. Kora realized she wasn't the only one looking five or even ten steps ahead.

Villette clasped her forearm, wincing when her fingers got too close to the flames. Kora didn't budge. While there was no pain for her, it still cost her greatly to make any kind of deal with a mortal enemy. But it was for Derek. Which meant Kora would do whatever she had to do. Even join forces with Villette.

When the Star Person spoke, her voice rang out clearly in the cavern. "I hereby vow that I will join with the hellhound, Kora, and anyone who enlists with her to locate Derek and get him out of my sister's clutches. I also pledge to assist in the battle to bring Miena down."

Magic sizzled over Kora's arm. It shimmered and turned iridescent as it slowly wound around Villette's hand and then over Kora's until it met the fire. Villette eyed Kora, waiting.

A thin stream of fire broke from the flames to begin its winding journey from Kora to Villette as she said, "I hereby promise to unite with Villette to locate and rescue Derek from Miena. I also swear to fight alongside Villette to kill Miena. This will all be done as quickly as possible."

Villette's eyes narrowed, but she nodded her blond head once. "As quickly as possible."

Their magic merged before sinking into their skin in an unbreakable, binding contract. Both released the other instantly.

"Lower the flames," Villette demanded.

Kora hesitated. Even with the vow, she was still wary. But they couldn't take the first step toward locating Derek until Villette gave them a direction to move in. Kora extinguished the flames. It hit her then that she might have very well allowed her one and only chance to kill Villette slip through her fingers. Out of the corner of her eye, she saw Merrill begin walking around everyone.

Villette took a hasty step back to put distance between them.

"Where is Derek?" Rhi asked.

Villette shrugged. "I might be powerful, but I'm not omniscient. I can't pluck that out of thin air."

"Then you lied," Alasdair declared.

Villette's nostrils flared as she cut him a withering look. "How dare you?"

"You made a binding vow," Con told her. "You are held to it."

"I know," Villette snapped.

"If you had no intentions of directing us toward Derek, then you lied in your vow," Lotti said.

Kora nodded as she took a step forward. She held out her right hand, palm up, as flames flared from it. "I knew I shouldn't trust you."

"Hold on," Villette said hurriedly as she took another step back, putting her even closer to Merrill. "I intend to help. I just wanted you to realize that I can't give you what you want this very instant. Besides, the binding would've known if I'd lied and wouldn't have worked. This proves I'm telling the truth."

Kora glanced at the fireball in her hand.

Villette gave her a pointed look. "The entire reason we're working together is because you need the power I bring."

"She's right," Lotti agreed.

Alasdair crossed his arms over his chest. "Nothing will stop you from leaving now."

Villette's gaze jerked from him to Kora. "I can't break our vow. Neither can you." She looked around in distaste. "One of you can remain with me at all times, if it makes you feel better. Merrill will do nicely. Especially since he's used to my bed."

The implication was clear. Merrill clenched his hands into fists, squeezing so hard his knuckles turned white.

"I won't subject Merrill to more of your company," Lotti said. "I'll shadow you."

Villette shrugged. "As you wish."

"Derek." Kora brought things back around to where they needed to be. "Do whatever you need to do to locate him but start doing *something*."

"As I said, I'm not all-knowing. If I was, I wouldn't need to go to the lengths I have to spy on the dragons," Villette said.

Kora frowned, wondering what Villette was talking about. Alasdair's nostrils flared, and fury sparked in his gaze. Lotti whispered something to him that calmed him down. Kora was grateful because she didn't want to take the focus off Derek.

Villette moved her blond strands to cover most of the burns on her right side, probably out of habit. "If I can locate anyone, it'll be Miena. And she won't be far from Derek."

"Then do it," Con ordered.

She sighed loudly. "Again, it isn't like snapping my fingers."

"I thought you were the most powerful being there is?" Merrill mocked. "Sounds like you're lacking."

Villette stiffened at the jab as if physically struck. She walked past them. Kora turned with her, watching to see what the Star Person would do. Villette halted next to the table and pressed her open palm to the edge where Derek's head had been, the same place Miena had rested her hands, then bowed her head.

Alasdair opened his mouth to say something, but Lotti shook her head to quiet him. The six of them silently watched Villette. There was no way to know if she was doing anything. It could all be a ploy.

"Miena is still on Zora," Villette said as she lifted her head and turned to them. She didn't release the table. "Pinpointing exactly where will take more."

Rhi eyed her. "More what?"

"Power." Villette looked at Lotti.

Everyone turned their heads to the other Star Person. She didn't hesitate to go to the table, simply walked around it until she stood facing Villette. There was no denying the animosity between them. This was how it would be going forward. But if they could get Derek back, it would be worth it. Everything would be worth it.

"What do you need from me?" Lotti asked.

Villette motioned to the table with her head. "Put your hand near mine. Search for magic. Miena was the last to use it here, so hers will be prevalent."

Lotti sucked in a quick breath.

"I see you found it," Villette said with a grin. "I did warn you that Miena was formidable."

Lotti exchanged a look with Alasdair. "Now what?" she asked Villette.

"Focus on Miena's magic. Put all your attention on it. I'll do the same. You'll have to stay fixated."

"As you said."

Villette's look was pointed. "The longer we sit here talking, the more her magic fades, and with it, any link we have to Derek. I say stay focused because we'll only get one shot at this." She paused. "It will take both of us to hold and follow the magic. You'll feel me, just as I'll feel you. We'll have to guide each other."

"You mean trust," Lotti said.

Alasdair made a noise that sounded like a growl. Kora understood his thoughts. She wasn't happy about any of this either.

Lotti said nothing as she closed her eyes. No one uttered a word or moved as Villette and Lotti fixated on Miena's magic. The seconds stretched to minutes. Each tick was a vise around Kora's heart, gripping tighter and tighter. It had to work.

It will work.

She closed her eyes, silently willing the universe or fate or whatever gods might be watching to let them find Miena. The fact that she was still on Zora was good news. But she could leave at any moment. Taking Derek with her.

If Derek left, Kora knew he would be lost to her forever.

"Lotti!"

The sound of Alasdair's shout snapped Kora's eyes open. Alasdair caught his mate before she hit the ground. Villette had dropped to one knee while a hand remained on the table to keep her upright.

"Lotti. Open your eyes, love," Alasdair called in a soft but insistent voice.

Villette laboriously pulled herself to her feet. "Give her a moment. She'll be fine."

A growl rumbled through Alasdair as he scowled at Villette. "If you've harmed her, I—"

"I'm all right," Lotti said, cutting off his words.

Kora looked away. It seemed wrong to observe the shared love between the couple. Her gaze collided with Merrill's. He came up beside her wearing a frown that hadn't smoothed from his brow since he'd returned to the cavern.

Alasdair got his mate on her feet. Lotti's hand trembled as she brushed blond hair from her face. Even Villette appeared shaken. Whatever they had done had cost them both.

Villette looked at Lotti, who nodded. Villette then cleared her throat and faced the rest of them. "Miena was in the north for some time. She's in the south now."

"Any particular location?" Con asked.

Lotti blew out a breath. "Not really. She paused at a few places but never stayed for long."

"Could either of you tell where they were headed?" Kora asked.

Villette's throat bobbed when she swallowed. "We need to head south. Lotti and I saw a general location. From there, it'll be easier to locate her."

"How?" Merrill asked.

Villette leaned heavily on the table as if it took everything she had to stay on her feet. Kora imagined it was hard, given the burns and magic it had taken to heal them. Not that Kora felt sorry for her. Whatever Villette suffered was of her own making.

"She didn't lie," Lotti said. "It took both of us to follow Miena's magic where we did. Even then, there were times I didn't think I could hold on. Villette guided me."

Alasdair whispered something in Lotti's ear that earned him a raised brow.

"South?" Merrill asked Kora.

She nodded as she squared her shoulders. "South."

CHAPTER 9

"Derek."

Her voice was right beside him, her breath on his ear. He reached for her, wanting to cradle her body against his, longing to feel her softness. Needing her on a level he couldn't fathom.

She slipped away. A roar filled him, but no sound escaped. He burned for her. It was a pain deep within, an ache that would remain until she was in his arms once more. His soul knew her.

If only he did.

"Derek."

Elation at her return made his heart trip over itself. He turned toward her. There was a note of urgency in her voice that hadn't been there before. His gaze was drawn to her dark strands of hair. It was parted on the side and hung in waves over her left shoulder to skim the side of her breast. The ends glowed red, reminding him of sparks. This time when he extended his hand, his fingers brushed the soft locks. He ran them down to the ends. The moment he touched there, they blazed hot and then dimmed.

"Derek?"

If he could see and touch her hair, then he could see and touch her. Yet he was afraid to look at her face. Afraid it would be blank once more.

"Derek...have...me."

She was trying to tell him something. He lifted his gaze to her face. Just as he feared, it was blank. But not all of it. This time, he saw her lips. They were moving, talking, but he couldn't hear all the words. He studied her mouth, trying to make out what she was saying, but as he watched, she began moving away from him again.

"Who are you?" he asked.

A firm hand on his shoulder yanked him from the dream. Derek jerked, startled to find himself staring into Ash's gray eyes. The tomte regarded him for a moment before straightening and going to stoke the embers in the hearth back to life.

"That must have been some dream to make you call out like that," Ash said.

Derek rubbed his palms along his thighs. He was shaken by the images that had filled his head. But especially the message the unknown woman had tried to share.

Small flames began dancing around the new log as Ash got the fire started. He dusted off his hands and faced Derek. "I didn't think it would take me so long to get word from the others."

Had it been that long? The fire had died, so it must have been. Derek remembered being content sitting in Ash's home to just be. It felt odd but nice. Did that mean he hadn't had such a place?

Surely, he had someplace he called his. He must have lost that memory. It was hard to tell. "Did they tell you anything?"

"Quite a bit, actually." Ash poured water into the kettle and put it over the fire once more. "That, combined with the wait, is what kept me."

Answers were right there. Derek could sense it. Impatience drove him, but he stopped himself from demanding the information. Ash had done him a favor. The least Derek could do was let him speak in his own time. But knowing the answers were close, things that had the potential to fill the gaping holes in his memory, was almost too much.

Ash walked to the chair from earlier and sat with a long sigh. He scratched his jaw and adjusted in his seat. "You wished to know about a skirmish with dragons."

"I did." Derek leaned forward, his muscles taut with anticipation.

"There was something recently."

The spike of elation at knowing Miena hadn't lied died a quick death the moment Derek discerned that Ash hadn't continued. "What is it?"

"Dragons were involved, but they didn't fight each other. They, along with other magicals, stood against a Star Person."

It was like being kicked in the balls. Derek slowly leaned back in his chair. "Miena?"

"The name they heard was Villette. That doesn't mean anything. People change their names all the time," Ash hurried to add.

But Derek knew it was someone different. He couldn't say why, but he did. "What color hair did this Villette have?"

"Blond."

"Miena has brown hair."

Ash's lips twisted. "Could be magic altering her appearance."

"Did they kill Villette?"

"No idea," Ash replied with a slight shake of his head. "Might've. Or she could've vanished herself. They move like that."

Derek looked into the fire and watched the flames dance around the kettle, slowly heating the water. It made him think about the woman in the dream and the ends of her hair. They had sparked just like the fire.

"I can see this news isn't what you were hoping for."

Derek grunted. "You could say that."

"That doesn't mean the battle you speak of didn't occur. It could've been deep in dragon territory."

"And I won't know if that's true unless I go and see for myself. Where I could potentially be attacked and killed."

Ash crossed his arms over his chest and shrugged. "You'd know then, though."

Derek glanced at Ash to find the tomte grinning. He shook his head and found a smile pulling at his lips, too. "Do you always look at the world in such a way?"

"It helps to get a different perspective. There's enough doom and gloom to go around without me adding any. I prefer to find the positive in things."

They fell silent until the kettle whistled. Derek watched Ash move around, making them tea again. He tried to decline, but Ash put the cup in his hand anyway. Derek shrugged and drank it.

"I've found that tea solves everything," Ash said, a grin curving his lips as he sipped. "If you're cold, it warms you. If you're hot, it cools you. If you don't feel good, it soothes you. If you're down, it revives you. In other words, whatever the problem is, make tea."

Derek could find no fault in Ash's words. The tomte seemed so sure of himself. About everything. Perhaps Derek had been the same before. Would he ever be so certain of things again? Or would he always have a kernel of doubt, waiting to rise at the most inopportune moment?

"What are you going to do?" Ash asked.

Derek lifted one shoulder. "I have no idea." But he couldn't remain with Ash. He had to take some kind of action. Besides, he wouldn't be the reason Miena entered Ash's home.

"Let's go over what you know for certain."

"Very little, I assure you."

Ash waved away his words. "Humor me."

"All right," he replied with a sigh. "I know I'm a dragon. I can shift from that form to this one and back again at will."

"What else?"

Derek searched his thoughts. "I know basic things, but I didn't even know my name when I woke."

"What about the dream? Did anything seem familiar?"

"There was a woman. I can't see her face. She's trying to talk to me, but I can't make out all the words."

Ash scratched his chin. "Hmm. You missed one. Miena."

"I suppose you could consider her a known fact."

"Of course, you can. Fact one: She's a Star Person named Miena. Fact two: She wants you to attack the dragons. Fact three: She was there when you woke and told you what she wanted you to know."

Derek ran a hand down his face. It was all the truth. The only thing he didn't know was if what Miena said was genuine.

"That's a lot of certainty, if you ask me," Ash said and sipped his tea. "Are you sure she's a Star Person?"

"I felt her power. It was...intense. Something about Miena warned me not to push her."

Ash grunted. "Then it sounds as if she was being honest about herself. What we don't know is if there was a battle, or if you received a head injury."

"What else but a head injury could take my memories?" A shiver ran down Derek's spine when Ash quickly looked away. "Ash? What do you know?"

The old tomte looked into his teacup, his jaw working. He waved his hand dismissively. "Talk. Hearsay."

There was no way Derek was letting this go. Ash knew something, and he wanted to know what that was. "From others, or your people?"

"It might be nothing."

That meant it could be something. "Tell me. Please. I have enough hidden from me. I'd rather face whatever you don't want to tell me than keep wondering."

Ash blew out a long breath and lifted his gaze to Derek. "A very, very long time ago, humans were found wandering. They didn't know their names, nor could they speak about their pasts. They knew how to walk, talk, and other basic things, but they didn't have a single recollection about anything before they were found."

"Just like me. Where was this?"

"Like I said, it was a long time ago. Thousands of years."

Derek set the cup on the floor and scooted to the edge of the chair. "Where?"

"Stonemore."

"That's the second time you've mentioned that city."

Ash wrinkled his face. "It's a bad place. Evil resides there."

"What happened to the mortals who lost their memories?"

"They had to build new lives. As far as I know, they never remembered their pasts."

Dread iced Derek's blood. He'd feared exactly that, and to hear it had happened to others was disconcerting. "Did anyone ever figure out what had happened to them?"

"There are some very formidable magicals out there. Some claim dragons could overpower all of us if they wanted. It is hard to know for sure since your kind mostly stays on their side of the barrier." Ash rested an ankle on his opposite knee. "To my knowledge, no one ever figured out who damaged the humans in such a way."

"Could it have been the Star People?"

Ash finished his tea. "Sure. It could've been anyone, really."

"We stated your facts, and it hasn't gotten me much of anywhere. What if everything Miena told me is true?"

"There's only one place you'll find answers."

"The dragons." The very place Miena wanted him to go.

Ash caught his gaze. "What are you going to do?"

"What I have to do."

"I'd go with you if I could, but I'm not much good in battle. I'd mostly be there for moral support."

Derek grinned despite himself. "With tea."

"Always tea."

They shared a smile. It felt like Derek had found a friend. He had enjoyed himself at Ash's, even if he was swimming in tea. He didn't want to leave the cozy home within the tree, but he couldn't stay. Miena might come looking for him, and Ash and his people didn't want to be near any Star People. The longer Derek remained, the more that became possible.

He pushed to his feet. "Thank you for your hospitality. I won't forget it."

"We tomte usually keep to ourselves unless we know other magicals. They know about you now. Don't be surprised if you see more of the tomte around."

"Only if they have tea."

Ash's face split into a wide smile as he got to his feet. "I'll make sure of it."

CHAPTER 10

Deciding to head south was easier than actually doing it. From the moment they'd agreed on the direction, the discussion on who would transport them began. Every time Rhi spoke up, a vein on Con's temple protruded a little more.

"The larger our group is, the more we'll stand out," Villette reasoned.

Merrill's withering look would've felled most, but Villette ignored him. "And the more we have to battle your sister, the better our odds."

"It's settled then," Kora said. "Let's go."

Alasdair jerked away when Villette reached for him. "No way am I going anywhere with her leading."

"I already said I would," Rhi added.

Lotti held up her hands. "This doesn't need to be so difficult."

"That's right. It doesn't. We need to go. Remember? Time is of the essence," Kora interjected in an effort to get things moving.

But no one listened.

"Enough," Con said without raising his voice.

Everyone still went silent. Even Villette. Con's black eyes flashed dangerously when Merrill's lips parted to speak. The two stared at each other for a long moment before Merrill crossed his arms over his chest and clamped his lips together.

"It willna take seven of us to locate Miena or Derek. Rhi and I will stay behind. The moment you find Miena, let us know," Con said.

Kora was surprised when his gaze turned to her. She knew what he would say before the words came. "Don't. Don't you dare tell me to stay behind."

"He has a point," Merrill said.

Kora shot him a glower then slid her gaze back to Con. "This happened to Derek because of me."

"Oh, I think we can safely say the blame lies with someone else," Alasdair said and pointedly looked at Villette.

Villette sighed dramatically. "For once, this isn't about me."

"As much as I hate to say it, Con's right," Rhi stated.

"If Derek gets your scent, he'll come straight for you," Lotti told Kora.

Villette lifted a finger. "I also agree with Con."

No one acknowledged her.

Kora couldn't believe everyone sided against her. "I could be what brings him to us."

"If he's near Miena, maybe," Con said.

Merrill shook his head. "I understand your need to be there, but you're no' thinking beyond that. You know what it's like to have Bryok and Gordon after you. It will take several of us to get you clear if Derek comes after you."

Everything he said made sense, but Kora still wouldn't relent. She couldn't. "We have Miena's general location. So? That doesn't mean Derek is there. We have to find him."

"We will," Con assured her. "But, as you said, we have a general location. This will take steps."

Villette wrinkled her nose. "If you don't want a dead hellhound, I'd keep her away from Derek until we know he isn't under my sister's spell."

"Nay," Kora said, but now she was the one being ignored.

And she hated it.

Worse, she understood it. It would be her argument if she were on the other side. That didn't make accepting it any easier, however.

Within moments, Lotti, Alasdair, Merrill, and Villette were gone.

"This isn't right," Kora said. "I'm meant to find him."

Rhi gently touched her arm. "Come. Return with us to Iron Hall."

Kora looked at the table, her stomach churning with apprehension. What if they found Derek with Miena? What if he attacked? What if he was on Earth, attacking everyone there? The what-ifs continued in a steady stream until her stomach was a ball of knots.

As she turned toward Rhi and Con, she suddenly remembered Daelya. "I promised Daelya I would come back for her."

"The mortal who can sense magic in others?" Con asked.

Kora nodded. "She was too fearful to come out of the room where Miena was held."

"No one here is stopping us." Rhi looked at Con and shrugged. "Let's go get her."

Con started to nod when he seemed to see something on the wall. He moved and trailed a finger down it.

"What is that?" Rhi asked, her brow furrowing as she walked to take a closer look.

Con's face was a mask of fury as his gaze moved around the cavern. "Claw marks."

"Miena hinted that Derek had been here before," Kora said. She then pointed to where Gordon had been sleeping. "The amethyst-colored one was there."

Rhi stopped Con when he would've looked. "Don't, my love. We can't change the past, but we can change the future."

"Aye," he murmured.

Rhi rubbed her hand up and down his arm before motioning Kora over. "Tell me where we need to go."

"The top. The section is destroyed. You can't miss it," she explained and took Rhi's hand.

Con grunted. "The place where Villette tried to kill Shaw and Nia."

"I've seen it from the outside. I can get us there," Rhi said.

Kora was getting used to being jumped long distances. Derek no longer had his cuff, which meant that wasn't an option for them anymore. If they even found him.

Her thoughts halted when Kora found herself standing outside the open doorway to Miena's prison. Kora released Rhi and rushed into the room, but Daelya wasn't there.

"Did she leave?" Rhi asked.

Kora shrugged and scanned the room again. "I hope so. She refused to leave before."

"Does Miena know about her abilities?" Con asked.

Kora nodded as she met his gaze. "They spent a lot of time in here together."

"We'll keep an eye out for her. It's all we can do," Rhi said.

Con grunted. "We should go."

Kora took one more look at the place where Miena had stood for a millennia. The chains were gone, likely melted once the flower was removed. Rhi was right. There was no changing the past. Mistakes had been made, and the only thing she could do was ensure she learned the lessons.

She turned to find Con and Rhi waiting for her. Kora walked to the couple, and within moments, stood in the center of Iron Hall. Someone called Rhi's name, pulling her away, and Con stalked away to who knew where. Kora imagined he was going to find the other Kings to...do whatever it was they did. She was left alone once more.

In a way, she was glad. She was still fuming about being left behind. Though she had been the one who'd said she needed help. The entire situation was her doing. If she were able to fix it on her own, she would.

What was she to do now? Sit and wait? Wonder? Plan? Hope? Pray?

She turned toward the stairs that led outside, then pivoted to another set of steps. Kora looked at the many other staircases that led to many other hallways.

"The city is enormous," a voice said behind her.

Kora turned to find a woman with long, black curls and hazel eyes. The long-sleeved, dark green tunic looked amazing against her brown skin. The top hung to her hips, and beneath it were tan trousers that clung to her legs. A wide leather belt showcased a narrow waist and the dagger strapped to her leg.

"I'm Tamlyn," she said. "I didn't get to introduce myself earlier. We're a large bunch."

Kora tried to smile but wasn't sure she succeeded.

"There's food if you're hungry," Tamlyn offered.

"I don't think I could eat right now."

Tamlyn's lips twisted. "I know that feeling all too well." She shrugged. "There are plenty of rooms. I can show you to one if you'd like to be alone. The beds are nice. Or maybe a soak in the tub. I could also take you on a tour of Iron Hall. We keep exploring and finding more of the city. Much of it is in ruins, but we're slowly putting it back together."

The moment Tamlyn said *bath*, Kora stopped listening. "The bath. I'd like that."

"I thought you might," she said with a grin. "Follow me."

They walked to a side stairway. The steps led to a corridor that widened where lights hung on the wall between painted murals. If Kora's mind weren't so scrambled with her current issues, she would've liked to look closer at the paintings. For now, she was doing well putting one foot in front of the other.

"I told Cullen we need to label the main corridors and especially the hallways that branch off them," Tamlyn said. "It's very easy to get lost. I've done it so many times it's embarrassing. If it happens to you, just call out. Someone will hear you."

Tamlyn took the first left and stopped at the third door on the left. She pushed the door open. "This is one of my favorite rooms."

Kora looked through the doorway and gaped at the beauty within. The far wall had a forest scene painted on it in greens, whites, and pinks. In the corner, a tree had been painted with an abundance of leaves and huge, pink flowers, its limbs contouring the ceiling as well as the walls. To her astonishment, someone had designed the tree to appear real as it jutted from the wall.

The bed was covered in different white fabrics. There were ruffles and lace, velvet and linen, cotton and silk. Three large, white pillows sat against the wall. There was a round, white pillow with ruffles, a rectangular one in white with pale pink dots, and a soft pink pillow that looked like a bow. A white and pink rug graced the floor.

To the right were gossamer curtains edged in lace. Kora was drawn to them. It looked as if there was a window behind them, with the sun shining through. But when she opened the curtains, it was a lighted glass panel that gave the appearance of the sun and showcased a second forest setting. She touched the glass in amazement. Kora turned to tell Tamlyn how beautiful everything was when she caught sight of the opposite side of the room.

There, along the wall, was another pane of glass arching high overhead. It was lit like the other, and another forest scene had been painted behind it. Just below the window was a freestanding, white oval tub. A pale pink drying towel had been folded and placed over its rim. There was a basket filled with pink and white soaps in different animal shapes and another white and pink rug running alongside the tub. Farther along the wall was a white pedestal with a bowl atop it, and a silver faucet protruding from the wall.

"I've never seen anything so beautiful," Kora said, awed by it all.

Tamlyn beamed. "We're all getting to play around with designs."

"I'm afraid to touch anything."

"Don't be. This is your space now. Unless you'd like to see another."

Kora shook her head. "This is perfect."

"Good," Tamlyn said. "I'll leave you to your bath then."

Tamlyn exited and shut the door behind her, leaving Kora alone. Just as she'd wanted. She sat on the edge of the bed and removed first one boot and then the other before staring at the tub. The full weight of everything crashed down on her in that instant. She curled up at the foot of the mattress and tucked her arm beneath her head as she pulled up memories of Derek. She imagined him molding himself to her back, his big hand resting possessively on her hip as his lips pressed against the sensitive skin behind her ear. A tear fell, rolling over the bridge of her nose and onto her cheek before dripping into her hair.

CHAPTER 11

Every step that led Derek away from Ash was a step closer to the truth. At least, he hoped that was the case. He had found a certain kinship with the tomte, and it was difficult to walk away from it. Especially since Derek didn't know what—if anything—awaited him.

Would it be death? Was there someone he had shared his life with? Was it the woman he kept seeing in his dreams? Did he have other family? Siblings, perhaps? Friends?

Enemies?

Ash's words came back to him then.

"You've been given a second chance. For some, that means starting fresh. You could live among mortals without them ever knowing who you really are. No one would blame you if you wanted to forget about the dragons, war, and the Star People."

It was tempting to set aside all the questions, but he wouldn't be able to do it for long. He had an itch within him. Like scratching at a scab. He *had* to find the answers. Even if he didn't like what he uncovered.

So, he kept walking east, all the while hoping he would one day return to share another cup of tea with Ash.

During his trek, Derek skirted villages and homes and kept his pace quick. Once the sun set, he shifted and spread his wings. He loved the feeling of the wind as it caressed his scales. He soared high to blend into the inky night, scanning the horizon. But he saw no sign of other dragons. He scanned the ground, mapping out the terrain and location of the cities in his mind. Just in case.

Maybe it was something he had always done. It certainly felt like an action a warrior would take. What did being a warrior feel like? He couldn't answer that. Hopefully, he knew since he was potentially about to face off against enemies.

As he flew toward the dragons' land, a feeling of unease grew. Nothing felt right. But it was where he belonged. Ash had said he could blend in with the mortals, but he couldn't. Not really. Derek couldn't imagine spending the rest of his life in his human form, foregoing the shape of his true self. And that was exactly what he would have to do to blend in.

There was only one place for him. One place he could be who he was without judgment or condemnation. *If* they let him return.

Derek covered five times as much ground in the air as he had on foot. It was an hour before dawn when he soared over a mountain range. He spotted a city built into the side of the mountain. He barely spared the forest a glance once he sensed the wall of magic up ahead. There was no denying the dragon magic. He had found the border.

He didn't get close. Not yet. Derek dipped a wing and turned south. He kept the border to his left until he sailed over a great body of water. He swung around once more. This time, he flew closer to the barrier. His journey took him over a canyon the border divided in two. The chasm eventually gave way to another forest and then another mountain range. After that, it was wild grassland that eventually turned into hills of sand.

Was one place better than another to cross over? Derek turned to fly back over ground he had already covered. He hadn't gone far when he looked to his left and spotted a dragon. Nay, many dragons. Some were perched on the mountains while others flew around and between the peaks. The first rays of sunlight broke the horizon and lit their scales. He stared in awe at the various colors. One of them could be a friend.

Or an enemy.

He almost went to them but changed his mind when he spotted a much larger dragon ahead, flying alone beside the border. Unlike the group he'd just seen, this one was only one color. The sea green scales contrasted starkly with the gray morning sky.

For reasons Derek didn't understand, he immediately dove into the forest. He tucked his wings to get beneath the cover of the canopy before the dragon spotted him. The trees were heavy with branches that scraped against his scales. Limbs tore off with a groan, followed by snapping and popping noises. Derek shifted in midair. There was no elegant landing this time. He plummeted to the ground, slamming into branches that twisted and flipped him. His hands groped for purchase and finally managed to grab hold of a smaller branch. Derek found himself dangling above the ground by one hand.

He let go and landed with bent knees, then looked back at the damage he'd done. He winced. His crash had been deafening to his ears. Had the sea green dragon heard it? Derek waited to see if anyone approached, but there was no sign of anyone.

The bark of the tree bit into Derek's bare back as he leaned against it. It bothered him that he had hidden at the sight of the lone dragon. Had Derek subconsciously recognized him? Remaining hidden wouldn't uncover any of the answers he yearned for. But did he want to immediately tangle with a potential opponent?

"This isn't where I thought I'd find you."

Derek stiffened at the sound of Miena's voice behind him. She came around the tree, plucking petals off a yellow flower. Her dark hair was parted down the middle and hung around her in a thick curtain. This time, she had chosen a peach gown. The long-sleeved top was sheer lace, showing her dark nipples. The plunging neckline emphasized her full breasts as the V tapered to just above her navel. The flowy, white skirt had a peach floral pattern and stopped at her calves to show black boots. Dark green fabric matching the leaves on the skirt wrapped around her waist several times and tied at the side so the ends fell against the skirt.

"Do you like?" she asked as she held out her arms and turned in a circle.

Derek shrugged. "Sure."

She huffed, her arms dropping against her legs. "Not exactly what I was going for."

He became acutely aware of her gaze centered on his groin. Derek immediately clothed himself.

Her brows raised, and her lips tightened. "You hurt my feelings."

"Your dress is fine. What is it you want?"

She flicked her fingers to the side, and Derek flew through the air, slamming into a tree before being jerked back, only to crash into another. He hit the ground, and pain radiated through him. His body promptly began to heal. He rose up on his forearm and scowled at Miena.

"That's the last warning you'll get," she informed him, her attention back on plucking the flower's petals. "I deserve respect. I saved you, after all."

Derek had detected her power and suspected he had only gotten a taste of what she could dole out. If that was a taste, he didn't want to feel the full force of her magic. He climbed to his feet and dusted himself off.

"I assume you found what you needed since you're finally here," she said as if she hadn't tossed him around like a leaf.

He scrutinized her in the silence. When she pinned him with her green eyes, he dipped his chin in affirmation.

"Good." She tossed what was left of the flower aside. "Just what I wanted to hear. What's your plan?"

"Cross the border."

"And then?" She made a sound at the back of her throat when he didn't answer right away. "Surely, you have more of a plan than that."

Derek raked his hands through his hair, pulling out a broken stick. "You've not given me much."

"I gave you all you needed to know. Go after the Kings."

"How many are there?"

She sighed loudly, irritation crossing her face. "It doesn't matter. You can take all of them."

"I couldn't before."

"Trust me. You can now."

He glanced through the trees toward the border. "Why are you sending me? You could easily remove them."

"You're right. I could," she stated with a haughty grin. "The Kings didn't wrong me. They wronged *you*. And while I enjoy... meddling with subordinates, I refrain."

Derek didn't buy a single word of it. If she was all she claimed to be, nothing would stand in the way of her doing whatever she wanted. There was more to the story.

"You aren't going to take my word for it, are you?" she asked in a flat tone.

"Nay."

She briefly turned her head away and blew out a breath. "I'd hoped I wouldn't have to tell you this part, but it seems you aren't going to leave things alone."

"Tell me what?" he pushed.

A pained expression tightened her face. "You were...with someone. A female you loved. Your...mate."

An image of the faceless woman who haunted his dreams filled his mind.

"She was protecting her eggs when a hellhound came upon her. They fought. The hellhound destroyed the eggs. And when your mate went after her, the Kings stopped her, choosing to protect the hellhound."

Derek's legs were unsteady beneath him. He grabbed the tree to hold himself upright. He waffled between outrage and disbelief.

"Your mate didn't relent. That's when...well, that's when the Kings killed her."

The world began to spin. Derek opened his mouth to suck in air, but his lungs refused to let any in. Miena was suddenly beside him. He saw her lips moving but no longer heard her. His mate had been killed. The eggs... He dug his fingers into the bark and felt talons sprout, sinking deep into the wood.

The moment Miena had mentioned the eggs, something snapped in him. He knew she spoke the truth. He had helped guard them. He had run his hands over them. That, combined with the woman he kept seeing, meant it was real.

"Do you understand why I told you to kill any hellhound you come across? It could be the one who murdered your children."

If he did find a hellhound, he would kill it. The entire species would pay for taking his family from him. He turned toward the dragons' land. And the Kings? They would get what they deserved.

He shook off Miena's hands and started toward the border. She called his name, but he ignored her and kept walking. Derek shifted before reaching the barrier and striding through it. His gaze lifted, waiting for the sea green dragon to appear. None came. Derek launched himself into the air and happened to glance back at Miena to find her standing within the forest, a smile on her face.

That probably should have bothered him more than it did, but he was being ripped in half by grief. Anguish this deep and painful had to be real. He had lost more than his memories. He had lost his mate and family.

Derek flew along the border, looking for another patrol. He grinned when he saw the morning sun glinting off sea green scales ahead of him. He flew faster, his focus locked on his target as he soared higher. When he was directly over the dragon, Derek tucked his wings and dove, talons at the ready.

The dragon jerked away at the last second. Derek spread his wings and beat them furiously to gain height once more. He turned to look for his foe when something slammed into him. Derek found himself staring into his opponent's eyes. They each grabbed hold of each other, clawing and ripping as they hovered in the air.

Until something barreled into them.

The sea green dragon let out a roar of pain. Derek couldn't even manage that. His body had gone stiff. Wind howled around him as he plummeted, scanning the sky for what had attacked him. The only thing he saw before he hit the ground was the sea green dragon falling with him.

CHAPTER 12

By sheer will alone, Derek rolled to all four feet and stood. His entire body spasmed with pain that alternated between stinging and throbbing. The agony seeped into his very bones. He scanned the area and strove to shake off the malicious feeling clinging to him. He had gotten a glimpse of an object floating in the air, but it hadn't been solid. Something dark swirled angrily within it. He felt it watching him, even though he couldn't discern its eyes. But Derek felt its rancor and uncontrollable rage. Then it suddenly took off with tendrils trailing behind it that made him think of spindly limbs.

Derek glanced at the sea green dragon who was now in human form but remained unmoving. Derek didn't waste any time unfurling his wings and launching into the air to fly after whatever it was that had attacked him. Pain in his left wing kept him from getting very far. Agony shot through him with every movement.

He glanced at his wing but couldn't see a wound. But he knew it was there.

He couldn't fly with only one wing. Derek bobbed clumsily in the sky, trying to reach a clearing within the forest. The throbbing became unbearable, and he dropped gracelessly through the trees, doing his best to miss as many branches as possible. It might have worked had he shifted to his human form, but he didn't want to. He was in dragon territory, and he would remain in that form.

The tumble was long, exhausting, and brutal, provoking his already pain-riddled body with even more suffering. The landing was jarring and sudden, but he was glad to finally be on the ground. He looked up to see the large hole he had created in the canopy.

Derek couldn't wait for his injuries to heal. He had to keep following what had attacked him. For all he knew, the Kings had sent it. And he wouldn't be taken unawares again. He slowly got his feet under him and attempted to stand. The muscles of his back seized violently. He bit off a roar and sank his talons into the ground, gouging it.

It seemed like an eternity before the worst of the pain subsided, and he could breathe easier. Too much time had passed for him to follow his assailant now, and that bothered him. Worse, he was still in no condition to fight.

The trees hid him, but for how long? Especially after the hole he had made during his fall. The healing process was happening, but it seemed slower than usual. Derek needed to kill the Dragon King before he woke—or alerted the others. His muscles began to gradually loosen. It was easy to get lost in the pain, but he retreated from it, shutting it out as he closed his eyes and began to plan how he would slay those responsible for destroying his family.

"Derek."

The sound of the woman's voice drew him. He wasn't sleeping this time, but she still came to him. It never entered his mind to shut her out or ignore her. He needed her.

She stood before him, and then she was in his arms. A sigh of contentment left him. Her touch healed like nothing else could. He held her tightly, her warmth familiar, comforting. He wrapped a cool wave of dark hair around his finger. It was soft and silky. He knew what it felt like to sink his fingers into it, how it draped like a curtain around his head when she leaned over him.

"Derek...have...me."

"I don't understand."

She leaned her head back, and he looked down into her face, his heart breaking when he found it was still blurred. There were dark spots now where her eyes should be. At least her lips were still visible. He brushed his thumb over the full bottom one.

"Say it again," he urged.

"Derek...have...me," she repeated urgently.

He shook his head "Why can't I hear all the words?"

"Derek...have...me!"

Whatever she said was important. He knew it, but no matter how hard he strained, he couldn't make out what exactly she tried to tell him.

Then she vanished like smoke from his arms. He grabbed at the air to keep her with him, but she was gone. Again.

A twig snapped. Derek kept his eyes closed and listened. Someone was coming toward him. Several someones.

"Is he dead?"

"I don't know. Poke him."

"You poke him."

"Get Jens to do it."

"Bollocks. You wanted to come see. You do it, Luc."

Derek listened to the young voices that had come up on his left. He had counted at least four adolescents. He cracked open an eye and found them huddled together while attempting to look brave. Their arguing continued, and by their conversation, Derek realized no adults were around. He lifted his head, pinning the group of four with a look.

They jerked back, their eyes rounded in surprise. They were about twice as tall as the average human male, their scales a myriad of colors.

The one with the lavender and pink scales glanced at the others and said, *"We saw you fall."*

"How did you make it as far as you did with that wing?" the dragon with mostly lavender scales accented with mauve asked.

"Did you see what attacked me?" Derek asked instead of answering.

The four looked at each other, confusion marring their faces. The first one spoke again. *"You fought one of the Kings."*

"There was something else there with us," Derek insisted.

The group backed up as one, their gazes darting around nervously. He heard one of them say something about an *invisible entity.*

"What is that?" he asked.

"It's been striking out against dragons for some time," Lavender and Mauve said. *"It killed dozens the first time it came at us."*

Anger churned in Derek as he got to his feet. The pain was

minimal now. Not gone, but nothing that would keep him down. *"Is no one doing anything about it?"*

"The Kings are. But no one can see it. Not even them."

That took Derek aback. If no one could see it, how could he? Or were the Kings lying? It was time they answered for a lot of things. *"Where are the Kings?"*

The adolescents frowned, looking at him with suspicion.

"I've not ventured from my home until recently," he told them. Hopefully, it sounded reasonable.

"You sound like my mum never wanting to venture out. Cairnkeep is in the mountain range to the south. You won't be able to miss it."

"You'll know they're Kings because they're all solid colors."

Derek tested his wing to make sure it could hold him, then nodded at the juveniles. *"Thanks."*

They began talking among themselves as he walked away, their attention shifting to other things. The moment he was in the clearing, he took to the sky and flew south. Dragons were everywhere. Many were in the distance, but some were closer. Others were playing in the lake, and even more were flying together in groups. He saw younglings of all ages, but it was the small ones just learning to fly that made him want to watch.

That could have been him with his children.

Grief hit him hard, followed closely by despair and a swell of anger that roiled within him, narrowing everything to a haze of red. He would have his vengeance.

His wrath was intense and terrifying. It shut out everything and everyone except the Kings. They might have gotten the best of him before, but not this time. His dead mate and children would be avenged.

Derek didn't look at the landscape. He didn't care about the other dragons. He sought Cairnkeep and any dragons with solid-colored scales. Everyone steered clear of him. Whatever kindness he might have had was depleted. His heart was gone, replaced by hardened stone that had been shattered into dust.

Ash had been right. He was a warrior. One who would wage war on the tyrants and oppressors.

The time of the Dragon Kings was finished. He would make sure of that.

CHAPTER 13

Kora's eyes snapped open. She lay quietly, listening for what had woken her. At first, she didn't hear anything. Then came the rush of footsteps running down the hallway. She pushed into a seated position, then ran to the door barefoot, pulling it open to look outside. She caught sight of someone's backside before they turned the corner.

Now that she was in the corridor, she could hear others. Something was happening. She ran after the person she saw, hoping she remembered how to get back to the main area. By the time she reached the stairs, a crowd was already gathered. She scanned the faces, looking for someone she knew.

She saw Tamlyn and Sian, but both were herding the children through a door. Con stood at the front of the group with a blonde whose hair was the same color as his. On Con's other side was a man with the same dark eyes as Con.

"Kora."

She spun at the voice coming up beside her. A sigh went through her at the sight of Rhi. "Is it Merrill and the others? Have they found Derek?"

"It isn't Merrill."

Three words, but they sucked all the hope from her. That was when she noticed that Rhi was watching her carefully. "What is it? What aren't you telling me?"

"There was an attack on a King patrolling the border."

They thought it was Derek. Maybe they even had confirmation. And that hung in the air between them. Kora wanted to ask, but the words were locked in her throat. She wanted it to be Derek. Didn't she? At least she would know where he was.

"We're still sorting out the details. Hector hasn't woken."

It took her two tries to find her voice. "It was Derek, wasn't it?"

Rhi pressed her lips together and glanced at Con. "Maybe."

"I don't understand. What do you mean, *maybe*?"

"There is an entity here that only Star People can see. It targets dragons."

Kora blinked a couple of times to digest that information. "If the Star People can see it, why doesn't Lotti kill it?"

"She tried. She thought she had succeeded, too."

"So, that's what attacked Hector this morning?"

Rhi dropped her gaze to the floor for a heartbeat. "There were indentations in the ground to suggest that two dragons had been hit. When we were alerted, we only found Hector. He had injuries that appeared to come from a battle with another dragon."

Kora swallowed. The up-and-down emotions were making her nauseous. "All right. What does this mean?"

"Others are looking for any sign of Derek. He has distinctive markings that will make him easier to find. Con healed Hector, and we're waiting for him to wake so he can tell us if it was Derek."

Kora heard Con talking but wasn't paying attention to his words. "I can't just sit here. Let me go out and look for Derek."

"It isn't that simple," Rhi said. "The dragons are getting irritated by the number of mortals on their land. They don't care that we're with the Kings. They don't care if we have magic. They even consider me human. Tensions are high. It's why the Kings with mates live at Iron Hall."

"The dragons hate us that much?"

Rhi's lips twisted. "If you knew the history, you'd understand. And I'll be happy to tell you the story one day. For now, come with me."

"Where are we going?" Kora asked as she trailed behind the Fae.

"To Hector."

Kora was shocked they would bring her to him, but she was delighted at the prospect of getting to hear Hector's account firsthand. She couldn't decide if she wanted him to have been attacked by Derek or not. On one hand, it would let them know where Derek was. On the other, it would prove that Miena had indeed turned him into what she wanted.

But there was more to be concerned about.

Kora hurried to fall into step with Rhi. "This other entity you spoke of, you're telling me it's invisible?"

"Unfortunately," Rhi said. "It took down fifty dragons and then went after my children. The twins were hit separately, but it was close for them. Con reached them in time."

"Everything can be killed. We just need to figure out how."

Rhi turned her head to her and smiled. "We?"

Kora shrugged. "Aye."

"It's good to have you join us."

"I've always hated dragons. It's been a change to see them as anything but my enemies."

Rhi slowed her steps and came to a halt. "There are good and bad people. Maybe I'll tell you about the horror that was my biological mother someday. My point is that it's easy to lump everyone into a single group. I'm not saying you didn't have a good reason, though."

"I understand. If Derek had told me early on what he was, I likely wouldn't have gotten to know him. And I would've missed out on…" She swallowed around the lump in her throat.

Rhi touched her arm. "I understand. More than you realize. Come. Let's see if Hector has woken."

Kora followed Rhi into the room. A man lay on a table in the center of the space. Along the walls were shelves containing books and jars of various sizes. There were more shelves with glass containers with small markings she couldn't read. Dried herbs were hanging from pegs. There was also a chart labeled *The Alchemists Table of Symbols* on the wall.

"This is one of Sian's workrooms," Rhi explained.

Kora turned her attention to the table once more. Hector lay unmoving on his back, a blanket covering him up to his shoulders. His wavy, light brown hair was tangled, and there was dried blood on his face and some on his shoulder that disappeared beneath the blanket.

"The Kings are all but immortal," Rhi said in a soft voice as she walked to the table. "On Earth, only another King can kill a King. We've only recently learned that Star People can kill them, too. This entity is getting close. Too close," she added in a whisper.

Footsteps sounded behind her. Kora moved from the doorway as Con entered, followed by the man and woman she had seen earlier.

"Any change?" Con asked. Rhi shook her head in answer. Con sighed before his dark gaze slid to her. "Kora, these are our children. Eurwen and Brandr. They rule the dragons here."

Kora offered them a nod of greeting. Eurwen had Con's blond hair and Rhi's silver eyes, while Brandr had Rhi's black hair and Con's dark eyes.

"I'm sorry we weren't here yesterday to greet you," Eurwen said. "We were out on patrol."

Brandr glanced at his sister and nodded. "If Derek is within the borders, we'll find him."

"That might be exactly what he wants. Especially if he was the one who attacked Hector," Kora said.

Con crossed his arms over his chest as he stood at Hector's head. "I explained the situation to the twins."

"When we locate Derek, we'll subdue him," Brandr explained.

Rhi's brows furrowed. "Will that work?"

"It will have to," Eurwen replied.

Con nodded once. "It will."

"How bad were Hector's injuries?" Brandr asked.

Con said nothing as Rhi grimaced. "Worse than yours."

"That thing is what we should be going after," Brandr said. "Fuck Villette. It willna stop until it kills one of us."

A groan came from the table before Hector said, "I do believe that's the intent."

"Doona move," Con said as he rested a hand on Hector's shoulder. "Rest."

The tension went out of Hector's limbs. His throat bobbed as he swallowed, then he opened his eyes. Rhi was the first to go to him. She took his hand and squeezed. Hector gave her a lopsided grin, then nodded to Brandr and Eurwen. His eyes locked with Con's. No words were spoken aloud, but something passed between them. Kora tried not to fidget when Hector's dark eyes turned to her.

"This is Kora," Rhi told him.

Hector pushed into a seated position, the blanket falling away to reveal a muscular body. "The hellhound." Hector flashed her a smile. "Good to meet you. Though I doona think you're here for an introduction."

"We saw evidence of another dragon when we reached you," Con said. "What happened?"

Hector swung his legs over the side of the table. As he did, clothes covered him, but it was no attire Kora had ever seen. The pants were a thick, dark blue color, the white shirt was plain with a round neck and short sleeves that contoured to his torso, and his boots were nothing like the ones she knew.

"I spotted him on patrol," Hector said.

Kora forgot about his clothes as she refocused. Words leaped from her. "Derek? You saw Derek?"

"I did," he told her. "He dove into the trees, so I kept my distance to see what he might do. It wasna long before he returned. I let him think I didna know he was behind me. He attacked, and I feinted to the side before I went after him." Hector paused and looked at the others. "The entity came at us almost immediately. It struck me first, but I think Derek got hit harder. We fell. I expected to get struck again, but then we slammed into the ground. I doona remember anything after that."

Brandr fisted his hands at his sides. "Fuck."

"The being hasn't been seen since the encounter with Lotti and the others," Eurwen said. "I really believed it had gone off to die."

Brandr cut his eyes to her. "We wouldna be so lucky."

"When we reached you, Derek was gone," Con told Hector. "The creature has never taken anyone before."

Kora's confusion must have shown on her face because Rhi said, "Hector alerted us that he might have found Derek. Con and a few other Kings went to investigate."

Without telling her. Kora shouldn't be upset, but she was. She wanted to see Derek. Maybe seeing her would be all it took for his memories to return. Then, this nightmare could be over.

She knew it was a foolish dream, but it was all she had.

"If the entity didn't take Derek, then where is he?" Eurwen asked.

Brandr ran a hand over his jaw. "The dragons will tell us if they see him."

Hector stood, tossed the blanket aside, and shrugged, his lips twisting. "All I know is there was murder in his eyes." Hector looked at Con. "The kind of vengeance we fought for too many years."

"Then we know what to do," Con replied.

Hector gathered his shoulder-length hair behind his head and tied it. "I'm no' sure he'll listen to reason."

"Then we make him," Eurwen said. "He'll have to calm down eventually."

Brandr grunted. "No' necessarily."

"Use me," Kora offered.

Everyone in the room turned to her.

"Let him get my scent. He'll come straight for me," she told them.

Rhi's face fell. "Only as a last resort."

"Do we have that kind of time?" Kora looked around the room. "I've known from the moment Miena took him that the only way I would find him again was to offer myself as bait."

Con stared at her with his black eyes. "He's a King, but he's a creation of a Star Person. We doona know the extent of his powers."

"He's saying we might no' be able to keep you alive," Hector explained.

Kora had wanted to die once. Now, she wanted to live, but she wanted that life with Derek. It wouldn't be much of one without him. "I understand and am prepared for whatever happens. Miena must be stopped. And Derek..." She blinked back tears. "He deserves to get his life back."

The mood in the room shifted to one of urgency and determination.

"We need Merrill," Con said and looked at Rhi. "We need to know every detail of what he knows about Derek's battle skills and magic." Con swung his head to Kora. "Until Merrill gets here, tell us what you know. Everything you can remember."

CHAPTER 14

"Derek has been spotted!"

Kora's heart dropped to her feet, and the hall came alive with movement. She had told them what little she knew or had witnessed of Derek's fighting skills. Merrill had arrived during her account and added his own. It hadn't taken long before they devised a plan. She didn't say anything. It wasn't as if she had much else to do but stand there. Derek had to get a whiff of her unique hellhound scent, and then he would come for her.

She curled her toes in the boots she had retrieved. Her feet were cold, but it had nothing to do with walking on the stones in her bare feet and everything to do with coming face-to-face with Derek again. She wanted this.

But she was scared of what she might find.

"Are you ready?" Rhi asked as she came up beside her.

There was a maelstrom of emotions spinning out of control within Kora. There was no denying their plan was dangerous, but no one could talk her out of it. They'd kept her from going with Lotti and the others. She wouldn't be held back from this. Not when there was a chance. That kept her going.

But she couldn't say all of that. Instead, Kora said the only thing she could. "I don't know."

"Remember, I'll be right beside you. You won't be able to see me, but you'll hear me."

Iron Hall's main room emptied quickly, leaving only Rhi and her. Everyone had a position, even if some were safely within the underground city.

"You don't have to do this," Rhi said. "Any of the Kings can stand in your place."

Kora shook her head. "I must do it."

"We won't let him get to you."

That wasn't something anyone could promise. Rhi's words were meant to offer comfort, and that was how Kora took them.

She and Rhi walked out of the city and into the canyon together. Kora didn't know how the others had crossed the border. It might have been discussed during the planning, but she had been too engrossed in deciding what she would say to Derek to pay attention. Now, she wished she had. They were details she might need to know.

"Derek is headed straight for Cairnkeep," Rhi said as she touched her arm.

Kora found herself at the top of the canyon, gazing across a boundary she couldn't see into the dragons' land. Cairnkeep. The capital where Eurwen and Brandr lived.

"The cage is ready and waiting for Derek." Rhi never broke stride as she guided Kora toward the obscure barrier.

Kora felt a growing resistance as she got closer to the border.

The dragons' home was a place she had feared beyond reason. It held the monsters of her nightmares. At least it had for a time. Still, she dragged her feet as she neared the barrier.

Rhi didn't push, simply stood with her and waited.

By going to Stonemore for Villette, Kora had faced her past. She had found love where it wasn't supposed to be. But the heart didn't care about fears or enemies. Derek had stood with her through it all.

If she could do all that, then she could lure in the man she loved so he could remember who he was.

Kora quickly stepped across the border. Magic slid against her skin as she passed through the barricade. Then, she stood on dragon land. It looked the same as it did from the other side of the border: wide-open landscape and mountains rising in the distance like knuckles on the hand of an ancient god.

"Ready?" Rhi asked.

Kora took a deep breath and nodded. She closed her eyes when Rhi reached for her hand. She didn't feel a change, but Kora knew she wasn't in the same place anymore. The air was crisp from the altitude. A cool breeze brushed her face, and the soft scent of rain lingered.

She opened her eyes and gasped at the beauty before her. They stood at the top of a mountain near the edge of a cliff. The sky was vibrant and clear, the sun a bright yellow dot rising over the distant peaks. She took in the trees and spotted evergreens mingled with the lush clusters of changing leaves. Mountains rose before her, even taller than the one she was on. Below was a steep valley where rocks protruded from the grass. Kora glanced behind her to find two identical stone cottages.

And all around her were roars and the *whoosh* of beating wings.

Kora turned to Rhi. "It feels wrong to be here."

"Because dragons hunted you?"

"Because this is their land."

Her lips twisted ruefully. "I know what you mean. But you are Derek's mate. You belong here just as he does."

"He won't remember that."

"We have to make him. If he unknowingly harms you and his memories return later...it will kill him."

Kora shook her head. "He's too strong for that."

"I'm not being metaphorical. I mean it. He will die."

The look in Rhi's silver eyes stopped Kora from arguing.

"A connection forms when a dragon finds its mate—one that binds them to their love much like the vow between you and Villette. The loss of a mate will destroy a dragon."

"Yet you put yourself in the middle of a battle while growing life."

Rhi's lips curled, and she placed a hand on her stomach. "Con and I have undergone the mating ceremony. While Fae live for thousands of years, the Dragon Kings can live much longer. I will live as long as Con does. The only way I can die is if he's killed. The magic of Earth chooses the Kings to rule each clan, and the dragons have been here. That means there hasn't been anyone to challenge him. Until we came here."

Villette and Miena. Everything always came down to them. Kora looked out at the Kings flying around them. "You and Con should return to Earth."

"He's the King of Dragon Kings," Rhi proudly stated. "And I'm his queen. We're not going anywhere."

Kora took the new information and set it aside. She couldn't worry about Rhi and her unborn child when Derek was on his way. "All of that is assuming Derek regains his memories. Even I have to admit that he might never."

"He will," Rhi insisted. "Which is why we cannot let him near you with dragon fire."

"It's a good thing I made that vow with Villette then." She grinned, even as the pit in her stomach grew.

Rhi's silver eyes held a note of worry. "Will that bond keep you alive if something should happen?"

"I guess we'll find out."

The Fae shot a quick look into the distance. "Remember, I'll be here."

Rhi vanished before her eyes.

"Can you hear me?" Rhi's disembodied voice asked.

Kora nodded. "I can."

"Call out if you need me."

Kora had learned a lot in the short time she had been with the dragons. Their senses were greatly enhanced, which meant Derek would see her before she saw him. It also meant he had probably already caught her scent. They were supposed to warn her when he neared Cairnkeep, but she wouldn't count on it.

Just as she wouldn't count on her binding vow with Villette to keep her alive. She knew the odds of her walking away from this trap were slim. Sure, the others had promised to protect and shield her, but they might not be able to do that *and* trap Derek. His survival was more important. He had family waiting here. A life where he could flourish away from Villette and Miena.

What did she have besides him?

Nothing. Her family was gone, and her kind had been wiped

out. Maybe more hellhounds would find their way to Zora, but she hadn't seen any in the time she had looked.

"He's close," Rhi told her.

Kora wanted to be sure to draw out Derek. Her scent might do it, but there was another way. She held out her arms and called the flames to her. Fire erupted over her skin—a blaze no one could miss.

CHAPTER 15

Cairnkeep was in his sights. Derek was surprised that no Kings had come out to divert him. Perhaps they planned to stand against him as one—as they had with his mate. He relished the thought of such a meeting. He would show them what retribution looked like.

He flew into a rainstorm, the droplets pelting his scales and spraying out in a stunning pattern as he flapped his wings. The storm was small, and he passed through it quickly, his speed dying him afterward. Then, the wind changed.

Derek caught a scent that shot through him and went straight to his brain. Something buzzed there, fiery and incessant. Menacing.

Hellhound.

Was it the one who had destroyed his eggs? He hoped it was because they had to pay for their cruel act. His lips curved into a smile when he realized the hellhound was at Cairnkeep. When he finished with the Kings, he would hunt down every hellhound on Zora and eradicate them once and for all.

The sight of flames shooting into the air drew his attention. He spotted the hellhound engulfed in flames as if beckoning him. They knew he was coming. Derek glanced around to make sure the Kings weren't silently surrounding him, but he was alone. They must have believed they were indestructible. He intended to show them differently.

He didn't have memories of seeing his dead mate or the crushed eggs, but he didn't need to. He felt it. It was an empty part of him that had been savagely ripped away and discarded. He was a shell of what he had once been. Not only were his memories gone. So was his heart. Now, a rage so ravenous he would never be able to stop it filled him.

The Kings had done this to him.

And to themselves.

The image of the hellhound became crisper as he flew toward the cliff. He saw the ends of long hair whipping in the wind as sparks flew. It was a female, standing naked at the edge of the cliff, flames licking her skin.

But that fire wouldn't save her from him.

He inhaled, feeling the blaze expand within him. She threw her arms outward and lifted her face. Something about that pose made him falter for a heartbeat. He shoved it aside and opened his mouth, dragon fire exploding and heading straight toward her.

Tears rolled down Kora's face when Derek came into view. The sight of his silver-tipped black scales was thrilling. And spine-chilling. He wasn't coming to save her this time.

He was coming to kill.

It was etched in every facet of his fearsome face and how his lips peeled back to reveal rows of sharp teeth. His was the visage her parents and villagers had seen the day they died. It was a face meant to terrorize.

And she was so very afraid.

Not for herself but for Derek—for what he might become if they couldn't keep him away from Miena.

She didn't take her eyes off him. The Kings were there. Rhi was somewhere nearby. Everyone stood on the knife's edge of anticipation.

"Come on, Derek!" Kora shouted as she watched his chest expand.

When he opened his mouth, his red eyes were locked on her. She held her breath, waiting for the heat of dragon fire to engulf her. Time stopped. Everything slowed to a crawl. It was just her and Derek, the man who had stolen her heart without her knowing it. The dragon who had become not just a friend but also her champion and lover.

Within a millisecond, Kora saw their possible future play out—the highs, the lows, and the love. A deep, unshakable devotion. One where they shared conversations with a look. The kind where they were joined from this life into the next.

And then it vanished, sound deafening her as a dragon with garnet scales struck Derek on the right side, shifting the blast of fire away from her. Kora dropped her arms when she heard Derek's roar of fury. More dragons came as he spun quickly and flicked his tail, lashing out at a teal dragon with a curved talon. Blood sprayed in an arc through the air.

"Kora! Now!" Rhi shouted.

Kora doused her flames, even as Derek inhaled again and headed toward her. The Teal, along with a Gold flew at Derek. He dove to counter and came flying straight up so fast and close to Kora that she fell backward from the wind gust.

"Come on," Rhi implored as she appeared beside her.

Kora scrambled to her feet, her gaze locked on Derek.

"Kora!"

She had done her part. She'd made sure Derek came to the right spot. It was time to leave and let the others finish the plan. But the sight of him left her in awe. After fearing that she might never see him again, here he was. Almost close enough to touch. She sighed and turned to the Fae.

A roar reverberated around her, making her cover her ears. The ground shook beneath her feet. She looked for Rhi, but the Fae was gone. It was then that Kora felt hot breath stir her hair from behind. She turned and found Derek standing there. The disdain in his eyes made her breath catch.

The other dragons were coming at him, tearing at his scales with their talons and tails, but he had found his target. And he wasn't leaving. The Kings wouldn't get closer to him for fear of hurting her. She should've gotten away when Rhi came for her. She had lingered too long and altered the plan.

She tilted her head back as Derek loomed over her. It was now up to her to get him into position. So, she did the only thing she could think of.

"Derek, stop!"

The sound of the hellhound's voice barely penetrated. Derek had intended to take out the Kings first, but he couldn't. Something within him wouldn't let go of the urge to kill the female. He didn't know why the Kings weren't damaging him more. What was it about the hellhound that made them all but withdraw? Why did they care about her so much?

Unless they didn't have the power they wanted everyone to believe they did. Miena was right. He could take them.

And he would. But first, the hellhound had to die.

He kept imagining her entering his cave and destroying the eggs. Had she been smiling? Had she enjoyed it? What had he ever done to deserve such actions? The hellhound would surely have come after him if he had done something. Those who targeted the innocent deserved a painful death.

"DEREK!"

He opened his mouth and roared to cut her off. He didn't want to hear anything she had to say. She covered her head with her arms and crouched, curling into a ball. Seeing her in terror thrilled him beyond reason. He wanted more of that. Much more. He wanted her to know what his unborn children had felt. What his mate had endured.

An enraged growl rumbled through him. She fell back on her hands and stared up at him. Something about this—about her— was familiar. Maybe he had known the hellhound before. Perhaps he had hurt her. Not that it mattered. She had sealed her fate. Her mistake had been going after his family instead of him.

The female scrambled back to the cliff's edge, looked up at him, and said something.

Then, she jumped.

Derek leaped after her. She wouldn't get away so easily. A blur of orange cut beneath him. Derek roared in outrage when the dragon grabbed the hellhound before soaring away. Derek twisted and flapped his wings to catch up.

Then, everything went black.

Kora looked between Merrill's talons to see the Kings blanketing Derek in magic. He went limp, his talons still reaching out for her before he faded out of sight as they carried him away. She curled into Merrill's hand and wept for the Derek he had been before.

Part of her had still believed that all he needed was to see her. That no amount of magic could make him forget their love. It had been naïve and foolish. Things couldn't be resolved so easily.

There was also another reality she had to come to terms with—and quickly. Derek might never be the man she knew. It was possible Miena had wiped away everything that made Derek who he was. Which meant he might never feel more than animosity toward her.

Everyone worried about what might happen to Derek if she died. No one had considered what might become of her if she lost him. Would the pain be any less? Would her suffering be diminished? What about the ache of never feeling his arms or lips again?

She would have to carry on, enduring the devastating loss for years. Dragons who lost their mates died. It seemed to her they got off easy. They didn't have to live with the emptiness or the yearning for something that would never be again.

When she felt Merrill landing, Kora hastily wiped her face. He opened his palm, and she stepped out. Rhi stood waiting, the border and canyon behind her. The Fae said nothing about her nakedness as Rhi touched her hand, taking them to Kora's chamber.

"It will be a while before Derek wakes," Rhi said softly. "You should rest and regroup before you face him again."

Kora was hollow. And broken. "I don't think it will do any good."

"Each time you said his name, he jerked. He's remembering." Rhi motioned to the already filled bath, steam curling up from the water. "Ease your muscles. Eat." She pointed at a table laden with food. "Then come into the hall."

Kora didn't have the energy to do more than nod. The door closed behind Rhi. Kora's gaze lingered on the tub. It did look inviting. She walked to it and found pink rose petals floating atop the water. A wooden tray lay across the tub, holding soap, a clear goblet filled with some kind of fizzy beverage, and a plate of tiny sandwiches and pastries.

She stepped into the water and slowly lowered herself. The moment her body was submerged, she sighed. Maybe this was what she needed. She closed her eyes and saw Derek's incensed gaze. Kora kept her eyes open after that.

If she was to speak to Derek, she needed to get her head in a better place. Right now, all she wanted to do was cry. So, she did. Better to get it out now than to weep in front of him. She wouldn't show him that vulnerability. She needed to be strong, confident.

She didn't know how long she cried before the tears dried. Her stomach rumbled. She reached for the snacks, and the moment the food hit her mouth, she realized she was famished. She couldn't remember the last time she had eaten.

Kora finished the sandwiches and reached for the goblet. The bubbles popping on her tongue took some getting used to, but she was enjoying the drink by the time she was on her third pastry.

With the snacks and drink gone and more food waiting, Kora washed. She emerged from the bath feeling renewed. The pink drying cloth was soft and plush against her skin, and she was loath to set it aside. There might come a time she went to Derek in nothing but the cloth, but not yet. The next time she faced him, she had to be mentally and emotionally ready.

Because the war to return the man she loved had begun.

CHAPTER 16

The tension was palpable as the trio walked through a meadow. Lotti had somehow found herself being a buffer between Alasdair and Villette, a position she'd never thought to be in. Yet, here she was.

Alasdair didn't think Villette had an honest bone in her body. Neither did Lotti. Still, she knew Villette spoke the truth.

Hence the tension building with every moment they didn't locate Miena.

Things grew worse after Merrill had returned to help trap Derek. To ensure Villette didn't learn of them, not much had been shared with Alasdair about those plans. It also meant that Lotti didn't know everything that was going on with the Kings. She didn't like that, but it was a small price to pay to keep Villette in the dark.

"This was a bloody waste of time," Alasdair said.

Villette spun to face him, her face tight with exasperation. "Fine. *You* locate Miena."

The argument that had been brewing was about to spill over. Lotti stepped between them. "We're all on edge. Let's remember that we all want the same thing."

She looked at Villette, who threw up her hands in aggravation. Lotti then slid her gaze to Alasdair. He ducked his chin. It was the only acquiescence she would get. But it was all she needed. She understood this was difficult for him. It was hard for her, too. Walking next to someone who had tried to kill you multiple times would never be easy. Or enjoyable.

Lotti didn't know how much longer she could keep the two of them from each other's throats. Neither seemed to realize she was doing her best to keep her own issues controlled. The only reason she remained calm was because she knew that if she didn't, no one would.

"Good," Lotti stated. "We've only covered five villages. We keep looking until we find Miena."

"Or I find you."

The voice registered behind Lotti. Alasdair's eyes narrowed, his lips parting, and then he was shouting. But there was no sound. Lotti whirled around to find a tall brunette standing before her.

"Miena," Villette said dispassionately.

Miena was even more beautiful than Villette. Her dark locks were parted down the middle and fell past her butt. Small sections on either side of her face were gathered at her chin with emerald clasps, the hair fashioned in a loose braid to the end and clinched with gold.

Miena's eyes were a striking shade of light green that reminded Lotti of the first buds on the trees come spring. A sleeveless gown in a deep emerald conformed to Miena's ample breasts and small waist before falling in soft folds to the ground.

She might be gorgeous, but the undercurrent of apathy and viciousness couldn't be missed. Unlike Villette, who attempted to hide her true intentions, Miena put them out there for the world to see. She embraced ambition and ruthlessness as tightly as she did power. Maybe it was the abject display, or perhaps it was Villette's acknowledgment that Miena was stronger, but whatever it was, Lotti knew it wouldn't be easy to bring her to heel.

And that wouldn't be enough for the Kings. It likely wouldn't be enough for Kora. But there had to come a time when killing wasn't the answer. Sadly, Lotti didn't think that would start with Miena.

Lotti looked over at Alasdair. He was pounding on some undetectable barrier that kept him in place and his voice from being heard. Fury darkened his features as he bellowed. The moment their gazes met, she tried to convey that everything was all right. It was far from fine, but she wouldn't worry if he was calmer. She must have communicated her desire because he lowered his arms to his sides and stopped yelling. Though his gaze, locked on Miena, told a different story. It was likely as calm as he was going to get. Lotti winked at him before turning her attention to the new arrival.

"He's a fine specimen," Miena said as she eyed Alasdair. "We've all had our share of dragons in our beds."

Lotti lifted her chin. "Alasdair is my mate."

Miena laughed, then sobered. "You're serious," she said in disbelief.

"We've been looking for you," Villette said, changing the subject.

Miena shot her a bored look. "I'm aware." She snapped her fingers, and three plush, green chairs appeared in a circle. Miena moved to sit in one. "Let's get this over with, shall we?"

Lotti looked at Villette, who glared daggers at her sister as she took one of the chairs. Lotti supposed they were both her sisters, too. She inwardly winced. It was easier if she considered them distant relations. *Very* distant.

She walked to the vacant chair and lowered herself into it.

Miena's smile was cold and calculating. "Now, let's get down to business. There are two options before you. One, join me. Two, stand against me and die."

"Still the same Miena," Villette replied.

Lotti watched the two glower at each other. "I've taken my stand."

"Pity," Miena replied without looking away from Villette. "And you, sister?"

Villette crossed one leg over the other, her arms resting on the chair's. "I can't believe you're even bothering to ask."

Miena rolled her eyes and made a sound in the back of her throat. "You've not changed. Still so whinny." She looked at Lotti. "She was the youngest until you. Villette always complained that we left her behind."

"You excluded me," Villette interjected indignantly. "On purpose."

"You were irritating."

"You were my family."

Miena shrugged. "You're the one who couldn't keep up."

Lotti didn't want to feel sorry for Villette, but she did. She knew what it was like to yearn for a family and want to be included. To know that Villette had felt that, too, was disturbing.

Villette was the enemy. Relating to Villette put her on a path to understanding—one Alasdair wouldn't be able to handle.

Frankly, Lotti wasn't sure *she* could.

"You. Left. Me."

Lotti inwardly grimaced at Villette's words spoken through clenched teeth. The depth of her hurt and resentment could be felt in every syllable.

"Until you became interesting." Miena smiled. "Your attempt to bring down the Dragon Kings is what caught my attention. I would never have invited you to join me here otherwise."

Lotti was going to be sick. Could Alasdair hear all of this? She wanted to look at him but thought it better if she didn't. It wasn't enough that the dragons had been slaves and gotten free. At least some of the Star People wanted to exact revenge for such an escape.

"Of course, then you betrayed me," Miena said in a voice laced with venom and ice.

One corner of Villette's lips curved into a smile. "I saw an opportunity."

"And you shall pay for it."

Lotti cleared her throat, drawing both their gazes. "We've all stated our intentions."

"Have we?" Miena asked with a laugh. "You certainly are young. You've no idea what you've stepped into, have you? You chose a side before you knew your family."

Lotti laced her fingers over her stomach, her elbows on the arms of the chair. "It seems taking sides is what our kind does best."

Miena's grin was anything but pleasant. "You are an infant compared to us. You know nothing."

"I know who found Zora, and it wasn't you." Lotti let that dig sink in. She bit back a smile at the hostility that filled Miena's eyes. Lotti had done it to see if Miena knew that Erith, leader of the Reapers, had created Zora. By her rage, she didn't.

"I've long thought it was Eurielle," Villette said.

Lotti didn't respond. Miena studied her, waiting to see if she'd reply, but there was no way Lotti would confirm or deny anything. There would come a time when Erith made herself known—and the fact that she was a Star Person—but it wasn't now.

Villette cut a look at Lotti as she told Miena, "Eurielle made herself known to Lotti and Alasdair."

"She did more than show herself," Lotti said. "She's the one who showed me what I am."

Miena pulled her lips back over her teeth. "She was supposed to kill you. It was punishment for—"

"For keeping Zora a secret from all of you," Lotti finished. "I'm aware."

Miena's stare was intense and pointed. "Eurielle's decisions have cut her from the family. I wouldn't advise following in her footsteps."

"Who should I follow?" Lotti looked from Miena to Villette and back again with raised brows. "One of you? Because you've both been so kind and generous?"

"If you want to be one of us, yes," Miena stated matter-of-factly. Then she scoffed, her derision clear. "Have you even left the planet? Do you know how to fly among the stars?"

Lotti told herself it didn't matter, but she felt the pull of the stars even now. "I'll figure it out as I have everything else."

"That's a very unwise choice."

Lotti shrugged. "You're not changing my mind."

"Soon, you'll beg me to spare your life and that of the dragon you've chosen," Miena replied.

Lotti pushed to her feet. "Since we're laying out promises, here's one of mine. Stop. All of it."

"Or?" Miena asked, one brow raised.

"Or it'll be you begging for life."

Miena threw back her head and laughed. "You've got courage, I'll give you that." She stood. "Nothing will make me stop what I began so long ago. Not you, not the dragons." She looked at Villette. "Not my sister. Not even the hellhound you're protecting. I have Derek, and my plan won't fail."

She was gone in the next heartbeat.

The chairs vanished. Villette teleported away so she didn't fall to the ground. Whatever held Alasdair disappeared, as well. He came up beside Lotti and wrapped his arm around her. She leaned against him, her heart thumping wildly.

"I heard everything," he said before she could ask.

Villette turned to them. "That went about as well as could be expected. Better than I thought it would, actually. There was no bloodshed. Though we had a chance to get her. Why didn't one of you call for Rhi?"

"Because the Kings have Derek."

Lotti looked at Alasdair in surprise. "Their plan worked?"

"It appears so."

"Then we're finished here," Villette said. "Let's get to Derek so we can return his memories."

Alasdair held out a hand to stop her. "You're not going anywhere."

"We're on the same team now, remember?"

He snorted. "Until you find a way out."

"There's no getting out of the vow she and Kora made." Lotti gave him a stern look. How many times must she tell him that?

Villette shrugged and tried to look indifferent. "I'll return to Stonemore then."

"The fuck you will," Alasdair stated.

Lotti had reached her limit for keeping the peace. "We can't bring her with us. Which means we stay with her."

"I doona like this," Alasdair said under his breath.

Villette turned her head away. "None of us does. At least I'm trying to do my part."

Lotti sighed when she felt Alasdair stiffen against her. "We found Miena, and we have Derek. That's two wins."

"Miena found us," Alasdair pointed out.

Villette glanced his way and nodded. "If I don't return to Stonemore, she'll take over there, too. If she hasn't already."

"I can no' believe I'm saying this, but Villette's right," Alasdair admitted.

Villette cupped her hand over her ear. "I didn't hear you. Can you repeat that?"

"Enough," Lotti snapped. "We're in agreement. Stonemore. But on one condition," she added when Villette began to smile. "You halt all executions of those with magic."

Villette hesitated.

"What possible excuse can you have to murder children?" Alasdair demanded.

Seemed she wasn't the only one who'd reached the end of their rope. Lotti crossed her arms over her chest. "Looks like you aren't going anywhere."

"She uses them." Villette's words came out in a rush as if it physically hurt to say them.

Lotti frowned, afraid she hadn't heard right. "What?"

"How?" Alasdair asked.

Villette swallowed, briefly closing her eyes as she looked away. "I found out that Miena had a secret. She wasn't always the strongest. It happened suddenly. I knew it wasn't natural and tried to figure out what it was. And I wasn't the only one. But she's devious. She hid it from me for decades while we were on Zora. It was only by chance that I came upon her with the child."

"Doing what?" Lotti was sure she didn't want to know, but there was no going back now.

"She stole the child's magic."

Alasdair jerked as if struck. "What the actual fuck?"

"How is that even possible?" Lotti murmured.

Villette shrugged one shoulder. "I don't know. It's always humans, and it's always children. I figured she'd discovered they didn't have the means to keep her from getting to it."

"She kills children for their magic, and you kill them for... what? Fun?" Alasdair was seething, his hands clenched at his sides.

"She didn't take their lives," Villette explained. "Just their magic."

Lotti shook her head in confusion. "Explain to me why you kill them then."

Villette looked away in aggravation. "When I caught Miena, she swore it was the first time she had ever done it, and it was by accident. I didn't believe her."

"I wonder why," Alasdair said sarcastically.

"It took a few years, but I discovered that in order to keep her secret, she'd learned to enter the kids' dreams and pull their magic that way. Even locked away as I had her, she could still get to a few of them."

Lotti swallowed the bile rising into her throat. "You kill them before she can."

"I didna think I could despise you more," Alasdair stated with a sneer.

Villette lifted her chin. "I did what I had to do to keep her locked away."

"We're not going to Stonemore unless the killings stop," Lotti announced.

Villette picked something off her skirt. "Fine. She's out now anyway. She can get all the magic she wants. Can we go now?"

"I hope we doona regret this," Alasdair whispered.

Lotti hoped so, too.

CHAPTER 17

Iron Hall

As she made her way to the main area of Iron Hall, Kora's heart felt like it would jump out of her chest at any moment. The bath and food had worked wonders in reviving her. She ran her palm against the soft, supple fabric of her black trousers. It wasn't a material she had seen before. The stitching was so precise and fine that it must have come from a highly skilled tailor.

There had been an array of tops and trousers to choose from, and even four different styles of boots. The tunic she'd chosen was a gray so dark it was nearly black, though it changed depending on how the light struck it. The fact that it was as soft as her pants was a bonus.

She hadn't known who would be in the hall when she arrived, but she hadn't expected Brandr. When he saw her, he looked up from the carving he was doing on a small rock and tucked it away in his pocket.

He got to his feet and nodded in greeting. "I'm to take you to Derek."

"Have they woken him?" she asked.

Brandr shook his head of black hair that fell past his shoulders. "No' yet."

Kora's apprehension intensified as she fell into step with him. "Are they sure he can be woken?"

"They used the same magic on Earth to capture four rogue dragons. It'll work."

She nodded, not knowing what else to say.

"Derek willna be able to hurt you."

Kora picked at a hangnail with her thumb. That was comforting, at least. Especially after seeing the hate in his eyes. "Good."

"Relax. Everything will be fine."

"You can't know that."

"Sure, I can," he said, shooting her a lopsided grin. "Believe it, and it'll happen."

Could it be that simple? Kora sure hoped so because she was barely holding it together. She had feared they would never find Derek. She hadn't thought too hard about anything else because she had believed their biggest hurdle was locating him and Miena. Things had seemed to happen so quickly that there hadn't been time to consider anything else.

She followed Brandr as he zigzagged through the underground city's corridors and hallways. She wasn't sure she would ever find her way back to the main room if he abandoned her. That was the point, though. They had put Derek in a remote section of the city, far from others. She and Brandr passed countless doors. Some sections of the walls had crumbled, but others looked pristine.

She didn't see any of it. Not really. She was too lost in thought. About Derek, about their time together…

About who he was now.

Brandr suddenly halted, then opened a door and waited for her to go through. Kora's feet felt encased in rock as she forcibly lifted one to move forward. The second step wasn't any easier. Then, she was in a room. She recognized Con, Rhi, and Merrill. There were other faces that looked familiar, but names didn't come to her immediately.

"Follow me," Brandr bade.

She once more trailed behind him as they wove their way through the spacious room to where Con, Rhi, Eurwen, and her mate, Vaughn, were talking.

Rhi smiled in greeting. "Nice clothing choice. How do they feel?"

"Wonderful. I may never wear anything else again."

"Good," Rhi said proudly. "By the way, the material will return when your flames extinguish."

Kora's mouth went slack. "That's…amazing."

"Every piece of clothing in your room is that way. You won't ever have to stand naked again. Unless you want to," Rhi added.

"Thank you. All of you," she said, looking around her. "For everything, but especially for listening to me and Merrill about Derek."

Vaughn's blue eyes met hers. "He's one of us. That makes Derek family."

"Assuming we can get through whatever Miena has done to him," Eurwen said.

Con caught Kora's eye. "Ready?"

"Now?" Her voice broke on the word.

Con smiled softly. "The sooner we begin, the sooner his memories will return."

He was guessing. Everyone was. The truth was that no one knew for sure. Kora felt the weight of expectation settle around her. She tried to adjust it, even to shake it off, but it wasn't budging.

"You can go in alone, if you want," Eurwen told her.

Kora nodded. "I think I'd rather do this without others watching."

"Can no' say I blame you," Vaughn said.

Con waited until she looked at him to say, "We'll give you a few moments before we remove the magic making him sleep."

Everyone was watching, but she didn't know where to go. She looked at Brandr, hoping he would direct her.

"This way," he said in a soft voice.

He took her to a door she hadn't noticed. As she stood outside it, she blew out a breath.

"You know him," Brandr said. "Better than anyone."

She tried to swallow, but her mouth was dry. "Do I? We were together for such a short time. And we both kept secrets."

"You *know* him, Kora," Brandr insisted. He touched his chest. "You two are connected. There's no turning back for a dragon who discovers their mate. If anyone can bring him back, it's you."

"What if Miena lied? What if he doesn't love me?"

Brandr glanced at the door. "There's only one way to find out."

Right. She needed to face Derek. But her feet wouldn't budge.

"We'll be right out here if you need anything," he assured her.

Kora clasped the handle but hesitated before opening the door. When she did and walked inside, it closed softly behind her. Her legs were wobbly as she made her way farther into the room. Balls of light hung in the air, casting a wide glow over the enormous room. A gigantic cage sat in the middle, and within it was Derek in dragon form. His rhythmic breathing was the only sound she heard. She watched the rise and fall of his stomach. It drew her forward.

The enclosure barely fit around him. His wing was squished against the bars. She walked to the cage and rested a hand on his arm. The warmth of his scales was as startling as the nearly metallic feel of them.

It wasn't her first time seeing Derek in his true form, but it was the first she'd been able to take her time looking at him. She let her gaze run over his long, angular skull where two silver horns sat. They were thick and straight. She moved to see more of his face and got a close look at the sizable teeth his lips didn't quite cover. Large, fan-like skin and bone structures ran along the sides of his jaw.

He had four limbs, and each had six digits, which meant six very long, very sharp black talons ready to tear someone to shreds. Wait. He had one silver talon on his back left. The silver-tipped scales on the upper part of his body were wide with rows of thicker scales running along his spine. The scales on his underbelly were broader, the silver along the edges wider.

Lastly, her gaze moved to his humongous wings. There was a curved wing spur growing from each like a giant scythe. His long tail was curled around him and had a matching, curved protrusion at the end.

She was so engrossed in studying him that it took her a moment to realize something had changed. It took even longer for her to comprehend that his steady sleep breathing was gone. Kora swung her head around to find his fiery red dragon eyes open and watching her.

"Derek," she said.

His growl rumbled the cage. She lurched backward. She wasn't ready for this. Why had she thought she could reach Derek? Their feelings had been new, delicate. Fragile. It wasn't a solid, sturdy bond that had endured years. What was she doing?

Kora turned to walk out but only got two steps before the memory of Derek shielding her from dragon fire with his wings stopped her cold. He had known the consequences of aiding her, and it hadn't stopped him. He had protected her and allowed her to get to safety. That was the same man who had held her in his arms as they slept. The same dragon who had given her his cuff, knowing it would leave him stranded.

He had shown her his love at every turn.

She had just been too blind to see it.

He deserved better than her fear and worry. He was worthy of so much more. And she would give him that.

Kora drew in a deep breath to calm her racing heart. She slowly released it and turned to face him. The dragon was gone. In his place stood the strong, commanding man who took her breath away.

Derek didn't bother to cover his nakedness. And Kora admired the stunning view. Powerful, defined sinew rippled from neck to ankle. Her palms itched to caress his broad shoulders and down his brawny arms. To stroke his thick chest and linger over his chiseled abs. She bit her lip at the cut of muscles just above his hip bones. The location was a particular favorite of hers, where she loved to lick him. Her gaze traveled to his thick cock that hung flaccid. She squeezed her legs together, recalling how his thrusts felt. Her eyes moved lower still to his muscular thighs dusted with dark hair.

Finally, she allowed herself to peer at his face. She knew every inch of his rugged visage from his thick, black brows, to the hollow cheeks, sculpted jaw, and amazing mouth. Those wide, full lips had kissed her senseless.

Kora made herself look into his pale olive eyes. Even though she knew the person looking back at her was different, it still made her heart catch to see what she did. The rage had doubled. And so had the promise of death.

How did she begin? A simple *hello*? An explanation, maybe? What did one say to a former lover who didn't remember anything? She licked her lips and noticed that his hands were fisted at his sides. If it weren't for the cage halting his magic, she'd likely be dead now.

"I'm—" She stared, but her voice came out a cracked whisper. She cleared her throat and tried again. "I'm sure you have questions. I can answer them."

His scowl remained in place.

"You know, the crazy thing is, I really thought you would remember me once you saw me. Remember *us*." She took a tentative step closer. "I told myself it would take more, but once that hope took root, it was bigger than I realized. Until you came at me on the cliff."

"No cage will hold me," he stated. "I'll get free, and when I do, your life is mine."

"You won't believe this, but a few days ago, you risked your life to save me. I hope to somehow return your memories to you. The ones Miena took."

He snorted. "Is that the story you're going with?"

Kora needed a way to reach him and get through the lies Miena had woven into his heart. No matter how many times Villette wiped his memories, he had always been the same person. There had to be something Miena's magic hadn't gotten to, something of the Derek who had chosen her.

But...something had to make him have such animosity. If someone hated, they also loved. And if there was love, then the Derek she knew was still in there somewhere. She would find him.

"The first time I saw you, I was leading some Stonemore soldiers into a secluded location," she told him. "I didn't know what you were. I simply saw a man and wanted to warn you to remain hidden so they wouldn't come after you. I unknowingly led them to your domain in the swamp and let them kill me because I knew it was the only way they would stop. As I lay dying, something stood over me, and I looked up into red eyes. Dragon eyes. *Your* eyes."

He crossed his arms over his chest, his glower intensifying.

"It was the last thing I saw," Kora continued. "I woke alone on the top of a mountain. You'd brought me up there. I raced off it and saw the charred remains of the soldiers who had attacked me at the bottom."

"You think I killed them for *you*?" he mocked.

Kora moved closer. "I know you did."

CHAPTER 18

The certainty in the hellhound's brown eyes did nothing to sway Derek. He tried to call his magic once more, but it still didn't respond. It was there, just beneath the surface, but something was blocking it. Likely, the cage.

He knew what the hellhound was. The others might not, but he did. It turned his stomach that she had looked at him with such appreciation. As if he would ever be attracted to the likes of her.

She stood confidently in her body-hugging attire, showing off her curves. She kept her dark hair long and loose, and there were no jewels to draw the eye. Her body did enough of that without her needing anything else. Her face was pleasing. If he didn't know what she had done, he might have considered her attractive with her oval face, high cheekbones, and plump lips. But he knew the darkness within her.

"Which one of them have you maneuvered into your bed?"

Her conviction slipped. "Excuse me?"

"Which of the Kings did you manipulate and coerce?"

"For what?" she asked softly.

He raked a scathing look over her. "To protect you. I saw them. Every move they made was to keep you from harm."

"You might have also noticed they didn't try to kill you."

"A warrior cannot be on the defensive and offensive at the same time. They were more concerned with ensuring your survival than removing me. How else do you think I got close to you?"

Her nostrils flared, and her gaze narrowed in anger. "We were trying to trap you, you arrogant arse."

He looked around at the cage. "This won't hold me for long. I'll get free. You would do well to run, hellhound, because I won't rest until I track you down."

"The Derek I knew wouldn't be so gullible as to believe everything a Star Person told him."

"You don't know me, so don't pretend otherwise."

"Did you not just hear the story I told you?" she demanded, her body rigid with frustration.

He dropped his arms to his sides and flexed his hands, imagining them wrapped around her neck as he released dragon fire over her. He could practically hear her screams now. "Were you talking?"

Her brown eyes searched his. "You cut your hair."

The words surprised him. He'd expected her to argue her point, not change the subject. And to one that caught him off guard besides. Derek fought to keep his arms at his sides instead of reaching for his hair. He remembered how he had run his hands through it and had been startled to find the length barely brushed the back of his neck.

"It's a pity. It looked good long." She turned and walked out of the room.

Derek remained still, counting off ten minutes. Then twenty. No one else entered. He shifted his attention to the cage. Now, he could focus on it and figure a way out. It had been large enough to hold his dragon form, which meant he had a lot of room as a human.

He walked the perimeter of the square enclosure. The magic was thick and heavy. There was more than dragon magic involved. It was a different kind of power. One he hadn't felt before—more than one, actually. The knowledge that the Kings had allies didn't deter him. He didn't care who he went up against. He didn't even care if he survived. All that mattered was making a stand against those who'd taken his mate and children.

And to think he had contemplated beginning a new life. Starting over by forgetting the past and all the unanswered questions he had. He was ashamed at even considering such a thing after what had happened to his family.

He felt a push in his mind and thought he heard a voice, but he couldn't be sure. Derek forgot about it as he rested a palm against the black bars. The metal was cool to the touch. The magic was just outside the bars, allowing him to curl his fingers around them. That wasn't enough, though. Derek held up his hand once more, palm out as he moved it between the bars. He encountered the barrier almost instantly. It was similar to the shield at the dragons' border.

His contact was light as he pressed his hand against it. The barrier gave slightly under his touch. He pushed a little harder, and magic zinged through his fingers and up his arm, sinking like hundreds of tiny blades into his shoulder and expanding outward. Derek yanked his arm back and shook it out. The instant he removed his hand, the pain stopped.

Everything had a weakness. Even a cage and a magical barrier. He only needed to figure out where it was. And once he was out, he would kill anyone who got in his way.

Derek checked different areas of the cage. He climbed to the top and tested that. He examined the floor. Then he took a long, hard look at the room he was in. The numerous lights left very little shadow. While he didn't have a good view of the ceiling, he guessed it was fairly high. That begged the question of how the Kings had gotten him into the cage.

He wished he could remember more about them. They didn't all lead. One of them had to be in charge. And why had they sent the hellhound to speak to him? They couldn't be afraid of him, surely. It boggled his mind why they protected her. They'd had a chance to take him out and hadn't taken it. Their oversight would be his gain.

His mind ran the gambit of ideas for why he was still alive. Many of them made sense, but he had to consider that he hadn't come to the battle with all his memories. The Kings potentially knew something he didn't. And they would try to use it. Maybe even attempt to turn him against Miena.

Derek lowered himself to the floor in the middle of the cage and sat with his legs crossed. He closed his eyes and went over the attack in his mind, dissecting his movements—and theirs—frame by frame.

"Derek."

Her voice again. But he wasn't dreaming this time. The voice was stronger now but still soft. Almost as if she was afraid of being discovered. He hadn't been there to protect his mate. Had she called out to him for help? Had she believed he would save her? Had her last thoughts been of him?

No matter how hard he tried, he couldn't recall her face or even the color of her eyes. The blow to his head had shaken those recollections loose. At least he still remembered the color of her hair and the way she fit against his body.

But what color were her scales?

Where was their home?

How had he met her?

"Derek...have...me?"

He clung to the sound of her voice, trying to pick up on any inflection that might form memories. His desperation to recall something—anything—more made his head throb. He didn't even know her name. Why hadn't he asked Miena?

That begged the question of why Miena hadn't told him about his family from the beginning. Why keep it from him at all? Especially when she had been so adamant about him returning to the Kings.

An image of two eggs, one a deep forest green and the other a bright magenta, filled his mind. They had been his. And they were gone. He knew that with such certainty that he must have seen it, but he couldn't pull up the memory.

Reflecting on his lost children hurt too badly. He tried to return to thoughts of the attack, but each time he fixated on the hellhound, he heard his mate's voice calling his name. It was a constant reminder of who was to blame for his family's deaths.

And the more his hatred swelled. Spread.

Burned.

He would not rest until the hellhound was nothing more than ash floating on the breeze. It didn't matter what it cost him. It didn't matter how long it took. She would die by his hands.

"Derek."

"I'm here," he whispered. "I'll always be here."

He had to remember her. Something, anything!

CHAPTER 19

Stonemore

It was wrong. All of it. Alasdair felt it in his bones. His mate was doing her best to ease the situation, he wasn't helping matters, and being back at Stonemore only made things worse.

Alasdair had insisted that Lotti teleport them into the palace over Villette's arguments. Lotti had brought them to the very tunnels beneath the city where they had battled Stonemore's army. The moments hidden in the catacombs had given him and Lotti a chance to spend time together without outside interference. He thought about the room they had located and the passion they'd shared within.

"Something isn't right."

Villette's voice broke into his musings, wiping away the good memories and opening him to the ones where he and Lotti had had to fight to get free. His gaze slid to Villette. Whatever she was up to was likely some ploy to catch them off guard. He glanced at

Lotti to see her frown of concern. His mate was smart. She knew better than to be taken in by Villette. Yet he hated seeing her interacting with the other Star Person as if the past had been wiped clean.

There was no washing that stain away.

Alasdair stiffened when Villette turned her blue eyes on him. She walked toward him. When she drew close, she walked around him. His gaze went to Lotti and he saw disapproval tighten her visage for a heartbeat before she took his hand and they turned to follow Villette.

She led them to a door. Inside was an empty room. A second door led to another passage. Villette walked across the corridor to a door cattycorner to them. Inside that room was yet another door. This time, they came out to squarial stairs. They were narrow and steep.

"Where are you taking us?" Alasdair called when Villette headed up the steps with purpose, Lotti right behind her.

Villette didn't look at him when she said, "I feel her."

"Miena's here?" Lotti asked.

Villette was silent for a moment. "Everything feels like it used to when she created the city."

"We're too late then." It was only a matter of time before they faced off against Miena. Alasdair was always prepared, but he wasn't keen on it being just him and Lotti. He couldn't count on Villette. She would likely run the first chance she got—or betray them, despite the binding spell.

Villette started to answer when something tossed her backward. She flew into Lotti, sending them both down the stairs. Alasdair stopped their fall. Even though he knew Lotti would heal, he didn't like her grunt of pain as her head slammed into the stone steps. She had taken the brunt of their tumble. Alasdair shoved Villette aside and helped Lotti to her feet.

"Wait," his mate said as she squatted beside an unmoving Villette.

"I doona suppose she's dead."

Lotti jerked her head to him and shot him a withering look. "Do you want to win against Miena?"

"You know I do."

"Then stop this."

"It's Villette," he argued.

Lotti briefly closed her eyes and released a sigh. "I know. It isn't something I will forget. But there are bigger issues than my feelings toward her."

"You're right. I'm trying, love. I really am."

She squeezed his hand and smiled. "That's all I can ask. But, nay, she isn't dead."

Alasdair looked up to where she had been. "I doona see anything."

"Me either. But there has to be something there. We should at least sense it."

"Unless it's a trap."

Lotti nibbled her lip as she stared at the spot where Villette had been. "We should go back the way we came."

"I suggest we leave. Now. Go anywhere but here," Alasdair stated. He saw grains of sand jumping on the stair next to Lotti.

His mate turned her head to him, her lips parting, but before she could answer, she went limp, her body sagging to the side.

Alasdair's heart jumped into his throat as he gathered Lotti into his arms. Her chest was still rising and falling, but she was pale. He turned to retrace his steps when he spotted Villette.

"Fuck," he growled and shifted Lotti over one shoulder as he flipped Villette over the other.

He then turned and hurried down the stairs. Every tunnel looked the same. He didn't know where he was going, but all that mattered was getting Lotti away from the staircase and figuring out what had happened.

Alasdair busted into a room and dropped to his knees. He let Villette slide down his arm then carefully laid Lotti on the floor before shutting the door. Once that was done, he turned back to them. What could have affected them and not him? The only conclusion was Miena.

"Fuck." He ran a hand through his hair and called for Rhi. When the Fae didn't show after a few moments, Alasdair opened the mental link. *"Con!"*

As the seconds passed without a response, Alasdair's fears were confirmed. Miena was preventing him from communicating with the others. Nothing good would come of that.

Alasdair knelt beside Lotti and gently tapped her face. "Come on, love. Open those beautiful eyes and look at me. Lotti?"

She didn't respond.

Alasdair glanced at Villette. He could get out with both of them, but he didn't know what might be waiting for them. Miena wasn't after him. If she had been, he'd already be dead. Her focus was on her sisters. For now. That gave Alasdair a little time to come up with a plan. And none of them involved leaving Lotti behind. Villette deserved whatever she got.

But did Kora? Because if he left Villette, and Miena hurt her, it would be Kora who felt the most pain. There was only one option.

"Fuck."

Alasdair wouldn't wait. He didn't know how long it would take him to find the main tunnel out the back entrance of the mountain—or how many soldiers would be waiting when he did.

He sat Lotti up to put her over his shoulder once more. She groaned. Alasdair searched her face. "Sweetheart? Can you hear me?"

Another groan.

"That's it," he said with a smile. "Come back to me."

Her eyes fluttered open, only to close again.

"Lotti, I need you to fight, baby."

"I am," she whispered.

He laid her back on the floor and watched her carefully. "Come on, love. Open your eyes."

Finally, she managed to lift her lids and keep them open. She smiled. "Hi."

"Are you hurt?"

Her face creased in pain. "Only when I breathe."

"I got us out of the stairwell, but we need to leave Stonemore."

"Where is Villette?"

Alasdair glanced at her, but she still wasn't moving. That was when he saw the grains of sand and dirt near the door begin to vibrate just as they had on the stairs. "She's still unconscious. Can you get us out?"

"I can try."

He grabbed Villette's ankle and dragged her closer. "We need to get out of here. Now, Lotti."

The murky room gave way to sunshine and dense trees. Lotti sat up and shook her head. "I figured Ferdon Woods would put us in the center of everything."

"You did good," he said and gave her a quick kiss.

Lotti grabbed her head with both hands and moaned. Alasdair

rubbed her back. He wished he could take away her pain. He slid his gaze to Villette, who had yet to wake. Alasdair shifted Lotti against a tree and moved Villette closer. Lotti drifted in and out as he paced the area, looking for foes of any kind.

"*Con?*" he called.

"*Aye.*" The King of Kings replied immediately. "*Is everything all right?*"

"*Miena has taken over Stonemore.*"

"*That doesna surprise me. Did you find her?*"

Alasdair quickly told him about their discussion with Miena.

"*About what we expected,*" Con said.

"*How are things there?*"

Con sighed. "*Kora is with Derek. I'll let you know how things progress.*"

Alasdair severed the link. He was doing one of his rounds when he returned and saw Villette sitting up and picking twigs out of her hair.

"Thank you for not leaving me there," she said.

Alasdair shrugged. "I didna want Kora to experience any pain Miena might have delivered to you. What happened?"

"It was Miena," Lotti answered.

Villette nodded. "It is a trap she's used on me before. It's highly specialized magic meant for only our kind. It incapacitates. She perfected it when we were still young and used it whenever she wasn't getting her way. Some of our older siblings learned to detect it, but I never could."

"I sensed nothing either." Lotti punctuated the statement with a shrug.

Villette smoothed her skirts. "She must have had it roaming the palace and mountain."

"That must have been what you sensed when we arrived," Alasdair said.

She wrinkled her nose. "Maybe. Had we remained, Miena would've found us."

There was no need for her to finish. All three of them knew what Miena would have done if she had come upon either Lotti or Villette.

"Now what?" Lotti asked.

Alasdair looked around the forest. "This is as good of a place as any. We wait here until we're needed."

The sound of a roar drew their attention.

"She's using Gordon," Villette said and climbed to her feet.

Lotti frowned. "Using him how?"

"To attack humans and draw us out."

Fury filled Alasdair.

CHAPTER 20

"It isn't working." Kora hadn't been able to get out of the room with Derek fast enough.

The antechamber had cleared out, leaving only Con, Merrill, Brandr, and Hector. The four of them stared at her for a moment before Con said, "We knew it wouldna be easy."

"Easy?" She choked on a laugh. "His words are cutting. The animosity is..." She turned her head away, her throat tightening at the memory of the hate Derek had directed at her. "I'm not the one who will get through to him."

Merrill leaned a shoulder against the wall. "I disagree. Keep talking to him."

"Maybe one of us should have a chat with him," Hector said.

Brandr slowly shook his head. "I agree with Merrill. Kora needs to go back in. That was just the first attempt. It could take hundreds."

"Hundreds?" she repeated in panic. "We don't have that kind of time."

Con tilted his head slightly and shrugged. "As long as Derek isna with Miena, we have time."

"You're guessing." Kora didn't bother to hide her ire. She didn't even care that any of the four could kill her on the spot. They didn't know any more than she did. That could be the very thing that cost Derek in the end.

Merrill pushed away from the wall, his face tightening with indignation. "You're fucking right we're guessing. It's what we bloody do! Do you have any idea how many enemies we've fought? Guess how many times others have tried to wipe us out. Go on," he demanded, his voice cold and low. "Guess."

"Merrill," Hector said in warning.

He ignored Hector and kept his dark blue gaze on Kora. "You want to know why we're still standing? Because we didna fucking give up at the first opportunity when things got hard."

"Merrill." This time, Con was the one issuing the caution.

But Kora wasn't about to back down. "Hard? You think this is hard? You have no clue what that is! The man I love is in there, but it isn't him. He doesn't remember me. All because I made a bad decision. It isn't that his memories are gone, or even that he abhors me. He wants to *kill* me. And not just because I'm a hell-hound. He thinks I did something. I can't reach him!" she shouted, fighting not to let the tears loose. "Do you know what that feels like? Have you loved like that?"

"Nay," Merrill answered calmly. "I can no' begin to know that feeling. But if you love him, then you'll get back in there and fight for him. Fight as he did for you against Gordon and Bryok."

Kora dashed away an escaped tear. Damn Merrill for bringing that up. She hated that he was right. She had run away because Derek had hurt her feelings. Nay. She had run because he didn't recognize her, and that felt like a dull blade sinking slowly into her heart. Every word and look of disgust had turned the blade a little more.

"We all knew this would be challenging," Con reminded her.

She nodded. "And that it might not work."

"Look, I'm not normally an optimist, but Derek is here," Brandr said. "That means he isna on Earth attacking the Kings. Miena lost her hold on him."

Kora looked at the three before her as a sudden fear sprouted. "What keeps her from coming to get him?"

"Good question," Hector said. "It's one we've repeatedly asked ourselves about Villette."

She frowned at the news. "Are you telling me Villette hasn't crossed the border?"

"Only recently," Brandr answered. "That was when we surrounded her up north."

"Crispy fried her," Hector said with a chuckle.

Kora had no idea what that meant, but she could guess. "What has kept her out?"

"Nothing, as far as we know. Lotti isna hampered by anything, which means none of the others are either," Con answered.

Merrill jerked his chin to the door. "Derek needs you. Let us worry about everything else. Focus on him."

Kora rubbed her hands together and faced the door. Derek had been prepared to die for her freedom. She had claimed the same for him. Standing on that cliff was easier than facing him now. The fact that he wouldn't listen to her made the situation so much harder.

So, she would make him.

Kora walked back into the room. Derek sat cross-legged in the cage with his eyes closed. She quietly shut the door behind her and made her way over, purposefully making the contact of her bootheels soft against the stone floor. She walked around the enclosure. Derek was calm for someone who had woken up confined. She would probably be pacing the space, demanding to know why she'd been detained.

"Derek."

He whispered something she couldn't make out. She continued her route around the cage, and as she came even with him, found his eyes open and following her, even though his head hadn't moved.

"It was wrong of me to begin by trying to convince you of... different things." Kora clasped her hands behind her back. "I should've known that wouldn't work."

"Why are you here instead of a King?" he demanded.

She stopped at the front of the cage and looked at him. "They think I can get through to you."

"Like you have them?" Derek snorted in derision. "Not likely."

"Why do you hate me?"

A muscle jumped in his jaw. "You know why."

"I want to hear it from you."

Kora was taken aback by his silence. It was difficult to have him so near and not be able to touch him. To look into his beautiful eyes and not see the man she'd fallen in love with. Miena had fulfilled her promise of cutting out all of Derek when she wiped his memories. What had she replaced them with? Something horrible about Kora, obviously.

"What is it you want?" she asked.

Derek blew out a bored breath. "Freedom. And to kill you and every King."

"Why?"

"You know why."

"You keep saying that. What is it you think we did?" she asked, hoping he would answer if she reframed the question.

Instead, he closed his eyes, shutting her out.

Kora dropped her head back and looked at the ceiling for a heartbeat. Then she turned on her heel and walked to the wall. She sat against it, keeping Derek in front of her. "I know you don't need sleep."

There wasn't even a twitch of agitation.

She hated the helpless feeling that threatened to swallow her. Everyone believed she knew Derek best. Maybe she did, but this wasn't her Derek. He was gone.

"No one here wants to hurt you," she said.

His eyes opened, but he didn't reply. Instead, he looked at the cage.

"We didn't have a choice. You were intent on harming us." She winced when his eyes closed once more. Kora rested her head against the wall and propped her feet on the floor, her arms on her knees. "I messed up. Badly. I did something I shouldn't have, and this is the result. You, there. Me, here."

"Seems to have worked out for you. For now," he said without opening his eyes.

She bit the side of her lip. "Miena isn't the first Star Person you've aligned with."

Now that was something interesting. Likely only a ruse, but Derek had to hand it to the hellhound, she knew how to get his attention. He still didn't look at her. It seemed to bother her that he ignored her, so he kept doing it. If he couldn't take her life now, at least he could agitate her.

"Do you remember Villette?" the hellhound asked.

There wasn't even the slightest inkling of such a name in his recollections. His foe could be making it all up. Or, as much as it pained him to admit it, the name could've been shaken loose with everything else. Not that he would give the hellhound the satisfaction of answering either way.

"What about Bryok?"

For just a moment, Derek thought the name sounded familiar, but it was gone just as quickly.

She sighed, the sound carrying in the silence of the room. "The man I know is in there somewhere. I'll reach you. I'm not giving up."

He could've told her not to bother, but she wouldn't have listened. When would the torture begin? As if she had read his mind, she launched into another story about their supposed trip over the mountain.

He realized the torment had already begun. She was the torture.

Derek found it easy to shut out her voice. He called to his magic but was filled with disappointment when he still couldn't use it. It was there, just out of reach. Infuriating. He thought about trying to reach out to Miena. He would if things got to the point where he couldn't handle it. He wasn't there yet, though.

"...Stonemore. The gates were huge."

The single word yanked him from his musings—Stonemore. Was it a coincidence that Ash had mentioned the city and now the hellhound had, as well? Derek listened intently.

"Yet you got us inside," she said. "It wasn't anything like I expected. It was dirty and smelly, but the worst part was seeing those living on the streets and starving. Nothing was being done."

Derek had thought the story might give him more, but he had been wrong. He tried to shut her out again, but his interests were piqued.

"The city has eight levels, and each has a gate patrolled by the army. The bottom four levels are for the underprivileged while the upper ones are for the wealthy. Somehow, you got us up there. No one questioned you. It was...incredible to watch. Surely, you must remember some of this." Another sigh at his silence. "You were there, standing right beside me. It was just last week."

Now he knew she was lying. He would've been with his mate and their eggs. "Stop wasting our time," he told her. "I'm done listening to your lies."

"They aren't lies," she insisted.

Derek opened his eyes. She had her knees up and her head bent forward as her arms curled up and over her head. Did she act as distraught and vulnerable in front of the Kings? Is that why they all went to such lengths to safeguard her?

The hellhound went back to her story, and he promptly closed his eyes. He listened with half an ear, mostly because he was curious about how good her lies might be. She gave just enough detail to make them seem plausible, but Derek didn't believe a word. She and the Kings were murderers. Someone needed to bring them to justice, and he was here to deliver it.

She droned on for hours before someone else entered the room. Derek was curious, but not enough to look just yet. The silence that followed was a relief. Yet he was aware of another presence. Something about this person was different. They had an air of something darker, something menacing. Savage.

Derek recognized what he saw within himself. He opened his eyes to stare into dark blue ones. Derek didn't need to ask to know that this was a King. His dirty blond hair hung past his chin and was raked back, like his fingers had just plowed through the strands. The King grasped the bars and leaned his weight into them as they stared at each other.

"She said she would go deep enough that nothing of you remained."

The King's voice was deep, the accent strange—and not one Derek had heard before. "Is this where I'm supposed to ask who you're referring to?"

"Aye. I'd be curious as hell to know where my memories had gone."

"It was a head wound."

The King grunted. "You could say that."

"Are you telling me we didn't battle?"

"No' each other. No' before yesterday."

Derek shook his head. "This isn't any better than her wretched stories."

"Her story is true. I was there for some of it. You'd be wise to listen."

"Why? To remember something that never happened?"

The King slammed his hand against the bars, rattling the entire cage. "To remember who you are!"

"And you know me?"

"We had just met when all this happened."

Derek was weary of this. "Stop with whatever this is and get on with whatever you have planned."

"This is the plan."

He searched the King's face for the lie but didn't find one. "You plan to talk me to death?"

"To remind you who you are."

Derek was up and at the bars in a blink. The King didn't so much as flinch when they stood nearly nose to nose. "Is that why you killed her? Is that why the hellhound destroyed the eggs?"

"What?"

The bewilderment in the King's eyes looked real. So did the color that drained from his face. But Derek didn't take the bait. "Don't play stupid. I know what the Kings did."

"You think we killed your mate?" he muttered and dropped his arms as he straightened and took a step back. "Bloody fucking hell."

Without another word, the King turned and walked out. Derek stared at the door for a long time afterward. He tried to shake off his adversary's reaction, but he couldn't. It stayed with him. The astonishment, the umbrage.

And he hated the King for the doubt it wrought.

Derek remembered the eggs. If they were real, then his mate must have been, too. If only he could recall her name. He turned to lean against the bars and tried to pull up her face in his mind. He searched his heart for some recollection of her other than her hair. How could he dredge up memories of eggs and not her? She was his mate, for fuck's sake! The one he loved above all others, their souls connected. He wouldn't forget her.

But he had.

Rage surged through him. At himself, at the Kings. At the hellhound. He curled his hands into fists and lifted them in front of his face. He wanted battle, to vent his fury on those who had earned it. And perhaps even himself.

The yearning to unleash agony and suffering on his enemies like they had never experienced consumed him. He sought pain, to feel the sting of a cut or the ache of burns that might chase away the gnawing emptiness of what he had lost. He needed to feel something other than grief and desolation. Something besides the endless anger.

He required blood for blood.

Derek turned and slammed his fists into the bars. The cage shuddered violently. He would never get to see his unborn children. Through his fury, he noticed the bars had bent outward where his fists had struck. He grinned. Maybe his anger was good for something.

He focused it all into his hands and grabbed the bars. He strained to pull them apart. The feel of them giving way propelled him to keep pouring his fury into his hands. He had known there was a weakness in the cage, and he had found it. There was no stopping him now.

He heard the door open as the bars gave way. His gaze locked on the hellhound as she skidded to a halt, her eyes widened in disbelief. Derek curled the bars back and turned to the side to move through them. He clenched his teeth, his muscles spasming when he met the barrier. It would all stop if he could get through it, but that was proving harder than he'd first thought.

Agonizing pain slid down his spine, up into his neck, and into his brain. He heard someone bellow and dimly realized it was him.

He reached for the hellhound. His arm was free of the barrier, but the rest of him was stuck inside. All he needed was to get clear. Then he would have her.

He stretched out his arm, his finger scraping the sleeve of her shirt just as everything went black.

CHAPTER 21

Kora stood frozen as she watched Derek fall to the ground unconscious. The room erupted with bodies that rushed past her, bumping into her on their way to Derek. Blood rushed in her ears, making their shouts seem distant and faint.

She stepped back, stumbling as she tried to get out of the way. She didn't stop until she made contact with a wall. There, Kora flattened her hands on the stone before slowly sliding down until she was on the floor. That's where she remained, her knees up to her chest, as Derek was examined before they turned their attention to the cage.

Though she was in the room, it didn't feel as if she was in her body. Time was disjointed, fragmented. Derek's face kept replaying in her mind. The way his gaze had lit with exhilaration at breaking free, to anticipation at reaching her, and then seething when he realized he hadn't.

Miena hadn't just erased Derek, she had made sure his disdain of Kora was so deep that nothing could repair it. Kora had been processing what Merrill had told them about the eggs when she heard Derek. No prison would hold a man such as Derek, especially not one who wanted revenge for the supposed death of his family.

Kora couldn't think of anything that would convince Derek that Miena had lied. There had been eggs. Though no one had gone to see if they remained intact. Kora had a sinking feeling they weren't. It would be just like Miena to destroy them to get back at Villette. All the while proving to Derek that she spoke the truth.

Kings and mates filed in and out of the room. Derek was back in the cage, which had been repaired. What was next? Starting all over? He hadn't listened to how they'd met or what they had been through at Stonemore. Nothing she could say would change his feelings toward her. She knew it as surely as she knew she loved him.

The residents of Iron Hall came into the room one by one and added their power to the barrier around the cage. She watched it pulse each time new magic was introduced before going still. Her attention got snagged on Lotti, who walked in with Alasdair.

Kora should probably talk to them to find out what was going on with Villette, but she couldn't get to her feet. It wasn't as if she could do anything. The binding vow prevented Kora from attacking Villette. Miena was out of her reach, and Derek...was lost to her.

The last time she had lost so much, she had withdrawn from the world. From herself. She had shut away her hellhound abilities and forgotten them. It had done nothing. Villette still perpetrated her evil, innocents had died, and the past never left Kora.

Retreating seemed her only option now. She wanted to go

somewhere, lick her wounds, and heal her broken heart. But that was the easy way out. Besides, she had told herself at Stonemore that she was done running. She had taken a stand, and she owed it to herself, her ancestors, and everyone else to fight.

Even if it was the hardest thing she had ever done.

By the time she got to her feet, Alasdair and Lotti were gone. A few people still milled about the room, checking on the cage's integrity. Con waved her over. She tried not to look at Derek as she walked to the King of Kings, but she couldn't help herself.

"It's your turn," Con said when she reached him.

Kora frowned up at him. "For?"

"To add your magic to the shield."

"I don't think you want mine."

His dark eyes held a wealth of kindness as he looked at her. "What happened wasna your fault."

"It isn't that. It's just that…I'm a hellhound."

Humor lit his expression. "Exactly."

"I don't think you understand. I can burst into flames, and I'm fast. We're apparently only good at killing Star People. We don't do much else." At least, that she was aware of. And after several hundred years of life, she should know.

Or would she? She had tried to forget that she was a hellhound for most of that time.

"Everyone at Iron Hall who has magic has added theirs."

Warmth spread through her at being included. Accepted, even. These people didn't know her, but they had taken her in and listened. They had worked with her and protected her. These dragons, who were supposed to be her enemies, were now people she called friends.

Kora raised her hand until she felt the vibration of magic from the barrier. Sparks flew as fire danced from her palm and moved up her fingers. She pressed it against the shield and watched it absorb the blaze. The flames wove through the barrier, giving it form before slowly diminishing until they were gone, and the shield was invisible once more.

She lowered her arm to her side as her gaze landed on Derek. "How did he break through?"

"He's a dragon, but he wasna born like the rest of us. He was made. By the Star People."

Kora swung her gaze to Con. "Meaning?"

"As I feared, he has some of their magic. It isna a lot, but it's enough that he got through our layers. We're hoping the addition of all the magic of those here will keep him inside until we can reach him."

"That won't happen."

Con's blond brows snapped together. "Why do you say that?"

"It's what I saw in his eyes."

"And what he told Merrill."

Kora nodded. "I know we have time to work on him, but—"

"We doona," Con interjected.

Her heart skipped a beat. "What do you mean?"

His black gaze briefly lowered as he crossed his arms over his chest. "Miena approached Lotti, Alasdair, and Villette. It appeared she wanted Lotti and Villette to side with her. But after Miena left, the other three went to Stonemore. Villette feared her sister would take over, and she was right to worry. Miena is there and has sent Gordon to attack the villages."

"Of course, she has." Kora tried not to think about the innocents dying, all because she had trusted the wrong person.

Nothing was going according to plan. Miena seemed to be ahead of them at every turn.

"Merrill was right, you know," Con said. "Even if he is surlier than he used to be. We've been victorious because we didna give up. We stand united. There are many of us, and only one of her."

Kora wrinkled her nose as a shiver ran down her spine at the thought of Gordon. "With a dragon who apparently can't be killed."

"He was Alasdair's brother."

And she knew exactly who was responsible. "What did Villette do to him?"

"Your guess is as good as ours. Right now, our focus is on Derek. You need to keep talking to him."

Kora shook her head. "It's a waste of time."

Con stared at her for a long moment, then asked, "You have something else in mind?"

"It's an idea. I don't know if it's a good one." She laid out the plan, and not once did he laugh or tell her it was absurd.

He briefly raised his brows as he twisted his lips. "I doona need to be the one to say it could backfire."

"What will happen to him if we can't return his memories?"

Con said nothing.

Kora looked at Derek's unconscious body. "Exactly. No one wants to be in a cage. He's had little control of things in his life with the Star People wiping his memories and directing him at every turn. He's uninterested in anything we have to say. So, we show him instead."

"And if that doesna work? If you die? He'll still come for us."

She nodded and slid her gaze to him. "Then that decision will be in your hands. I'm open to other ideas."

"I'd like to try something where there isna a chance of your death."

There was always a chance of her death. Kora wasn't sure when she had accepted that. Maybe when she decided to find Villette. Or perhaps it was when she first stepped foot in Stonemore. All she knew was that there was only one place she had ever felt safe: Derek's arms. Nothing that had happened to him was his fault. He was a pawn in a vicious game where he was always the loser.

And it was time someone set him free.

CHAPTER 22

Nothing would have happened if Rhi hadn't been on her side. Each time someone asked Kora if she was sure about her plan, she wanted to say *nay*. She wasn't sure about anything anymore, but they were out of options.

Kora had to give it to those at Iron Hall, though. Once a decision was made, they went to work. There wasn't much to do, thankfully. Yet that meant the time where she would face Derek again drew nearer with each passing moment.

The first time on the cliffs hadn't gone well. She'd held on to that shred of hope until the very last second. The second time when Derek broke free of the enclosure, she had frozen. If he hadn't been knocked unconscious by the barrier, he would have gotten her. Everything hinged on this next effort.

Rhi came up beside her and gently nudged Kora to fall into step with her. The Fae glanced at the Kings busy weaving their magic. "I won't say this in front of anyone else, but I'm worried about the plan."

"Then why are you helping me?"

Rhi halted, dropping her arm as she smiled ruefully. "Because I know what it feels like to think you might lose the one you love."

Kora followed her gaze to find it locked on Con. The King of Kings suddenly looked up, and the two shared a silent look. Kora dropped her eyes.

Rhi turned her head to her then. "Besides, I recognized that look in your eyes."

"What look is that?"

"The one that says you intend to do this whether we're with you or not," Rhi answered with a grin. "I've worn that look many times, and I'm sure I'll wear it again."

Kora returned the smile. "My brother called me reckless."

"Reckless, rash, impulsive, impetuous. I've been called it all." She shoved her black hair out of her face. "I'm still standing. And so will you be, if I have anything to do about it."

"Then there are some things you need to know about hellhounds."

"This is when I should probably tell you that I've met another."

Kora smiled. "Xaneth. Con told me about him."

"Good. Once Miena and Villette are taken care of, I'll make sure the two of you meet."

Tears burned her eyes, but Kora quickly blinked them away. "It's been a very long time since I've seen another of my kind."

"He's never met any other either. It'll be good for both of you."

Kora grinned until she looked around her. "But first, Derek."

"First Derek," Rhi agreed.

A warm body brushed against Derek's. He knew her instantly. His arms wrapped around her as her lips brushed his throat. His hand splayed on her back, holding her close as her bare breasts met his chest. Desire wound through him, sending blood straight to his cock.

He captured her lips and kissed her. The feeling of their tongues tangling caused his balls to tighten. He grabbed her hip with one hand and rolled her onto her back. He ground into her, aching to be inside her once more.

This was his mate. He might not be able to recall her name or the features of her face, but he *knew* her body. He recognized the feel of her, the heat, the soft curves.

Her hands softly skimmed up his back, her nails gently raking over his skin as he kissed along her jaw and down her neck. "Derek."

Her raspy whisper made his blood heat. An inferno was building. She did that to him. Her and her alone. He cupped her breast, massaging the globe before circling her nipple with his thumb. Her back arched, and her ragged breaths filled the air as she rocked her hips against him. The friction of their bodies was delicious, but it wasn't nearly enough. He needed all of her. Even if it was only in his dreams.

He moved a hand between their bodies and touched the junction of her thighs. She sucked in a quick breath when his fingers grazed the folds of her sex. He groaned at how wet she was and guided himself to her entrance to slowly enter her.

She pulled his head down for another kiss as he began slowly moving inside her. He briefly opened his eyes and saw dark lashes against her skin. His heart began to beat faster. He was remembering!

Derek ended the kiss and raised up to look at his mate. A bellow of refusal began deep within him when he found himself staring at the hellhound. He shoved her away and came awake in the same instant.

Derek didn't move for several moments. The thought of touching the hellhound quickly rid his body of any remaining desire. He was disgusted with himself. It repulsed him that he couldn't get her taste off his tongue. How had her face taken that of his mate's? It had to be some form of magic. A new torture, most likely.

As he got his dismay and anger under control—and the dream shoved aside—he recalled breaking through the bars to get to the hellhound. Derek looked around for the cage, but it was gone. He slowly sat up and found himself in what looked like an arena. The seating encircled him, and the dome above him was painted to look like the sky.

Derek slowly got to his feet and turned in a circle. He used his enhanced senses to scan every inch, looking for anyone. He had nearly turned all the way around when he saw movement. Of all the people he'd thought would come to face him, it hadn't been the hellhound.

She walked out of a doorway with her head held high. She was dressed in all black, her dark hair falling free. Her gaze didn't move from him. She walked with purpose, her steps unhurried and confident.

No cage held him now. Nothing would stop him from ending her life. He glanced behind her, waiting for the Kings to file out, but there was only her. Derek immediately shifted. He grinned at the jolt she couldn't suppress. By the time he finished with her, she would be doing more than trembling.

The hellhound came to a stop and craned her neck to look up at him. "This is what you wanted, isn't it?" she asked, her arms out wide. "It's just you and me. What are you waiting for?"

It would be easy to kill her. He could exhale fire before she knew what was happening. It would engulf her, but it also meant a quick end. He was death, and he had come for her, but it would be slow and agonizing. He wanted her begging for him to end her life. Not that he would grant it. She hadn't considered the innocent lives she'd taken when she destroyed the eggs. And the Kings hadn't deemed his mate's life worth anything.

But he did.

This arena was inside somewhere, likely a place the Kings guarded. After their united front at Cairnkeep, he didn't believe for one instant that they would leave her to face him alone. They were here somewhere, waiting to make their entrance. He wanted them to come. He didn't care about living. How could he with all the grief?

Derek let out a roar filled with wrath and anguish—and the promise of death. The hellhound didn't cover her ears. She closed her eyes as the sound blasted her hair back. Then she looked at him.

"After such a display earlier, breaking through the bars, that is all th—"

He batted her away with his hand. Her words were cut off as she tumbled through the air and landed with a bone-jarring crunch against the wall that lined the arena. Derek feared he might have broken her neck when she didn't stir. Finally, she moved her leg, curling in on herself. She coughed and pushed up onto her hands. Her head lifted, and she swung her deep brown eyes to him. She didn't mask her pain, or maybe she couldn't.

Good. He was just getting started.

Shite, that hurt. Kora had known goading Derek would get a reaction, she only wished she had thought about what he might do. He hadn't tried to douse her with dragon fire. That had to mean something, didn't it? Unless he wanted her to suffer. The madness she saw in his red eyes confirmed that fear. Her body was healing, but it wouldn't mend fast enough to stay ahead of him.

Or even remain alive.

Kora had known there was a chance Derek would kill her and wait for her to come back before repeating it all over again. She had made Rhi and the others promise not to interfere unless Derek used fire. Not that she expected them to reach her in time. She had fought hard against death when she stood against Miena and Villette, and she wanted to live, but if giving her life meant Derek's freedom, then she would do it.

She got to her feet, holding her left arm against her broken rib. "I guess we're done talking then."

Her eardrum ruptured on his next roar. Blood trickled from her ear onto her cheek. Strands of hair stuck to the warm fluid. She kept her eyes on him to guess his next attack. He was massive and couldn't move as quickly as she did.

So, when he nimbly lunged at her in the next breath, it took her by surprise. Kora tried to step out of the way, but his reach was extensive. His talons raked her back as she spun. A cry of pain escaped as she tumbled forward onto her hands and knees.

He didn't wait for her to get to her feet this time. He tossed her into the air once more, knocking the breath from her. The ground and ceiling twirled so fast she didn't know which way was up. She didn't know how to right herself or even if she could. Then it didn't matter because she slammed into the ground. Dust wafted up around her. She opened her mouth for a breath and inhaled a mouthful, making her cough, which sent pain shooting through her body.

Another rib was broken. Maybe several of them. Three fingers on her right hand were out of joint, and given how one of them was bent at an odd angle, it was likely broken. Blood poured into her eye from a cut on her head. She couldn't stay down, though. She had to get up and face him.

Somehow, she got to her feet, only to realize that she couldn't put any weight on her left foot because it had snapped at the ankle. Kora kept her balance on her right and looked at Derek again.

He was playing with her—and enjoying every second.

CHAPTER 23

The scent of blood hung heavy in the arena. Derek had struck the hellhound hard enough to bring the Kings, but her protectors hadn't come pouring out. He turned and abruptly unfurled a wing. The end smacked into her chin, snapping her head back with a crack. She stumbled back onto her broken ankle, and her knee gave out.

Derek swung his wing and swept her up and into the air. There, he batted her with his wing a few more times just for the fun of it. His anger only swelled, though, because there were no screams of pain. Only a few moans had fallen from her lips. That meant it was time to get more forceful. He could hear his unborn children's screams in his head. He would hear hers, too.

Blood dribbled from her mouth to mingle with that from the cut on her temple. She rose to her knees and lifted her chin defiantly. His gaze scanned the area for the Kings. They still hadn't come. Perhaps they had turned their backs on her.

Derek waited until she was standing, then slashed a talon across her body, carving cloth and skin. Blood gushed from the wound. She stumbled, fighting to stay upright. He then whipped his tail around and embedded the end in her back, severing her spinal column.

The scream he had been yearning for finally filled the arena. But it did little to ease his grief.

He yanked the blade from her back and watched her body buckle and fall into a heap. Her chest rose and fell rapidly, her breaths wheezing as she clung to life. He moved to stand over her. Her eyes met his as a single tear rolled from the outside corner into the blood.

"It's all right, Derek. Do what you need to do."

Blood spilled onto the ground. Her dark hair was tangled and fanned around her. The light was fading from her eyes. Toying with her hadn't been as satisfying as he had thought. He should end her now with dragon fire and go find the Kings. Derek drew in a deep breath, fire stirring within his lungs.

But as he stared at the hellhound, the edges of his vision blurred and shifted. The sandy earth gave way to dark, packed ground and wild, green grass. The two scenes flickered back and forth several times. And with it, the hellhound. She was lying, bloodied, looking up at him in both. But her clothes were different, as was the emotion in her gaze.

Derek shook his head, hoping it would clear away whatever was happening. But the scenes kept fading from one to the other until he didn't know which was real. He tried to hold on to one, but there was no stopping whatever was happening.

He looked around. In one scene, there were empty seats, in the other, six blackened bodies.

In one, the silence of the arena. Then the sounds of a…marsh.

Inside. Outside.

Arid. Damp.

The hellhound. Kora.

The minute her name filled his mind, the memories flooded in with searing urgency. His talons plunged into the ground as agony racked his body. He never took his eyes from Kora, even as the life drained from hers. He had shredded her body. He, who had sworn to keep her safe, had brought her misery.

Voices broke through the haze. Derek immediately lowered himself over Kora to protect her as others spilled into the arena. He roared, warning them to stay clear. They halted. All except one.

Merrill slowly moved away from the group. "Derek? We're no' going to let you kill her."

Kill? Derek looked at Kora. It was what he had wanted, what he'd yearned for. All because Miena had said she'd destroyed the eggs. Another roar rolled from him as he fully comprehended what had been done to him. Derek returned to human form on his knees and touched Kora's face, but she was gone. The one person he had never wanted to hurt.

It didn't matter that she would revive. He had caused her immense pain, and she had taken it. She had told him it was okay. To do what he needed.

Sorrow cut through him as he gathered Kora into his arms and rocked back and forth, his face buried in her neck. His anguish had been real, but not directed at Miena's fictional adversary. His heart, his very soul, had tried to tell him who Kora was. If only he had *seen*.

Even his mind had conjured Kora. Her body, her voice. Why hadn't he put things together? Why hadn't he figured it out?

"Derek."

He stilled and lifted his head enough to see Merrill. "Don't touch her."

Merrill lifted his hands, palms out. "I can take you to her room where we can get her cleaned up."

"No one is touching her but me."

"As you wish." Merrill lowered his arms and took a step back, waiting.

Derek noticed the others watching. He only cared about Kora, but her eyes were closed. Her beautiful, warm brown eyes that had gazed at him so lovingly as he stood over her, ready to engulf her in flames. By the stars! He had nearly ended her life for good.

He adjusted her body and got to his feet. Derek didn't look at the others in the arena as he followed Merrill to an open section of the wall. More Kings were there. They had stood by and let him hurt Kora, and there was only one reason for that: Kora had asked it of them.

The sand gave way to cool, smooth stone beneath his bare feet. Kora's blood dripped from her body, leaving a trail in their wake. Merrill said nothing. No one followed, and they didn't encounter anyone else in the many corridors they traversed.

Derek should have studied the hallways in case he needed to get out. It wasn't as if he had his cuff anymore. But he couldn't think of anything but Kora. How she'd stood before him in the arena. Talked to him when he was caged. Used her fire to call him at Cairnkeep. She hadn't given up. Not once. Not even when he'd hurled hurtful words at her.

Not even when he attacked her.

He had felt it when she breathed her last. Everything went blurry as his eyes filled with tears. At least she would revive. But what if she wasn't able? What if his memories hadn't returned? What if he had burned her? He didn't like the dark turn of his thoughts. It was better not to linger on those lest he fall into the pit of despair that waited.

It felt as if they walked for hours before Merrill opened a door and stood aside. Derek halted at the doorway to look inside.

"Blood washes out," Merrill said. "And if it doesna, things can be replaced."

Derek still hesitated.

"What do you need?" Merrill asked.

What did he need? He needed time. Forgiveness. But that wasn't what Merrill wanted to know. He was asking about Kora. Derek held her tighter. "The greater the injuries, the longer it takes her body to recover. It took nearly a full day the last time. These wounds are worse."

The wounds *he* had given her.

"You doona have to tend to her alone," Merrill said.

"I need to do it on my own."

Merrill nodded. "I'll be close if you change your mind."

They didn't trust him. He wouldn't either. But they had trusted Kora. What it must have taken her to travel to the very creatures she feared. It demonstrated her courage once more. Not that he had ever questioned it. He had appreciated her bravery from the very beginning.

He walked into the room and gently lowered Kora into the tub. Derek went to the bed and moved the pillows so it would be ready after he cleaned her. When he turned around, Merrill was gone, and the door was closed.

Derek returned to Kora and turned on the water, filling the tub halfway. Then he began the process of tenderly cleaning her body.

When the water became too stained with blood, he drained it and repeated the steps until she was clean. Then he focused on her hair.

The activity took awhile, but it was better than sitting in a chair and doing nothing. So, he washed her hair twice, keeping her reclined against the back of the tub as he combed out the long strands. Only then did he carry her to the bed and smooth the covers over her.

Now came the part he hated the most. The waiting. Because he feared there might be another way to kill a hellhound besides dragon fire. Alone in the chamber, there was nothing for him to do but worry and think. His moods swung between rage and dread.

But he knew one thing: Miena had to die.

Derek grew restless after sitting for hours and moved about the room. He didn't know where he was, and he wasn't sure he would get an answer if he asked. He hadn't seen any large buildings when he was at Cairnkeep. There was also the fact that he hadn't seen any real windows to the outside. It made him consider the possibility that they were underground.

It might be better if he didn't know the location. That way, neither Miena nor Villette could pull the information from him. He hated how easily they could mess with his head. They cared nothing about who he was. It was only about them and what they were after. Derek never wanted to see another Star Person in his life, but he didn't have that option. He owed it to those he had unknowingly—and knowingly—harmed on their behalf to rid Zora of any and all Star People.

Derek halted next to a bench that had clothes laid out for Kora. All were made of the same material in different colors. He rubbed the fabric between his fingers. It was soft but also strong. He looked down, just now remembering that he was naked. He used magic to clothe himself.

A soft knock on the door pulled his attention. Derek glanced toward the bed, but Kora didn't stir. He made his way to the door and opened it to find Merrill holding a tray of food.

"How is she?" he asked.

Derek opened the door wider to let him see the bed.

Merrill lifted the tray. "This is for both of you."

"Thanks." Derek took the tray and brought it to the table.

"How are you?"

He shrugged as he turned back to the door. "I'm fine."

"That's shite. You can try that with Kora when she wakes, but no' me. I saw you in that arena."

Derek ran a hand down his face and looked away from Merrill's dark blue gaze. "I hurt her."

"She isna dead."

"She was about to be."

"Nay, she wasna."

Derek frowned. "What do you mean?"

"Con's mate, Rhi, is a Fae. They can veil themselves. She was there. She saw you about to breathe fire and was at Kora's side to get her away."

"Why didn't she?"

Merrill gave him a pointed look. "She saw what we did. Kora thought that if she could recreate the first time you saw her die, it would bring you back. Few of us believed her. But she was right."

"You shouldn't have let her do that."

"There was no stopping her."

Derek turned his head to the bed. "What happened after Miena took me?"

"More than you're going to like."

His gaze swung back to the Dragon King. "Tell me."

"We're working with Villette."

Derek's suspicion was short-lived. He nodded as understanding dawned. "She's helping you find Miena."

"And you."

"Don't trust her."

Merrill crossed his arms over his chest. "We doona. She and Kora made a binding vow. It was the only way Kora would let her out of the flames."

"Kora had her?" Derek asked in surprise.

Merrill nodded. "She did. The only reason she agreed to work with Villette was to find you."

Derek found his eyes seeking Kora once more.

"You need to tell her," Merrill said.

"Tell her what?"

"That she's your mate."

Derek drew in a deep breath and slowly released it. "I'm not someone she should want."

"Tell that to your heart. Or hers," Merrill replied before walking away.

CHAPTER 24

Freedom. Miena stood at the edge of the lake and watched the soft ripples as fat raindrops splashed into the water. In all the endless years she had wandered the vast universe visiting different realms, she had never been afraid, had never feared. She had only known certainty and might. Being a Star Person meant that everything was there for the taking.

But to have what she coveted, she had to be intrepid and bold. It was something Miena had learned early in life surrounded by so many siblings. Especially when each tried to outdo the other. There had been no mother, no father, no elders to guide or teach. They had learned as they went. And destroyed many worlds in the process.

Zora was meant to be different. It was meant to be hers.

But she had been betrayed.

It galled Miena that she hadn't anticipated Villette's move. Little, annoying, never-bright-enough-to-think-up-her-own-plan

Villette had bested her. Locked away in that room, wearing the same dress, staring at the same walls, surrounded by the insufferable heat, Miena had imagined all the ways she would retaliate against her sister. Her anger had festered, and her indignation had chafed. Rankled.

Miena prided herself on always being several steps ahead of others. And when she wasn't, she went her own way until she was the brightest and quickest. The cleverest. It was why she had chosen Villette to partner with. She had believed with absolute conviction that her little sister would never attempt to betray her.

She looked down at her wrists, rubbing them. She could still feel the weight of the manacles. It infuriated her that Villette had duped her, but along with her outrage was humiliation. To add insult to injury, none of her siblings had come to free her. Not a single one. It proved what she had always feared: She could only count on herself. Never again would she align with another. Never again would she trust.

The rain beat a slow, steady rhythm upon the lake. She tilted her head back and closed her eyes as the water pelted her face. She had hurriedly escaped the rain so many times, but that was before her imprisonment. After yearning to feel something different for thousands of years, she now greeted the change in weather with open arms. She didn't even care that her gown was getting drenched.

Miena lowered her head and walked along the shore, her shoes dangling from her fingers. The sand eagerly soaked up the rain, turning it from dark gold to bronze. Her feet sank gently into the sodden shoreline, the grains greedily clutching at her bare toes. A blaze of fiery red was cast upon the shore by the sinking sun hanging between the two mountains.

But she didn't pay attention to the sunset. She was plotting. The talk with Villette and Lotti had gone exactly as she had predicted. Miena was still peeved at Kora for getting the cuff off Merrill. He would've been a great asset to have. Not only had Gordon not killed Kora, but Miena didn't have Merrill under her control. That had been a double blow, but she had adjusted accordingly.

It had been a simple enough feat to get Derek to target Kora. She wanted to be there when he tracked her down, but Miena had other adversaries to deal with. Kora's death would be nothing compared to what was coming.

Derek had been Miena's prized possession. Bryok had been a close second, but Derek was special. He had been her first creation. He was also her greatest accomplishment—and he would give her dominion over Zora in epic fashion and make her siblings take notice.

The rain tapered to a light mist. Miena's hair was wet and stuck to her face, but she loved the way it felt. The crispness in the air made chills race over her skin. Temperatures barely registered for Star People, and only occasionally did they react. But when it happened, it was glorious. She stopped and soaked in the sensation before it faded.

When she opened her eyes, she found herself staring into a face she had thought never to see again. "Eurielle."

"Hello, sister."

Her straight, dark hair was gathered high on the back of her head with strategically placed gold fasteners down the length to create the illusion that her hair was bubbling. Gray eyes watched Miena with wariness. Eyes that had always seen too much. Miena had hated that about Eurielle. That and the fact her older sister had always thought herself better than the rest of the family.

Miena was the one who told their siblings about Eurielle's intention to keep Zora—and the dragons—a secret. The result had been Eurielle's punishment to remain on Zora indefinitely. Even now, after such a sentence, she stood defiant. The sinking sun created a halo behind Eurielle, setting her dark hair alight and outlining her silhouette in gold.

Eurielle had always had a quiet, still beauty about her. One Miena was embarrassed to admit she envied. Eurielle hadn't wanted to be the best or the bravest. She had simply wanted to *be*. Only once had Eurielle interfered on a realm, and she had felt so bad about it that she'd retreated deeper into herself.

Miena had assumed she would go off into a cave somewhere and hide away. But that meek, disgraced woman wasn't who stood before her now. Her elder sister had changed. There was a toughness about her now, a sense of uncompromising resilience that hadn't been there before. Maybe it was in the cut of her attire. The dark mauve gown with its long sleeves and high neck contoured to her upper body. The shoulder points stretched past her shoulders with silver flower embroidery that reminded Miena of armor. The front laced down the middle with string of the same color, and her waist was cinched tight. The skirt fell softly to her calves to reveal her knee-high boots. Yes, her sister had definitely changed.

But then, so had she.

"This is a surprise," Miena stated.

A gently arched dark brow rose on Eurielle's forehead. "It shouldn't be." Her face slackened as if something had just occurred to her. "You must not have spoken to the others."

"I've been otherwise occupied." Miena didn't have time for her siblings. Any of them. And that included Eurielle.

"Then let me warn you. Leave Zora. Right now."

Too bad Eurielle hadn't shown this side of herself long ago. "I don't think so."

"This realm has been claimed."

"By you?" Miena asked with a bark of laughter. "I took it from you easily before. I'll do it again."

Eurielle's smile was slow, amusement lighting her gray eyes. "You never change, do you?"

"But you have."

"Perhaps."

"You still don't have the power to take me on." At least Miena didn't think she did. That was part of the problem in not interacting with the others. Eurielle's confidence gave her pause, but Miena had never backed down from anything. She wasn't about to start now.

Eurielle tucked an errant strand of hair behind her ear. "You won't win this time. Leave. Find someplace else to play your games."

"Are you attempting to save Villette?"

Eurielle laughed. "She can take care of herself."

"Then why the urging to leave?"

"Maybe I'm trying to save you."

It was Miena's turn to laugh. "You don't seriously think I'll believe that, do you?"

"Perhaps you could try."

"Did you come get me out of the prison Villette put me in?"

Eurielle blew out a breath. "I did not."

"Then I have no reason to believe anything you say," Miena stated.

Eurielle shrugged. "Don't say I didn't warn you." She started to turn away before she paused and met Miena's gaze once more. "How are things going with your new plan?"

Miena didn't have a chance to respond before Eurielle vanished. Her sister's words caused disquiet to slither through her. She had been so lost in her thoughts that she hadn't realized how long it had been since she'd last tried to contact Derek. He hadn't responded then, but she had assumed he was in battle since he hadn't replied. She had seen him when he crossed onto the dragons' land. Nothing would deter him from his mission.

"Derek," she called through their mental link.

The silence that followed made her agitation grow.

"Derek! Answer now!"

Still nothing. He would answer if he could. Had the Kings killed him? If they had, he hadn't gone down alone. She should've been there to see it. She should've stayed in contact with him. Because, as powerful as he was, and as deep as she had dug into his mind, she hadn't been able to get rid of everything that made him who he was. If she had, it would have ended him. So she'd had no choice but to leave some. She had thought she'd only left enough, but what if she had left too much?

Miena teleported to the border at the start of Raynia Canyon and looked across to the countryside. The dragons steered clear of the barrier since it was so close to Stonemore. Just thinking of the city she had taken back from Villette made her grin. But this wasn't about her sister. It was about Derek.

She walked the last few steps to the concealed barrier and moved to cross it when she was thrown backward, landing unceremoniously on her butt. Miena clenched her jaw and got to her feet. She tried to dust herself off, but the dirt clung to her wet clothes. With a wave of her hand, she traded them for a three-quarter-length-sleeve teal velvet wrap gown, then tried to cross again.

Miena was prepared when she was thrown back this time. She stayed on her feet but only just. Dragon magic couldn't keep her from crossing. Could it? Had the former slaves developed more potent abilities during their time on Earth? She hadn't asked Villette if she had crossed the border. Miena just assumed she had. There was no reason her younger sister wouldn't.

Unless she couldn't.

Magic from another of her kind could keep her out. Eurielle's warning came to mind. Perhaps Miena had been wrong to disregard it. She hadn't thought Eurielle's power was that strong, but she had been away for a very long time.

"Not even you can protect the dragons, Eurielle," Miena said aloud.

She had wanted to make them suffer and have some fun before creating more like Derek, but Eurielle had ruined it. So, she would wreck things for her sister once more. Miena snapped her fingers, a move meant to wipe out all dragons—even Derek, if he was still alive. She didn't have to worry about Gordon since he lived because of star magic.

"Same old Miena."

She whirled around to find Eurielle. "You should know better than to try and keep me from crossing the border."

"Oh, that wasn't me."

Miena was ready to call her a liar, but something in her sister's gray eyes made her stomach drop to her feet. "Who?"

"I could tell you, but what would be the fun in that?"

"I'm not in the mood for games," Miena replied tersely.

Eurielle grinned. "Everything is a game to you."

"It doesn't matter. The dragons are gone."

"Hardly."

Miena knew the extent of her powers. The dragons were dead.

"Look behind you," Eurielle said as she pointed over Miena's shoulder.

Miena didn't want to do it, but she turned and saw the distinct silhouette of a dragon in the distance. Her gaze swung back to Eurielle. "Tell me who is doing this? Which of our siblings dares to interfere?"

"You mean like you've meddled so many times before?"

"Who?" she bellowed.

Eurielle ignored her outburst. "Last warning. Leave Zora. It is protected. The dragons are protected."

"Then how has Villette been killing them?"

"That was then."

Miena didn't believe a word of what she was hearing. "This is you, Eurielle. I know it."

"We've done enough to the dragons. Our brother freed them and gave them a home. Villette ruined it. Zora became their second home, and I won't allow either of you to do more damage."

"It *is* you." Miena couldn't believe her mild-mannered sister had developed such audacity.

Maybe more had changed than Miena had first thought. She wasn't used to being defeated. She needed to regroup and reevaluate. More importantly, she needed to boost her magic. She had gorged herself when she first got free, but there was no such thing as too much.

"You can't protect them forever," Miena taunted.

Eurielle didn't take the bait. "Get used to losing, sister."

Miena shot her a glare, but a thought took root. Eurielle might have won this round, but Miena didn't intend to lose any more. And she knew just what to do.

Eurielle's knees gave out a heartbeat after Miena left. She caught herself with her hands and let her head hang. It had taken everything she had to create the bubble around Miena to keep her from killing the dragons. Keeping her out of their territory had taken much more than Eurielle had estimated. She had goaded Miena here, but it wouldn't work a second time. Eurielle should've stayed hidden. Miena might have believed herself inferior and left the dragons alone.

Eurielle shook her head at the thought. Miena would never give up. It wasn't in her nature. But people changed. She had. No more standing in the background watching. No more slights of hand in hopes her siblings didn't notice. She wouldn't hide anymore. She had taken a stand, and she didn't care who knew it.

CHAPTER 25

The surge of breath was like a punch as it yanked Kora back into the world of the living. Her muscles seized as her lungs filled and deflated. Slowly, the tension ebbed from her body. She had to try three times to swallow to wet her dry mouth. Her vision was blurry, causing her to blink until things came into focus.

The sight of the chamber was comforting. On the heels of that was the memory of what had happened in the arena. Kora scanned the room in hopes of finding Derek, but no one was there. Not Derek greeting her. Nor anyone telling her that it had worked. Which meant her plan had failed.

The grief was unfathomable, the anguish endless. She wanted to scream in denial and release the flood of tears, but another emotion skimmed along with the others: rage. She gripped it tightly and held it close. Her ire would get her up and moving so she could take down Miena.

Kora sat up, grimacing at the pull of muscles and organs in

their last stages of mending. She swung her legs over the side of the bed and sat. The cuts and contusions were healed. Even her bones had knitted back together. But nothing could be done about her broken heart.

She was clean of all blood. It was only the second time she had woken thus. The first was when Derek had washed her. That was the day she had told him she was a hellhound. A secret she had never told another soul. That day seemed so long ago, yet it had only been a week. There was no use reliving those memories and wishing for a different outcome. The only thing left now was to get dressed, find the others, and figure out the next steps.

After she asked about Derek.

She needed to prepare herself for the answer. Though she wasn't sure how much worse she could feel, knowing he was gone forever. Did it matter if he still lived? He wouldn't be Derek, and he wouldn't be with her. Kora didn't care what others said. If she hadn't freed Miena, she wouldn't have taken Derek. But Kora would rectify her mistake.

One way or another.

She got to her feet with a sigh. Her legs wobbled for a moment but held. She wanted a long soak, but she had no idea how long it had taken for her to recover. There would be time to linger in the tub later. She turned to get dressed when movement in a corner drew her attention. A tall form moved out of the shadows.

The sight of Derek drew her up short. Her heart missed a beat. She blinked, unsure if her mind was playing tricks on her. He stood rigid, his brow furrowed slightly as his pale olive eyes watched her.

"Derek?" she whispered, hoping against hope.

The lines on his face eased. "It's me."

Relief flooded her, making her dizzy. His face blurred as her eyes filled with tears. She hurried to him. He was before her in two strides, one hand tangling in her hair at the back of her neck and the other winding around her as his mouth came down on hers. Kora clung to him, touched his face, his shoulders, his back.

He bent her over his arm and deepened the kiss, almost as if he were trying to meld their bodies. His hand smoothed down her back to cup her bottom and bring her flush against his arousal. To have him in her arms again was everything, especially when she had thought him lost forever. But he was here. The only thing wrong was that his clothes were between them.

She yanked at his shirt, but his clothes suddenly disappeared, and she was pinned between him and the wall. He lifted her so she could wrap her legs around his waist. His cock rubbed against the folds of her sex. She groaned, needing more.

Needing *him*.

He ended the kiss and looked at her. The blunt head of his arousal pushed against her entrance. He held her gaze as he slowly filled her, holding her still with his large hands when she tried to move. Then he gradually pulled out until only the head of him remained. It was maddening. It was exhilarating. She held her breath, waiting for more. Craving him and the ecstasy that awaited.

With one hard thrust, he filled her. Kora cried out from the pleasure. His mouth seized hers again as he began to drive in and out of her. She gripped his shoulders, the thick sinew moving and bunching beneath her hands. His body was powerful, potent. And she couldn't get enough of him. Would never get enough.

He was the balm to her soul, the fever to her passion, the fire to her yearning.

The strength of her purpose.

Desire tightened, throbbed. It swelled and surged. She tore her lips from his as she orgasmed. Kora rode the wave of pleasure as ecstasy swept her up in its embrace. She was slowly returning to awareness when Derek's fingers dug into her thigh. He buried himself deeply inside her. She could feel him shuddering as the walls of her sex pulsed around his cock.

He carried her to the bed, gently putting a knee on the mattress and laying them across it. He pulled out of her and propped up on an elbow on his side. She ran her fingers over his cheek to scrape against his whiskers.

"I'm sorry. For everything. But mostly for the pain I inflicted upon you."

She shook her head and put her finger to his lips. "You have nothing to apologize for. None of it was your fault."

He gently moved her hand away. "They were my actions."

"Based on lies."

"I didn't have to attack. I certainly didn't need to torment you."

She rolled to her side to face him. "You thought I killed your children."

"I nearly..." He looked away for a moment. "I nearly used dragon fire."

"But you didn't. There's no need for us to linger on *nearlys* or *almosts*. It didn't happen. Let's focus on that."

His brow furrowed as misery filled his eyes. "I promised I would never hurt you. I broke that."

"*You* didn't. Miena took what made you you." She rose on her elbow so their faces were even. "I don't hold you responsible for any of it. It's Miena who needs to pay."

"The sooner, the better."

She pressed her lips to his. "That, we can agree on."

He blinked, and his face tightened as he leaped to his feet, pulling her with him. "We need to get dressed."

"What is it?" she asked as she rushed to her clothes.

"Merrill is waiting."

"What happened?"

"Miena."

That was all Kora needed to hear. Derek used magic to call his clothes then stood waiting anxiously as she hurried into hers and tugged on her boots, jumping from one foot to the other. He threw open the door where Merrill was standing just outside.

"Follow me," Merrill said as he turned to start walking.

Kora hurried to keep up with their long strides. Her gut twisted as she thought of the private time she and Derek had taken when Miena was out there. It felt selfish to have taken those few precious moments, but she had needed them more than she realized.

She expected Merrill to take them to the main area, but he led her and Derek to a room already packed with people. Some were noticeably absent, however. The children. After watching Stonemore's priests kill the girl, Kora was hyperaware of all the children around her. She refused to allow another to die on her watch.

While she and Derek remained near the back, Merrill continued toward the front where Con and his children stood.

Kora leaned close to Derek. "That's Con. With him are his children, Brandr and Eurwen."

"They favor him."

"They're able to have children on their world," she explained. Just then, Rhi came into view. "And that's their mother, Rhi."

Something passed over Derek's face, but he quickly tucked it away. She wanted to ask, but Kora knew he wouldn't say anything when surrounded by so many. Instead, she slipped her hand into his. He turned pale olive eyes to her and they shared a wordless look—one where she didn't need to voice how happy she was to have him there.

And he didn't need to tell her how glad he was to be standing beside her.

Sharing the same looks other couples had that she'd envied. That longing had been fulfilled. She wanted to jump for joy. She wanted to spend days in Derek's arms. Instead, they had an enemy to take down.

"Kora. Derek."

The sound of Con's deep voice with his strange accent drew their attention. Con motioned them to the front. Kora was about to politely refuse, but Derek squeezed her fingers.

"We're indebted to them," he whispered.

Kora couldn't argue with that. It wasn't the first time she'd had so many eyes on her, but it wasn't as nerve-wracking as before. Derek appeared outwardly calm, but she felt the stiffness in his hand that remained twined with hers.

Derek halted before Con. "I owe you all a great debt."

"You owe us nothing. You're one of us," the King of Dragon Kings replied.

Derek bowed his head as the two clasped forearms. Kora released Derek to stand beside Merrill as they got down to business.

"Gordon has to be stopped from taking more innocent life," Eurwen announced.

Someone from the back asked, "Why are we standing here talking? We need to stop him."

"That's exactly what she wants," Merrill said.

A muscle worked in Derek's jaw as the room erupted in voices. Kora knew he had something to say. And she wasn't the only one who noticed.

"Say what's on your mind," Brandr urged.

Derek grimaced. "She wants to draw us out to put us in a specific situation of her making."

"I agree," Con replied.

Rhi wound her long, black locks behind her head and fastened them. "I'm not going to sit around and watch innocents die. We don't have a choice but to stop Gordon."

"We do," Kora said. She bit her lip when they looked at her. The conversations dwindled, then quieted. "We have Villette. She wants Miena gone more than we do."

Merrill grunted. "I hate to admit it, but Kora's right. We need to use Villette."

CHAPTER 26

It felt wrong not to take to the skies and go straight for Gordon. It's what he would've done before. But things were different. *He* was different. Derek looked at Kora, who stood at his side, listening intently. Rhi had brought them and a small group that consisted of Con, Brandr, Merrill, and Hector to meet Villette, Alasdair, and Lotti. Other Kings had been divided into groups to patrol the borders in case Miena launched an attack against the dragons.

Alasdair, Lotti, and Villette had followed Gordon. The trio had tried to distract him from his rampage across the land, but it hadn't been successful. Now, all of them stood in the ruins of a village Villette's army had destroyed.

Derek had learned a lot in a short time. There had been the fact that Lotti was a Star Person, which had been difficult to acknowledge after swearing the doom of all like her. Kora liked her, and that went a long way to softening his reaction. Then there was Iron Hall, confirming his suspicions about them being underground.

There hadn't been time to learn more of the Kings' names, but Derek hoped he got a chance later. Kora had whispered a promise of them exploring Iron Hall together when all of this was done.

All of this. War. She meant war. No one wanted to say it, but they all knew that was exactly what it was.

Villette's gaze finally turned to him. Derek prepared himself, but she looked away without comment. Maybe she was interested in getting rid of Miena. He still didn't trust her, but he would rather have her on their side than against them. At least they had a chance with Villette. She knew how Miena thought.

"I'll ram Gordon and force him to fight me," Alasdair said as they stood in a circle. "He can no' ignore that."

Villette crossed her arms over her chest. She wore gold armor on her upper body over a sky blue gown. The armor was so thin the blue could be seen beneath it. The metal covered her upper body from her neck to past her hips. The shoulders were triple layered with armor running down her arms. Elbow guards and gauntlets completed the ensemble. Her blond hair was gathered in braids to fall down her back. "You can't kill him."

"Everything can die," Rhi said. "We need to find what takes him down and keeps him there."

Merrill looked to Derek. "We faced him before. Let's do it again."

"That would be a mistake," Villette said. "Miena needs to see Derek. He will be the one to divide her attention."

Kora nodded. "I agree. She went to a lot of trouble to take Derek, and she'll want to make sure he's still on her side."

"She reached out. I didn't reply." Derek saw Kora frown. He

hadn't told her or anyone that until now. Not to hide it, but because there hadn't been time before. "I'll find her."

Villette's blue eyes swung to him. "She'll demand you prove your loyalty."

"Do whatever she wants," Hector urged. "We can take it."

Villette shook her head. "It won't be against any of you."

"Then the answer is nay. He shouldn't have to hurt anyone else," Kora stated.

Derek couldn't help but grin at the way she protected him. No one had done that for him before. He hadn't told her about his feelings. He hadn't said the words, at least. He had shown her, but he should have voiced them. He would. Before he went into battle, he would find a few moments alone with her and say the words. "I'll minimize what I can, but we have to convince her."

Villette nodded. "If Derek makes her believe he's still loyal, we'll have an opportunity to double-cross her. But it'll have to be *very* convincing."

Derek knew what she meant. He had killed without hesitation when he believed it was to help the dragons. The truth had been revealed now, however. Could he so easily take life again? Even if it would end the suffering of so many in the long run?

"We doona have time for this shite," Brandr said. "People are dying."

Derek blew out a breath. "Then I'll go now."

"Not until we have a plan," Kora said urgently.

Villette was quick to point out, "The less he knows, the better."

"It won't work," came a new voice. "She'll expect a betrayal."

Derek looked over his shoulder to see woman standing on a fallen door. Tall and dark-haired, with a slender, delicate frame garbed in a simple maroon tunic and matching trousers tucked into black boots. Her gray eyes briefly met his before returning to Villette.

"Eurielle," Lotti said, a smile in her voice. "I was hoping you heard me."

Derek knew without asking that Eurielle was another Star Person. How many more were on the realm? And why Zora? If the universe was as big everyone kept saying, what brought them to this world? He glanced at Kora to see her reaction. If anyone knew if someone was evil, it was her. She gave him a small shake of her head.

"Does this mean you're joining us?" Alasdair asked.

Eurielle and Villette stared at each other for a long time before she nodded her head of dark hair. "I am."

"Three against one," Villette said. "This should be interesting. Why, though? Why come out of the shadows now?"

Eurielle stepped into the crumbling ruin of the building and made her way to their circle. She stood between Lotti and Hector, who couldn't take his eyes off her. "I chose a side when I disregarded my family's orders and helped Alasdair and Lotti. I saw Miena recently. We spoke, and after, I followed her. She went to the border." Eurielle shrugged a slim shoulder. "She intended to cross to find Derek but I stopped her."

"A bold move," Villette stated, respect in her blue gaze.

Eurielle's throat bobbed as she swallowed. "It infuriated her. She then attempted to wipe out all dragons on this realm."

There were varying reactions. Most, Derek noted, were shocked and appalled. A few, like Con and Brandr, were outraged. It was Villette's awed expression that caught his attention.

"You were able to stop her?" Villette said in a voice low with wonder.

Eurielle's lips flattened. "Barely. If she had attempted it a second time, I wouldn't have been able to do anything."

"We owe you," Brandr said.

The two shared a silent look. Derek watched the exchange with interest. "Does Miena know it was you?" he asked.

"She does," Eurielle admitted.

Villette smiled, a real smile that took everyone aback. Even Derek. She looked...pretty.

He didn't like this side of her. She appeared too human. Too relatable.

"Up!" Alasdair suddenly bellowed.

Everyone looked up through the damaged roof to see amethyst scales headed their way. The three Star People calmly walked outside. Rhi teleported to jump onto the back of a gold dragon. The Kings rushed from the building and shifted, jumping into the air to fight. Derek watched, wanting to join them.

"Go," Kora said.

"I—" he began, wanting to tell her of his feelings.

She smiled and touched his face. "Me, too."

He took one last look at her before running out. Derek didn't immediately shift. He went to touch the cuff out of habit, only to remember that it was gone. He headed in the opposite direction toward Stonemore and Miena while the Kings fought Gordon. How had Gordon found them? But he knew. Miena.

All he could do now was hope she hadn't seen him with the Kings. Derek ran like the wind, the ground rushing beneath him so quickly it was a blur. When the roars grew distant, he leaped into the air and shifted, unfurling his great wings. He soared into the air and looked back at the battle. He hesitated, hovering as he wondered if he should return to the Kings. Then he thought of

Kora and how she had looked up at him with such trust and passion.

He didn't want to leave her side again, but he had to. Derek looked toward Stonemore. He hated everything about the city. He wouldn't just destroy Miena, he would turn Stonemore to dust.

Derek covered miles with a single flap of his wings. His gaze locked on the Tunris Mountains and the peak where the palace was. Miena was there, waiting. As he made his way to the city, he thought about the lies he had been told, the manipulation used to control him. Miena was his creator, the one who had given him life. He wanted to be the one to take hers, but no matter how hot his dragon fire was, it wouldn't kill her.

Though she could take his with a thought. Or remove his memories again. Derek yearned for a chance at a real life. One with Kora. If he didn't guard his thoughts, words, and actions, Miena would make sure he never got a future. He had hung onto a bit of Kora before. He knew in his heart that nothing Miena or anyone else did could ever make him forget her.

By the time he swept down from the clouds, he had locked away his hate and resentment. But not all of it. He had to be convincing in his aversion to the Kings and Kora.

He flew over the city and heard the inhabitants' screams as they spotted him. Miena walked out onto a large balcony and lifted her head to him. Derek circled her, spiraling lower and lower until he shifted and dropped to his feet behind her.

She turned to face him, her eyes raking over his nude body before he clothed himself. Miena said nothing as she stood in white and silver armor from head to toe. Unlike Villette, she chose trousers, though her armor wasn't any less ornate.

"Well?" she asked.

This was the test. He had planned on one thing, and she likely expected another. But he did neither. "The Kings claim you lie."

Fury flashed across her face at the affront. Never mind that she had, indeed, lied. "I thought you were more intelligent than that. Of course, they say I'm lying. They fear you attacking them. Which, I take by you standing here, didn't happen."

"Oh, I did."

She turned her head slightly, her green eyes narrowing. "And?"

"It was only after I took some of them down that they wanted to talk." If she could lie, so could he.

"Why would you listen to them?"

He shrugged indifferently. "I had the advantage."

"Obviously, you gave it up."

"I got my revenge." Sadly, that was partly true. And in the process, he'd nearly lost the only person who meant something to him.

Her eyes lit with curiosity. "Tell me."

"They tried to protect the hellhound, but I got her."

"Did you kill her?"

Derek nodded as an image of Kora's bloodied body flashed in his mind.

"You burned her?"

Derek nodded, unable to say the words.

Miena smiled triumphantly, but it dimmed immediately. "But not the Kings."

"They have no knowledge of me or my mate. Without my memory, I must have facts."

"You didn't need them to go after the hellhound."

"I remembered the eggs."

Alarm crossed her face but disappeared quickly. "You remember them?" she asked carefully.

He'd thought that admission might unsettle her. Miena thought she had scoured his mind of everything, but she had missed that. At first, he had believed it intentional to make her story believable, but after seeing her face, he knew that wasn't the case.

"What else do you remember?"

"Flashes here and there." He wanted to tell her that he recalled everything, to yell it into her face. But that would come later. For now, he had to convince her.

Eurielle's doubt made him question every emotion that crossed Miena's face and every question out of her mouth.

"Head wounds are tricky," Miena said. "I think you'll get all the answers you're looking for very soon."

Unease swirled in Derek's gut. He tried to reach out to Con, but he didn't answer. Neither did Merrill. No one did. Miena was making sure he couldn't communicate with them.

She held out her hand, and a helmet formed in her palm. She slipped it onto her head. It was white with white metal contouring her nose and across her cheekbones. Silver shielded her ears and jaw, and a white strap held her chin. The back of the helmet was plain, but the four, silver, finger-like barbs jutting backward with three-inch blades at the ends caught his attention.

"You have a second chance to get your revenge on the Kings. Come, we'll fight them together."

Derek wavered for too long, and it earned him a sharp look. "Shift. I will ride upon your back into battle."

CHAPTER 27

Kora hurried outside to watch Derek fly away but couldn't do it for long. It was too painful to have him leave again. Roars reverberated through the air, drowning out all other sounds and dragging her back to the present. She swiveled her head to the six dragons locked in battle.

The sight of Rhi lobbing large, iridescent orbs from atop Con's back was mesmerizing. She remained seated, no matter how Con dove, twisted, or whipped around. They worked seamlessly together, as did the other Kings alongside them. The group knew battle. Understood it on a level she could only imagine. There was a real chance of success with them on her side.

Kora turned her head to where Lotti, Villette, and Eurielle stood. They were in a semi-circle, their hands held out before them, touching. Their eyes were open, staring at the dragons—Gordon in particular. Kora had seen him die, so she didn't get her hopes up, even when he faltered against the five Kings, Rhi, and the sisters.

She was useless against a dragon. Her flames did nothing to them, so she didn't bother to join in. She had no other magic to make up for it, either. But she was here for Miena. Kora eyed Villette. Perhaps her, as well. But not now.

Kora looked just in time to see a tail coming toward her. She dove to the side before rolling to a squat out of the way, then looked up to find the Kings attempting to keep Gordon from flying away. It caused them to move back and forth and up and down in the air. Gordon tumbled from the sky with a thunderous roar. He desperately tried to flap his wings, but both were ripped and hung uselessly. Kora shot to her feet and turned to run. A shadow fell over her. She wasn't going to make it.

Suddenly, she was on the opposite side of the village from where she had been. When she looked over, she found herself staring into Villette's face. Villette said nothing as she walked away. Kora could only stand in shock as she watched her rejoin Lotti and Eurielle.

Kora drew in a deep breath and caught a whiff of evil from Villette. It wasn't as strong as before, but it was still there. Remembering that Villette hadn't changed helped to center Kora. She had likely only helped because of the binding vow, though Lotti or Eurielle could've helped. It caused confusing emotions that Kora didn't have the time or wherewithal to contemplate at the moment. Not when the Kings were decimating Gordon.

Kora almost felt sorry for the Amethyst, but she understood what Derek had been through. Perhaps Gordon was being manip-ulated like Derek had been. Then again, he could also be like Bryok and welcome Miena's actions. It was difficult to tell.

The Kings abruptly launched into the air again. Gordon lay unmoving. She held out hope that he wouldn't rise again—there wasn't much of him left *to* rise—but she was living proof that it took certain ways to end someone's life for good.

"Kora, hide!" Villette shouted.

Kora looked over her shoulder and saw a familiar black and silver dragon approaching quickly. A fist gripped her heart and squeezed. While none of them had said it aloud, everyone knew Miena might wipe Derek's mind again. Maybe he had convinced her of his loyalty. Or perhaps she would demand that he prove it now.

Villette shouted her name again, and Kora looked around for a hiding place. The logical spot would be in one of the building's ruins, but she chose a small grove of trees instead. It was easier to see what was going on around her.

Kora's heart thumped painfully against her chest. She gripped the bark of two trees and peered between them to watch Derek draw closer, the silence broken only by the flapping of wings. Her breath was loud in her ears. She felt her flames just beneath the surface of her skin, begging to be released. She didn't understand why until Derek drew close enough that she saw something white on his back.

But it wasn't something. It was some*one*.

Miena. In armor.

The reek of evil slammed into her. She had to tuck her mouth into the crook of her elbow to hide the sound of her gag. There was no way for Kora to know if Derek had fooled Miena or if she had taken control of him. And she probably wouldn't. It was tough to accept after all they had been through to bring Derek back.

But she had to trust him. He had endured the worst of it

already. He had willingly gone to face Miena, knowing the dangers. Being in his arms once more, even for the brief period they'd had, let Kora see how relieved he was to be himself again. He was a warrior, and he would fight with everything he had. Just as she would.

Kora glanced at the Kings. They remained close, flying in a tight formation as if they had done it before. Her gaze moved to the trio of Star People standing serenely as they waited for Miena to make a move.

As for Miena and Derek, she straddled him as he flew in wide circles. Kora peeled her lips back in a hiss when Miena leaned over Derek and patted his scales like he was her pet. Flames shot up around Kora's hand. She hastily doused them and scowled at the burn mark on the bark where her palm had rested.

"Emotion drives us and our fire. You cannot let it control you, or you'll lose before a fight even begins."

Her knees went weak as the memory resurfaced. She replayed her brother's voice, savoring the deep timbre while remembering her training. It wouldn't be easy to keep control of her emotions. The man she loved was out there. But if he could do it, so would she.

"Good hiding spot," Rhi said as she appeared beside her.

Kora jumped in surprise. "Is Derek still Derek?"

"I don't know. I could tell Con was trying to reach him, and I think the others were, too, but I can't tell if he heard them. Villette kept Merrill and the Kings from communicating with each other, so it's possible Miena is doing that, too."

The air was thick with tension and hostility.

"This is the worst part before a battle," Rhi murmured.

Kora shot the Fae a glance. "Battle is better?"

"Not in the least," Rhi said with a soft chuckle. "But there's no time to think about it. You're in it."

"I've not really been in one."

Rhi met her gaze and nodded once. "Trust your instincts."

Their conversation ended when Miena suddenly stood before her sisters. Lotti, Villette, and Eurielle stayed shoulder to shoulder—Villette in her armored gown and both Lotti and Eurielle in tunics and trousers. Across from them was Miena in her white and silver armor.

"How close do you need to be?" Rhi whispered.

"Close. I can throw fire, but not this far."

Rhi made an indistinct sound. "Good luck."

"You, too."

Rhi touched her arm and was gone. Kora didn't know if she had veiled herself or teleported back to Con.

"This is ridiculous," Miena stated. "You can't honestly expect to win."

Eurielle threw a quick look at the other two. "It's three against one."

"I've seen those odds before," Miena said, indicating Derek flying above her. "And I have him."

Lotti cleared her throat and motioned to the Kings. "Five to one there."

Miena laughed. "A babe walking with the adults. You know nothing."

"But I do," Villette said.

Miena's green gaze slid to her as she smirked. "I know what you really are, little sister. Scared of being alone, of being left out, of not being good enough. Because you never were."

Kora expected Villette to react, but Eurielle threw up her hand.

Miena stumbled back before bracing with one foot forward as she was dragged back. The look she directed at Eurielle made Kora swallow nervously.

"When this is finished, and I stand over your bodies, you'll wish you'd made a different choice," Miena stated as she straightened.

Villette took a step away from the other two. "You always did talk too much."

The moment the words left her mouth, a rush of magic that even Kora felt came. Then the battle was in full swing. Lotti, Eurielle, and Villette took turns attacking Miena. To Kora's shock, Miena deftly dodged and blocked them all. A flurry of color in the sky pulled her attention from the Star People to the dragons. She saw a ball of scales twisting in the sky as the air filled with snarls and roars once more as the Kings—and Derek—fought.

Kora wanted to be out there with the others. When Miena had her back to her, she saw an opportunity to attack, but as she was about to rush out, Miena turned around. Had Kora gone then, she would have come face-to-face with Miena.

But staying hidden was worse than being in the middle of it all. From her spot, Kora saw everything. Every missed strike, every hit against her friends. She heard Derek's pain-filled roar permeating the air. Her heart lurched, and fear snaked around her.

"Keep calm." Kayden's voice was in her head again. How could she have forgotten all the times her brother had told her that when they were growing up?

Kora tucked away the fear and locked her gaze back on the battle at hand. Something snagged her attention. She did a double take when she found Gordon rising to his feet. He was in the air before she could alert anyone and crashed into the ball of dragons.

Another startled cry rose, this one human, and pulled her attention. Eurielle was on the ground, holding her arm as Villette and Lotti closed in on her. Villette suddenly winced as her magic bounced off her left hand. Almost immediately, Kora's left hand throbbed, and every bone felt as if it had shattered. The pain made her double over. She squeezed her eyes closed and clamped her lips shut. She wouldn't cry out and draw attention to herself.

There wasn't time for this. Kora leaned against a tree, sweat running down her face. She looked up at Villette, but it didn't appear as if she even had a wound on her hand. Kora then looked at Miena, who sported a few injuries, though not nearly enough in Kora's mind. She had to get closer if she wanted to trap Miena. That meant she had to move.

Kora needed to come up behind and around Miena. It was the only way. She scanned the area, noting two places she could reach. Her gaze lowered to her hand cradled against her body. Even looking at it hurt. Running would be agony.

She swung her gaze back to the Star People and found Villette pulling herself off the ground as she looked at her. Kora pointed to the bush she needed to reach. Villette nodded and sent a blast of magic at Miena's right shoulder, spinning her away. Kora burst from the grove, moving as fast as she could. She slid behind the bush before Miena launched her next strike.

Just as she'd expected, the movement had been pure torture. She bit her lip so hard she tasted blood. All she needed was one hand to throw her fire. She had that. Now, she just needed to get a little closer.

Kora glanced at the battle in time to see Miena send a blast straight at Villette. Kora held her breath. If Miena struck Villette again, Kora wouldn't be able to move. Thankfully, Lotti blocked the magic before it reached Villette. That forced Kora to move from behind the bush to a tree. She plastered her back against it and waited. The pain had dimmed a bit. Or maybe she was becoming numb to it. Regardless, she would take it. Her mind needed to be focused, not split.

She peered around the tree. Two more moves, and she would be behind Miena. The problem was, there were no good hiding spots.

"I'm done hiding, remember?" she told herself.

Kora watched Miena. The way she dodged and sidestepped and how she shifted forward on one foot when she flung her magic. She was quick, fluid. She adapted rapidly. But all of that dimmed in comparison to the force of her magic. The smile on her lips told anyone watching that she expected to win.

Kora moved from behind the tree. She locked her gaze on Miena, and everything else fell away. She didn't know how she got from the tree to her enemy. Flames exploded around her hand as a ball of fire formed. Kora pulled back her arm, ready to launch it, when Miena spun to face her.

The impact of Miena's magic smashed into Kora, doubling her over. Her breath left her in a whoosh, and she slammed into the ground. She saw a blinding white light...

Then, nothing but darkness.

CHAPTER 28

Kora's yelp of pain cut through the roars and the clash of bodies, piercing Derek's heart. He jerked his head toward the sound and saw her soar through the air before landing awkwardly. Miena was over her in a heartbeat.

Then Miena's green eyes leveled on him as her voice filled his mind. *"Did you think I was that gullible?"*

He snarled in fury as he pulled away from the others and flew straight at her. He didn't care what she did to him. The only thing that mattered was Kora. Derek extended his hands, talons outstretched. Just before he closed his fingers around Miena, she vanished, taking Kora with her.

Denial was a bellow reverberating in his head. He landed in a panic, staring at the spot where Kora had been as if his thoughts could rematerialize her. There were only a few drops of blood.

"You think you know loss," Miena's voice said in his head.

"You've only begun to understand what it means. It's time the two of you get acquainted."

Derek recoiled at her triumphant laughter bouncing in his head. He should've known. He should've recognized that Miena hadn't believed him. But he wanted it so badly that he had missed the signs. Because he wanted a future.

He wanted Kora.

"Derek!"

Lotti's shout scattered his bleak thoughts. He turned his head and found her pointing up. Derek lifted his gaze and saw dragons flying at them from all sides. Gordon pulled away from the Kings long enough for the wave of dragons to reach him. Then the bombardment began.

With Miena gone, Derek heard the Kings' voices again. Con barked orders to everyone, including him. Derek was torn. He wanted to go after Kora, but he was doomed to fail if he faced Miena alone. She expected him to chase her. And while it killed him to remain, he had to do it.

Derek launched himself into the air, joining the Kings so they were wing to wing—a barricade that would make anyone think twice. Below, the three sisters—Lotti, Villette, and Eurielle—positioned themselves.

He became lost in the battle as he moved from foe to foe, attacking and evading, striking and dodging. He took out two, then a third. He had just raked his talons across a fourth's throat, killing it, only to have a dozen tiny dragons with pink scales swarm him.

They covered him from head to tail, slashing and biting. He swiped at them with his hands, knocking them away, only for them to return. They ripped at his wings and clawed at his belly.

He tucked and rolled to the left before snapping out his wings. It dislodged several of the Pinks.

He captured a few, but a roar of pain ripped from him as more sank their claws into his neck and a still-healing wound. They went for his eyes with teeth and talons. The more he flung off, the more appeared. As suddenly as the Pinks had arrived, they were gone. Derek looked from the small dragons plummeting to the ground around him and spotted Villette staring up at him. She nodded before turning to face another attack. Derek didn't have time to think about that as he saw Hector battling three dragons. He hurried to join the King.

Derek glimpsed Rhi on an enemy's back, plunging a sword into their neck before teleporting to another. Trees burned with dragon fire. Scorch marks cut through the canopy and the ground. Derek welcomed the bitterness that fueled his rage. Every swipe of his talons, hit of his wings, and stab of his tail got him closer to going after Kora.

He welcomed the pain of his wounds and the sensation of his enemy's blood. It fed the beast of battle, the one that would fight for its mate until the end of days.

Derek turned to look for his next opponent, but there were none. He swung to the other side but only saw Kings. He looked down and spotted Con and Brandr in human form with Rhi. Merrill flew low over the dead. Alasdair, still in dragon form, stood next to Gordon, whose head was barely attached to his body. Villette, Eurielle, and Lotti walked among the fallen.

Exhaustion finally reared its head. Derek drifted to the ground, shifting just before he landed. The sight of so many dead dragons sickened him. They shouldn't be fighting among themselves. They should have joined forces against Miena. There was another worry, though. Where had Miena gotten the dragons? His gaze slid to Villette. Her clothes were stained with dirt and blood, but he couldn't tell if any of it was hers. As if sensing him, she met his gaze.

"She knew," Derek said. "Miena knew I lied."

Eurielle replied, "I tried to warn you."

"Where did she take Kora?" Brandr asked Villette.

But Derek knew. "Stonemore."

Villette nodded slowly.

"Then what are we waiting on?" Lotti asked. "We should go."

A long, low growl rumbled from Alasdair. Derek turned and saw Gordon's body healing. Alasdair sank his teeth into Gordon's throat and ripped his head completely off his body.

"The others are healing," Rhi called out.

Derek looked around to see that the dragons' wounds were, in fact, mending.

"Villette. Is this you?" Eurielle asked.

All of them turned their attention to her. She flinched. It was slight, but Derek saw it, nonetheless. As did everyone else.

"Bloody fucking hell," Brandr bit out. "These are the dragons captured in the thorn forest."

Derek frowned, his attention divided between the developing commotion and the dragons twitching and coming back to life.

"What did you do?" Con bellowed.

Villette wasn't cowed. She held the King of King's gaze. "Do you think we created Derek and the others out of magic alone?"

"That explains why our magic isn't working on them as it should," Eurielle muttered.

Lotti's face flushed with anger. "You should have told us."

"Yes, I should have," Villette admitted.

"How are you controlling them?" Lotti demanded.

Villette shot her an incredulous glare. "I'm not. I'm on your side. The last I saw of these, they were dead. Miena has control of them. They're like Gordon. Shells. Everything that made them who they were is gone. They're soldiers. They take orders, carry them out, and return."

"How do we kill them?" Derek asked. That was the only thing that mattered right now. They would deal with the rest after Miena was gone.

"You can't."

Con was wrath personified as he stalked to Villette, not stopping until he towered over her. His nostrils flared. Violence rolled off him in great waves. His words dripped with venom when he said, "Everything can die."

"Take their heads," Alasdair said into the charged silence.

Everyone turned to see him standing beside Gordon's headless body. Behind Alasdair was dragon fire, and within the flames, amethyst scales.

"Like the Warriors," Con said.

One side of Alasdair's lips quirked in a grin. "Just like the Warriors."

Derek had no idea who or what they were talking about, but it didn't matter. He began taking the heads of dragons around him and threw them into a pile. It was repugnant. These were the kin he had fought so long and hard to free. Except they hadn't been across the border. They'd been right where he was all those years. The only thing that made it less sickening was the knowledge that the dragons were already dead. He told himself they were allowing them to finally rest in peace as they always should have.

They weren't quick enough, though. Half the dragons healed

before they got to them and began another assault. Derek took to the sky. The moment the Pinks came at him, Derek went for their heads. It felt wrong to kill dragons that reminded him of younglings due to their size, but they were intent on carnage. He had no choice.

The group had a system now. The moment one of them killed an attacker, someone was on the ground to take their heads. It wasn't long before Derek and the others were triumphant once more. But it didn't feel like a victory.

Brandr and Merrill set the three piles of heads ablaze. Derek glanced at the sky. Would more come? He turned his head to Villette.

"How many more dead dragons do you have?" Hector asked her.

Apparently, Derek wasn't the only one wondering.

"It isn't as if I counted," she answered.

Rhi wiped the blade of her sword clean on her pants. "Katla said she caught thousands of dragons in the thorns. There are only forty-three here."

"Then more will come." Villette paused. "Though if I know Miena, she'll send them when we least expect it."

Eurielle twisted her lips. "Villette's right. We're prepared for them now. Miena won't send more yet."

"Then we go for Kora," Derek stated. Either they went or he would. But he was going. Period.

Villette's face scrunched in rebuttal. "That's exactly what Miena wants."

"It's what she's going to get."

Con came up beside Derek. "We'll get Kora, but let's be smart about it. She worked hard to get you back. We doona want to lose you again."

Derek didn't want to wait. "You speak with wisdom, but I have to go to her."

"Kora isn't hurt," Villette said. "I would know. I would feel it. Miena hasn't hurt her."

Yet hung in the air. It was coming. They all knew it.

Eurielle said, "We played into Miena's hands already. We shouldn't do it again."

They were right. But knowing that and accepting it were two different things. Derek kept seeing Kora's body on the ground, twisted and bent. He nodded in agreement. It was the best he could do.

"What does Miena want?" Hector asked.

Villette started to laugh before her face creased in pain. She cried out as she fell to her knees and then onto her side. Eurielle was the first to reach her. When she turned Villette over, she was unconscious, and blood soaked her gown beneath the armor. Eurielle ripped it away to reveal a large gash across Villette's stomach.

The *yet* had come sooner rather than later.

"The binding vow," Lotti murmured.

Eurielle frowned at them as she pressed her hand over the wound. "The pain delivered on Villette will be five times what Kora experiences. It will also take Villette longer to heal."

"Allow me," Con said.

Derek watched as Con put a hand on Villette. The blood halted, and the wound closed before his eyes. Derek wished Con would've gotten to Kora in the arena before she died. She might come back from death, but she also experienced unimaginable pain before and after.

"Should you have done that?" Merrill asked.

Derek understood his reservation because he couldn't—and wouldn't—forget that Villette was the enemy.

"She can't help if she's unconscious," Eurielle replied.

Alasdair grunted. "I'm not sure if she'll be much help when awake."

"I disagree," Villette said as she opened her eyes.

Her gaze went to Eurielle first. The sisters said nothing as Eurielle got to her feet and moved away. A flare of surprise widened Villette's lids when she noticed Con beside her. He, too, straightened and stepped back.

Villette pushed herself into a seated position and looked down at the blood-soaked material. By the time she stood, the ruined gown and armor had been replaced by a flowy, pale yellow dress. She tipped her head to Con. "Thank you. That won't be the last time Miena hurts me and Kora. We need to find them quickly."

"I just said that." Derek balled his hand into a fist.

Villette briefly looked at him. "And I said it's what she wants. That doesn't mean I didn't agree with you."

"Then what do you suggest?" Rhi asked.

Villette look at Eurielle and Lotti. "We three should go to her."

"The fuck you will," Alasdair declared. "No' without me."

Lotti put her hand on his arm. "Hear Villette out."

He looked askance at Lotti but held his tongue.

"Well?" Merrill urged.

Villette adjusted her hair to cover the burns on her face. "There's no use trying to deceive her. She'll expect everything we come up with. The best thing we can do is go at her with the truth."

"And what might that be?" Eurielle asked.

Villette grinned. "That we've come—alone—to get Kora." Just as Merrill parted his lips to speak, she turned to him and said, "Remember what just happened to me. Anything done to Kora, I feel, and vice versa. I want Kora away from my sister more than any of you do."

"You want us to stay back and wait?" Derek asked. Because that wasn't happening.

"On the contrary," Villette replied.

CHAPTER 29

Miena surveyed the room that had once been her prison. Returning had been tougher than she'd anticipated. Even without a door, the chamber sent shivers down her spine. She rubbed her wrists as if the heavy manacles still restrained her hands. Standing in one place century after century, unable to move. To sit. To lay.

Or turn.

Her gaze had burned a hole in the wall across from her—at least, she had pretended it had. But her magic had been taken from her. A single mistake had stripped away all her triumphs and victories.

Nay. A *betrayal.*

It would haunt her for eternity. No matter how many times she hurt Villette, it would never make up for what her little sister had done. Villette had stripped away Miena's defenses and erased everything she had worked so hard to attain.

Miena stopped and faced the new occupant. Kora stood upon

the knoll in the middle of the room. Her arms were spread out at her sides, the manacles and chains locked around her wrists stretched across to the wall at either end. Her ankles were also bound, but that was only to prove a point. There would be no movement for Kora.

Blood continued to drip from the slice across her abdomen. A cut Miena knew Villette would feel deeply. Too bad Kora didn't. Yet. She was still unconscious. She would wake soon, though, and Miena would delight in hurting not just Kora and Villette but also Derek. Because each time Villette cried out, he would imagine it was Kora. Miena smiled just thinking about the anguish she would cause all three.

She had made a mistake in sending him after Kora. Miena had believed her magic stronger than the link between a dragon and its mate. It had amused her to convince Derek to hunt her, but it had come back to bite her. The moment Miena knew he loved her, she should've kept him far away from Kora.

Those kinds of blunders couldn't happen again. The misstep had nearly cost her everything. If she hadn't anticipated a ruse, she might have been fooled. She still wasn't happy about three of her sisters opposing her. None of them were in good standing with their other siblings. Thankfully, that meant the rest of their large family wouldn't intervene.

A soft groan drew her attention. Miena waited for the hellhound to open her eyes. Kora blinked, trying to focus. Comprehension soon dawned, however. Miena didn't move as she watched Kora's gaze scan the chamber and land on her.

"It's an uncomfortable spot, I know. I made a few changes just for you," she said.

Horror skidded across Kora's face when she found herself

standing in frozen water. Kora tried to move her legs, but they wouldn't budge. Miena had made sure they wouldn't. Kora began to tremble.

"Hellhounds despise the cold," Miena continued. "Personally, I love it. Since I know the torment of being surrounded by something I hate firsthand, I thought it fitting that you should experience it, as well. You're probably wondering how you can possibly survive."

"This won't kill me for long," Kora said through chattering teeth.

Miena smiled. "It made sense for Villette to want to work with your group. She's not strong enough to take me on her own. She got lucky the first time. What I couldn't wrap my head around was why you agreed to it. Villette is responsible for the deaths of not just your family but also all the hellhounds on Zora, after all. There is only one way the two of you would work together. A binding vow. It isn't something known to many. We began it. Trust isn't something that comes easily to my kind."

"Imagine that."

"I tested my theory when we were in battle. It took me a while to locate you, but once I did, every time Villette was injured, so were you. It confirmed everything. You might have guaranteed that Villette wouldn't betray you by committing to that vow, but you also put yourself in an untenable spot. Sure, you feel her injuries, and she feels yours, but your life forces are linked. Hers will help keep you alive and force you to feel every unbearable second while you're here. Not forever, but long enough."

"For what?" Kora asked.

Miena pursed her lips and tapped her finger against them as she looked Kora over. Then she held out her hand and flicked a finger downward. Kora's sleeves vanished, leaving her arms bare to the frigid air. "You really don't want to know. Besides, it'll give you something to mull over instead of the cold."

"You won't win."

"I already have."

Kora barked a laugh. "Sure."

It was a brave show, setting Miena's teeth on edge. "I always get what I want."

"Maybe. But at what cost? Your sisters have turned against you."

"I don't need them."

Kora tried to shrug, only to wince when her arms held firm. "Keep telling yourself that."

"You would've made a good Star Person with that kind of fortitude."

"I would never want to be one of you."

Miena bent and smoothed her hand over the thick ice. "You have no idea what you're missing. The power is inconceivable."

"I freed you, and this is what I get in return? It's no wonder no one trusts you. You never keep your word."

Miena's gaze cut to Kora as she slowly straightened. "I did what I had to do to get free. It's the same thing you'll try to do. The same as you're *attempting* now." She blew out a breath. "Yet, you're right. I do owe you. Tell you what, ask me anything."

Kora's lips were tinged blue now. "As if I can believe anything you say."

"Do you want to ask something or not? And don't be so incredibly asinine as to ask me to release you."

"Oh, I know better than that." The teeth chattering grew louder. "Tell me why you have it out for the dragons? You can create your own, and the ones here aren't the same as those that were freed—by your brother, I might add."

Miena had to give it to the little hellhound. Of all the questions she could have asked, Kora had voiced the one she would answer truthfully. Miena shrugged a shoulder. "Because they're happy. Because they don't need us."

"No one needs you. None of the other Star People seem to have a problem with the dragons being free, but you and Villette certainly do."

"Ah," Miena said with a wide smile. "Villette didn't tell you, did she?"

"Tell me what?"

Miena held up a finger and tsked. "You asked your question. I won't answer another."

"Did you ever think there is something bigger out there than you? Something that ensures the dragons keep defeating you?"

"There is nothing else out there. Trust me. I've looked."

Kora's lips cracked when she smiled. "Maybe they didn't want you to find them."

"It was you, wasn't it? Derek saw you and remembered who he was."

"Not at first," Kora admitted. "But eventually."

Miena had never experienced that kind of sentiment with another. It was as foreign to her as death. "What does it feel like? Love."

A dreamy look filled Kora's eyes, and her lips curved softly. "Exhilarating. Like you can do anything. It's a state of bliss I didn't know existed. But there's a sinking terror, too."

"Why?" Miena asked, her curiosity deepening.

A look of sadness fell over the hellhound's face. "Because once you love someone, and they love you in return, once you have that connection where words aren't needed and can see and feel their emotions, you'll never be the same without them. The thought of losing them, of never holding them again, is impossible to comprehend. The agony is unbearable. As if someone has reached into your chest and ripped out your heart."

Kora painted a vivid picture. Miena tried to imagine feeling something like that with another, but she couldn't. She would say Star People weren't meant for trivial emotions such as love, but Lotti had proven differently. Except Lotti had been raised with humans. Perhaps that's what made her different.

"Humans throw around the word *love* a lot," Miena said. "It seems to rule lives as much as it ruins them."

"Says someone who has never experienced it."

Miena chuckled. "I'm not the one who bound myself to a dragon. You have no idea what you've done there."

"I know what I feel."

"In the heat of the moment. What about a year from now when there are no more battles to fight, and it's just boring, day-to-day life? How much time have you actually spent with Derek?"

Blood seeped from Kora's cracked lips when she grinned. "I'll never spend enough time with him."

"You're pathetic."

"You're jealous."

Miena was surprised to find that perhaps she *was* envious that Kora had found a way to return Derek's memories and that he was, even now, plotting to get to her. Miena's *family* hadn't even come to free her from Villette.

"He's suffered enough," Kora said.

Miena quirked a brow. "Has he?"

"First you, then under Villette's rule all those years. And then you again. Both of you messing with his mind as if he didn't have a say in any of it."

"He doesn't. I made him. Therefore, he's mine."

Kora's gaze filled with loathing. "He isn't a thing. He's a person. You don't own him any more than you own the dragons. Derek has been enslaved, just as the dragons used to be. Imagine if he had remained because he *wanted* to instead of being manipulated and coerced. Imagine what it might be like to have that kind of ally. I hear Villette had that in Bryok."

"Both of them were mine," Miena snapped before she could stop herself. Kora had struck a nerve—and it hit deep.

Kora studied her. "If you're going to kill Derek, do it quickly. He's given enough."

"That isn't for you to decide."

"You want revenge against Villette, then take it. I'm right here. Use me. But leave Derek out of it."

Is that what love did? Did it make someone weak and reckless? Miena was glad she didn't know what the emotion was.

Miena almost blurted out that she had tried to kill Derek during the battle. It hadn't been Eurielle who stopped her. Something else had. Miena needed to figure out what it was before the next time.

"The more you ask me to spare him pain, the more I'm going to hurt him," Miena said.

Kora's entire body trembled. "Love always wins."

"Excuse me?"

"It's something my mum told me long ago. Love always wins."

Miena walked to the door. She paused and said over her shoulder, "Not when I'm involved."

She walked out and snapped her fingers, placing and securing a new door in the opening. Miena lifted the ends of her purple gown and stepped around the servants busily cleaning the room. Villette had kept her identity and power a secret, but Miena had shown everyone what she was the moment she arrived in the city.

Her next stop was the temple on Stonemore's fourth level. She appeared in the nave of the building. The central part of the temple stretched from the entrance to the altar, the area free of chairs and benches to allow more standing space. Her arrival startled the red-robed priests, who quickly bowed at the waist.

"Have they been readied?" she asked.

Another priest walked into her line of vision. His dark hair was cropped short, and his pointed face reminded her of a bird. There was determination in his narrow-set, dark eyes. "I'm Aksel, my queen. I will take you to them."

"I don't need accompaniment."

He bowed his head. "Of course not."

She studied him for a long moment. He wanted something. Men like him always did. It was better if she discovered what it was now and put an end to whatever aspirations he had. "Lead the way."

Delight lit his eyes as he walked toward the stairs that switched backed to the top. The red sandstone steps had been traveled so much there were depressions in the middle of each. She watched the priest try to look at her without turning his head.

"How many did you round up?" she asked.

His lips curved as only someone who took great enjoyment in their work could. "Three. The woman you provided has been most helpful. After some coaxing, that is."

"Good. Daelya continues to give you names, I take it?"

"She does, my queen. Just a few moments ago, I sent a group of soldiers for another."

Miena would have to stop by and see Daelya on her way out. Though she knew how the one-sided conversation would go. Daelya had thought to escape her fate, but she had sealed it the moment she divulged her secrets to Miena.

They finally reached the top of the stairs. Aksel turned and bowed while holding out his arm toward the door. Miena paused beside him and gently touched his face. She liked him. She would have to keep him around. As long as he didn't overstep. He had aspirations.

Her gaze moved to the door. She opened it. There, her gaze landed on a black-haired woman who stood defiantly as three children huddled behind her.

"Come for them and die," the woman declared.

Miena eyed the female who'd dared to stand against her. "You have no idea who you're dealing with."

"Oh, but I do know," she stated before lifting her hands.

Magic pelted Miena, throwing her back as the room exploded with a blinding light.

CHAPTER 30

"I doona know about this," Brandr murmured.

Derek stood beside him as they looked at the small entrance at the base of the mountain.

Hector came up on Derek's other side and squatted to gaze into the hole barely big enough for them to squeeze through. He straightened, his lips twisting. "Do we have a choice?"

"There's always a choice," Villette said from behind them. "But if you wish to defeat Miena, then that's where you need to go."

Merrill joined them and caught Derek's eye. "Does this look familiar?"

"It does not," Derek replied.

Villette blew out an audible breath. "It will. This entrance will take you down the tunnel. You've used it countless times."

"For what?" Con demanded.

Villette made a sound of impatience. "Many things. We don't have time for this. Trust me."

"You ask the impossible," Alasdair told her.

Derek wasn't sure about the opening, and taking Villette's word contradicted his feelings about her. But she was on their side. This time. Then there was Kora. If it would save her, then he would do whatever Villette asked.

"I'm going in." He shot Villette a warning look.

"The tunnels were dug after Miena was imprisoned," Villette told him. "She won't know about them."

There was a chance it was a trap, but that could be said about anything when partnering with someone like Villette. Derek drew in a deep breath and jumped into the opening. He folded his arms over his chest, but his shoulders still scraped the sides, the stone tearing at his shirt and raining dirt and rocks upon him.

The drop was short. He landed and moved out of the way as his night vision took over, allowing him to find the only passageway out. Within moments, the other Kings and Rhi stood in the cramped room.

Derek peered down the shaft. "This way."

"Hold up," Con said.

Derek swung his head around. "What is it?"

"We're no' all going," Merrill said.

Derek looked at each of them, his irritation spiking at yet another hesitation that kept him from Kora. "Fine. You've done enough."

"We're still with you," Con stated. "It's better if we split up in case it's a trap."

Brandr looked up through the hole to the darkening sky before he spoke. "What's the plan then? Just split up?"

"Something like that," Rhi replied with a grin.

Con looked around at them. "We know more dragons will

come for us. Villette might have helped to this point, but I doona put it past her to set a trap. We doona know what's down that passage," he said, nodding toward the tunnel Derek stood beside. "I willna leave any more of our kind behind in this place."

Derek suspected that the last bit was directed at Merrill.

"I'm going with Derek," Con announced.

Merrill inclined his head. "Me, as well."

"Then it's decided," Alasdair said.

Derek didn't wait for the others as he hurried down the narrow tunnel. It cut through the ground in a straight line, and the walls were smooth to the touch—even the rock had been honed down. He heard Con and Merrill catching up to his long strides. No one said anything as the passage spit them into a low-ceilinged cavern. There was nothing inside but rocks and an impressive stalactite formation in the center.

He had hoped something would look recognizable, but once again, he found himself gazing at unfamiliar walls.

"Here," Merrill said.

Derek swung around to see Merrill disappearing behind a boulder. He trailed Con to the huge rock and walked around it to feel air against his face. Neither of them hesitated to follow Merrill.

The path was tight and winding but short. They moved into another opening with yet another tunnel. They navigated three more with nothing looking even remotely familiar before they spilled into a cavern with a soaring ceiling that domed above them.

Merrill grunted. "There're no doors here."

"Anything?" Con asked as he glanced at Derek.

It was the same question every time they came out of a tunnel.

Derek turned in a circle to look about the place. He was ready to give the same answer as before when he suddenly stopped. There was nothing particularly interesting about the wall, but something about it caught his attention.

Merrill came up beside him. "You recognize something?"

"Maybe," Derek said.

Con walked to where he had been looking for a closer view. There wasn't anything at eye level. Derek could see that. He lifted his gaze. His heart beat faster when he found the dragon carved into the rock by talons—*his* talons. The illustration was clumsy and awkward, but it was his. Instantly, the memories came tumbling back.

"I know where we are," Derek declared. Both Kings turned to him. He pointed to the dragon. "I drew that."

Merrill gazed up at the carving. "Why there?"

"In case I ever forgot about this."

Derek shifted, standing tall in his true form. He released a short burst of fire at a section of the wall. After returning to his human form and covering himself with clothes, he walked to where the fire had hit the stone and ran his hand diagonally from the right down to the left. A hidden door slid open, big enough for a human to pass.

Kora couldn't stop shaking. She couldn't even press her arms against her sides for warmth. Her flames wouldn't answer, but she kept attempting to call them to her anyway. She tried to imagine them covering her, warming her, but nothing could penetrate the cold.

Miena's words hung in the air long after the door had slammed closed. Kora tried not to think about how long she might be locked away. The binding vow wouldn't be fulfilled until each promise had been satisfied. That meant she could be here for decades. Centuries, even.

Unless Miena killed Villette.

Kora's link to her nemesis kept her from dying over and over again. Though if she succumbed to the cold, at least she would get a little relief. The way things were now, she was stuck in it, suspended in an endless glacial climate with no end in sight.

She hoped someone would think to come and look for her here. Surely, they would come to Stonemore. Kora had no idea if Miena had returned to the battle or if it had been suspended. The not knowing was almost as bad as the temperature.

Her gaze dropped to the ice that held her from the knees down. She couldn't see her feet through the cloudy, frozen water. The lava had been sweltering, but she could handle the heat. The cold was a different beast. Her muscles stiffened and cramped, and her reaction time dwindled to nothing. Even her thought processes had slowed to a crawl. She enjoyed nothing about glacial climates. It might be pretty, but its havoc on her body wasn't worth it. It seemed Miena had found the perfect torture.

Yet even as Kora's body suffered, her heart felt the deepest ache. She was once more parted from Derek. They had gotten lucky with his memories, but she wasn't sure they would be so fortunate this time.

Though she hated to admit it, Miena was right. She and Derek hadn't spent a lot of time together. They had talked and shared things, but not nearly enough. Even when Derek was once more himself, she had lost precious hours because she had been healing.

The few moments she and Derek had snatched for themselves were ruined by the knowledge that innocents had died as she moaned in pleasure.

At least Derek had the Kings now. He wasn't alone. He would never be alone again. He needed a home and a family. Con and the others would give that to him. She wondered if they would take him to Earth one day. Kora couldn't imagine going to another realm to see the people, taste the food, and experience the differences. She probably wouldn't get that opportunity, but Con would make sure Derek did. And that pleased her immensely.

"I love you," she said aloud, hoping the words reached Derek.

Words she had never spoken to him but should have.

She had thought they weren't needed because she felt it in his actions and saw it in his eyes, but she was wrong. She needed them. And he likely did, as well. They'd gotten a second chance, and she had blown it.

Just as she had blown her opportunity to catch Miena unawares.

Kora would never forget the look of triumph on Miena's face as she was battered with magic. Her teeth chattered loudly. An ache began in her neck from trying to clench her mouth closed. She let her mind drift, creating a world where there were no Star People, one where she and Derek were free to live together in peace. She would tell him her deepest, darkest secrets. He would share his in return. Then they would forge a solid foundation that carried them through the eons.

She could picture it all. A cottage in a flower-filled meadow with a river running alongside it. Mountains rising on either side. She imagined him soaring among the peaks, his magnificent form backlit by the setting sun. Or maybe flying so high she could only see his silhouette against the moons.

They would argue but then make up with wonderful sex then lie in each other's arms for hours afterward. He would be by her side when it was time for her to hunt evil. They would live as passionately as they loved.

Kora let her fantasy expand to include those at Iron Hall. A family for both of them. Friends to share things with. There would be large gatherings for celebrations, and perhaps her and Derek's family would include one of the children who'd been saved from Stonemore.

Derek would be an amazing father. She could picture him in the meadow with the spring sun rising on the horizon and a little girl laughing atop his shoulders. He might be at the river in the last days of summer with a young boy at his side, teaching him to fish. Or perhaps they would be blessed with both a girl and a boy.

Kora was so immersed in her imagined world that she almost felt the sun on her face for the briefest moment.

But the cottage and meadow cracked and shattered like ice. The children iced over, and then, so too did Derek. Leaving her with nothing but her frosty prison.

A tear dropped onto her face and immediately froze. The pain was intolerable, but it was only just the beginning. She wouldn't give in to the wail of hopelessness rising inside her. She would fight. For Derek. For love.

For herself.

CHAPTER 31

Derek, Con, and Merrill paused at the tremor that shook the mountain.

"Tell me that's normal," Con said.

Merrill shook his head. "No' that I'm aware of."

The two looked Derek's way. "Nay, that isn't normal."

"Miena, perhaps?" Merrill offered.

Derek motioned to the open door. "Only one way to find out."

"Lead the way," Con told him.

Derek stepped through the doorway. The plain walls of the mountain gave way to designs etched into every available space. The walls, ceiling, and even the floor. Illuminated in soft blue, the graceful swirls didn't have a beginning or an end and connected from one pattern to another. Some were small, some large, but all part of one enormous design.

"Did you do this?" Merrill asked.

Derek lowered his gaze to the floor, where the pattern indicated the way forward. "Nay."

They followed the path from that stunning space into a tunnel with scrawled waves on either side. The ceiling was dotted like stars. The ground beneath them was etched to look like water, and the light moved in such a way that it appeared real.

"What happened on Earth to send the dragons here?" Derek asked.

Merrill said, "Humans."

"It was much more than that," Con added. "On our world, the dragons were segregated by color. Those clans each had a King who was chosen by the magic of our realm."

Derek glanced over his shoulder at them. "How does that work?"

"The magic knows our strengths and heart," Merrill explained. "If one in a clan was stronger than their current King, the magic propelled that dragon to challenge the leader."

"To a fight?" Derek asked.

Con made a sound in the back of his throat. "To death. There were times that a King died in battle, making the transition easier, but most of us had to slay the King of our clan to take his place."

Derek looked at Con. "Did you?"

"Aye. I slayed the King of Golds to take his place in our clan. Until we met the Star People, the only ones capable of killing a Dragon King was another King."

It sounded vicious to Derek. "And how did you become the King of Kings?"

"The strongest of each clan leads. The males are bigger than the females, which is why we never had Queens. It requires even more strength to be the King of Kings. The largest dragons are the

Golds and Silvers. Throughout our long history, either a Gold or a Silver has led the Kings."

Derek nodded as he took in everything while traversing the tunnel. "If all of you were so powerful, what went wrong?"

"Fucking humans," Merrill replied.

Con said, "When mortals arrived, we took pity on them. The Kings approached them. It was the first time any of us shifted. It allowed us to communicate with them. We carved out space for them, taught them to hunt, and showed them what plants were edible."

"But it wasna enough," Merrill said. "They always wanted more."

Con was silent for a moment. "Aye. They did. Most of the Kings had given up land for the humans. Many of us even walked among them, taking them as lovers. The man I called brother then, the King of Silvers, believed he had found his mate in a human. Ulrik's uncle believed *he* should be King of their clan and conspired to turn the female against Ulrik. I discovered her plan to murder Ulrik, and the Kings stopped her. Ulrik didna take it well."

"He was angry at us for no' letting him deal with his lover, but he wouldna take it out on us. Instead, he went after the humans," Merrill said.

Con nodded. "Once the war began, it was difficult to stop. Ulrik and his Silvers attacked the humans, and that set them after others. We were no' just battling mortals but also our own. I commanded the Silvers and Ulrik to return to Dreagan, our home base. Ulrik and four of his largest Silvers ignored me. While I was trying to reason with Ulrik, the humans were hunting down the smaller dragons and decimating them."

"Because you ordered us no' to kill any of them."

Derek heard the animosity in Merrill's voice and glanced at him. Merrill kept his gaze forward, not looking at Con or Derek.

"We made a vow the day the humans arrived," Con said. "We said we would protect them."

Merrill grunted. "Over our own."

"You could have killed all the mortals. Why didn't you?" Derek asked.

Con blew out a breath. "It would make us murderers, making all of us incapable of being Kings. The magic would've replaced us."

"So, we trapped the Silvers with the same magic we used on you," Merrill told him. "Then we sent our dragons away because we knew the conflict would continue endlessly."

Derek realized they'd not mentioned something. "What happened to Ulrik?" he asked.

"We bound his magic and banished him." Con paused. "It was the worst day of my life. But he found his way back. He's leading the Kings at Dreagan while I'm here."

It felt as if doors were opening in Derek's mind with each step he took, allowing old memories to surface. He knew that he would reach another hidden door in exactly thirteen steps. "You sent the dragons away, but the Kings remained? Why?"

"Someone had to protect Earth. We hid away on Dreagan until dragons fell into myth and legend among the humans. Then we walked among them," Con answered.

Derek walked to a waist-high boulder and stopped. He stared at it. "The mortals didn't know what you were?"

"They're oblivious to much," Merrill replied.

Con raked a hand through his blond hair. "I always hoped we might bring the dragons home someday."

"I always knew that was never possible."

Derek glanced at the two Kings, who stared at each other. He returned his attention to the boulder and wrapped his fingers around a small rock atop it. Magic filled his palm and moved into the rock. Light filled the carvings that rose from the floor to intertwine in an elaborate motif before meeting at the top in another flourish. The door slid open silently. Derek walked through the opening as a cool blast of air greeted him.

"Bloody hell," Merrill murmured.

Three tunnels sat before them. Derek looked at each of them. It had been a long time since he had seen these tunnels. Villette had kept him out of them for a reason. Maybe she knew the memories she'd locked away would be revealed the moment he stood here.

"What are they?" Con asked.

Acid burned in Derek's stomach. He didn't want to be here. He didn't like the memories that inundated him. But there was no holding them back or ignoring them. Faint screams reached him, but they were echoes of the past, not something from the present. They were the same screams that had assaulted him when he lay injured in the cavern.

Merrill had said the dead were talking to him. But he didn't hear any words. He heard cries. If only that was all. He also felt pain, anguish. Fear.

"Derek?"

He found Con standing before him. Derek wished Con and Merrill weren't there. He wanted to erase this part of his history, but there was no escaping the past.

"This is where Villette brought the dragons." Derek's voice was gruff from the emotions now choking him.

A muscle ticked in Con's temple—the only response on his carefully restrained visage. "And?"

Did he have to give details? Wasn't it better to leave things as they were? Con didn't budge. Neither did Derek. "It's where she killed them."

Fuck. Saying the words aloud was like having his stomach sliced open.

"What did you do?" Merrill demanded.

Derek didn't take his eyes off Con. "I fought her. Or tried to. Afterward, she wiped my memories for the first time."

"You remember that?" Con asked, skepticism dripping from his voice.

"Coming here triggered something."

Merrill came to stand beside the two of them. "How many times did she mess with your mind?"

Derek swallowed as he turned his head to Merrill. "I don't know. I know this place, though. I remember finding a dragon here and being elated. And I remember watching her kill it." He closed his eyes, the memory playing as if it were happening right then. "She told me a lie I didn't believe, and I got between her and the dragon." He opened his eyes and pointed to the right. "I stood there. There was a flash, and then nothing." He pointed to another place on the left. "I stood there once. And there, and there." He indicated all the places. "All with the same outcome."

Con blew out a breath as tension eased from his body. "Where do the tunnels lead?"

"The one on the right will take us to a dead end. The left will bring us to Stonemore."

Merrill glanced at the middle one. "And that one?"

"The cavern we were in," Derek answered.

Miena shoved rubble from her as she climbed to her feet. She was covered in dust. The top of the tower was no more, blown away. The roof and walls were gone, leaving her staring out at the city. The floor was cracked, and every piece of furniture had splintered into tiny pieces or was gone.

"My queen."

She glanced over her shoulder at Aksel, where he stood on what was left of the stairs. He was bleeding from a head wound. Half his face was coated in pink dust from the sandstone. Miena scanned the debris for signs of the woman and children.

There were no appendages sticking out, no blood.

No bodies.

"Who was that?" Miena demanded as she faced Aksel.

He swallowed, his eyes darting about nervously. "Someone suspected of doing magic."

"Suspected?" she asked in a soft voice that belied her wrath.

Aksel nodded hastily. "She looked out of place. So, I had her picked up and brought here."

"Did she use magic to try and get away?"

He shook his head and swallowed again.

"You fear what you don't understand," she said as she slowly walked to him. "Do you know what I am?"

His hands shook as he clasped them together. Whether it was in fear or pain, she didn't know or care. "You have claimed the throne."

She waited until she stood before him before leaning close and whispering, "But do you *know* what I am?"

"Magic," he replied softly.

Her mouth curved into a smile. "You've been killing everything with magic in sight. Are you going to try and take my life?"

"N-nay."

"You wouldn't be able to if you wanted." She turned back to the destroyed room.

Behind her, Aksel's voice wobbled as he said, "I don't understand. You asked us to find those with magic."

"So I did." She looked down and wiped some dust from her arm, but it was all over her. She touched her cheek, and her fingers came back pink. She intended to find out who the woman was.

"If I may be so bold, why?"

Miena sighed and spun to look at the priest. "Because I want them." She pointed to the top of the palace. "Do you see that portion of balcony to the far left? I was locked in that room for thousands of years by my dear sister." She returned her gaze to him. "The one you called The Divine."

His brow furrowed.

"She discovered my secret and betrayed me." Her stomach clenched thinking about it, even now, all these eons later. "Our kind thrives on power. I was determined to be the strongest. Do you know how I did that?"

Aksel slowly shook his head.

"I found a way to acquire it. There are many, many beings out there with magic, but the weakest of all are the humans. And the purist are their children. The younger, the better."

The priest's frown deepened.

"I take their magic. I can't believe none of my other siblings have done such. Not even Villette. Stupid of her when you look at how things turned out." Miena shrugged. "Villette might have found a way to lock me away, but it didn't stop me from getting to the children through their nightmares. My sister learned of that quickly enough and devised another plan. She made all of you fear magic. You turned on each other, just as she knew you would. There needed to be a rule while making sure I couldn't get to the children. What better way than to use religion?"

His face went pale.

Miena laughed. She could well imagine Aksel's internal struggle at learning that everything he believed in was a lie. But she was done playing. "The point is, I've been starved for so very long. I need magical kids, and I need them now. Get to the other names on your list."

Aksel said nothing as he hurried down the steps so fast his heel slipped on the edge of a stair and he landed on his back. He glanced up at her as he got to his feet and ran.

Miena anxiously rubbed her finger along the outside of her thumb. After her clash with Eurielle and the battle, she was depleted. If she was to come out on top, she needed more power. And fast. She had been counting on the children. Three wouldn't have been enough, but it would've been something.

The woman was a concern, but she was something Miena would handle once she put Villette in her place and killed the Kings. Miena looked toward the palace as her thoughts turned to Derek. He was a masterpiece, but he had to die. It had taken her countless attempts to create him, but she had done it once, and she could do it again.

What troubled her was his strength. She had purposely made him fast and strong, but he shouldn't be able to resist a hit from her. Yet, he had. It had to be because she had gone so long without the children's magic. Once she had satiated herself, she would once more reign supreme.

And once she had set things on Zora to rights, the rest of her siblings would have to acknowledge what she had done. They would have to accept that she was the strongest of them. And she would do what none of them had been able to do before. She would lead them.

"Then we go to the left tunnel," Con said.

Merrill walked toward the shaft. "The palace is huge. Miena could be in any number of places, including the labyrinth of passages in the mountain."

"Nay," Derek said, his gaze still on the center tunnel. "We need to go here."

The two Kings looked at him. It was Con who asked, "Why?"

"I don't know. Something is pulling me."

Merrill peered into the middle passage. "There's nothing in that cavern. Unless there's a way to Stonemore."

Derek shook his head. The soft screams that had battered him now came at him from one direction—the central tunnel. "There are answers there."

"You hear them again," Merrill said.

Con looked between them. "Hear what?"

"He can hear the dead."

Con's eyes widened. "That is a rare gift. If the dead have something to tell you, listen."

Derek hesitated.

"What are they saying?" Merrill asked as he came up beside him.

Derek pulled his gaze from the passageway to look at first Merrill and then Con. "Screams. They're just screaming."

"Follow it," Con urged.

He knew little about this so-called *gift*. Had he always had it? Or was it something new like breathing ice? A search of his memories brought back nothing. Unless he could only hear dragons that had died. That would make sense. He hadn't been around other dragons except for Bryok. And Villette had kept him away from the tunnels and the cavern.

Derek started toward the middle tunnel with Con and Merrill a few steps behind him. The moment he entered the passage, the shrieks became louder, the pull harder. A shout behind him drew him to a stop. Derek turned to find Con and Merrill standing at the entrance.

"We can no' get in," Merrill said.

Because whatever was here only wanted him. He could return later. After Miena was defeated, and Kora was by his side once more. Derek pivoted to return to the Kings when mist churned from the wall, and the head of a dragon rushed him. Derek lifted his hands, the fog scattering as soon as it touched his skin.

"Go," Con bade. "We'll head to Stonemore."

Derek barely heard him over the screams. He nodded and turned on his heel to continue down the tunnel.

CHAPTER 32

The air was cool, the night silent. Too silent. Rhi didn't like it. This game had too many moving parts, and the Kings were separated. On Zora and Earth. The Kings were strong apart but virtually invincible when facing a foe together. She had seen it, had even been a part of it. This thing with Miena reminded her too much of Usaeil.

Her mother had been as merciless and single-minded as Miena and Villette.

The enemy of my enemy... It was a popular human adage on Earth. But would it work with a viper like Villette? Rhi knew from experience that a person could change. All she had to do was look at one of her closest friends, Balladyn. He had gone from a general in the Light Fae army, to a Dark Fae, to King of the Dark, to a Reaper.

Then there was Usaeil, who was a completely different kind of animal. Some could—and willingly did—change. While others showed the world their true colors from the very beginning.

Which one was Villette? And would they discover the truth before it was too late?

"I doona like waiting," Hector mumbled as he paced.

Alasdair stood morosely off to the side, arms crossed and silent as a sentry. His sherry-colored eyes flicked to Hector, but he didn't reply.

Rhi's gaze moved to her son. Brandr sat upon a rock at the base of the mountain. He had one leg stretched out while he braced the other foot on the rock as he leaned on a forearm. His dark eyes lifted to her. Con's eyes. There was much about her mate she saw in each twin, but Rhi saw more of Con in Brandr. It was in the way her son held himself. Brandr also had the same habit of concealing his emotions. Like now.

But she didn't need to see them to know he was as edgy as she was.

As they all were.

"Doona worry, Hector. There will be another battle," Brandr said.

Rhi wished that wasn't the case. This was supposed to be a time of peace. After everything the Kings had endured on Earth, they had believed it had culminated in them locating the dragons. Instead, it seemed trouble had followed them. Con wasn't the only one doubting if they should have come. But she knew they were meant to be here.

If only all the Kings were together. She didn't like this. Any of it.

She walked to Brandr and leaned against the boulder near his feet. "You wanted to go with Derek."

"We all did."

"But you really did."

He looked down at his hands at the dried leaf he slowly picked apart. "Aye."

"Because you want to be the first in battle?"

"Because anything can happen. I'd rather be there to help, rather than here, waiting."

"Your father will be fine." The words were like sand on her tongue. It didn't matter how many times Con had been in battle, the worry of losing him would forever remain.

Brandr suddenly went rigid. In the next moment, he was on his feet, his gaze on something in the distance.

"What is it?" Rhi asked. A Fae couldn't see as far as a dragon could.

Alasdair dropped his arms and scanned the horizon. "Dragons."

"Looks like you're getting your battle," Brandr told Hector.

Rhi exchanged a look with her son. She could only hope that whatever Con had to face was easier.

Derek continued down the tunnel with slow, measured steps. The shouts continued but at different resonances. Some high, some low. A few close, but most far away. He felt, more than heard, their agony and anger. Their distress.

More ghostly dragon figures wavered before him. He sensed eyes watching him, scrutinizing. The dead were all around him. And more were waiting. Did they intend to punish him for not saving them? Maybe they blamed him for their painful endings. He held himself responsible.

He had known in his gut that the dragons were in danger. But not from the Kings or humans. They had been slain by the one he had killed for. All those times Villette had wiped his memories, and he hadn't been able to hold on to anything that would've led him here to save even one. It chafed that he had failed them.

More so that he had taken so many innocent lives in the name of freeing the very ones Villette had slaughtered.

How could he make it right? What could he do to make up for his failures? Because they wanted something. The number of ghosts flying around him confirmed that.

Finally, the tunnel ended. Derek didn't immediately step into the cavern. He looked across the way to the table he had lain on just days before as poison ate through him. He had expected to die there, unable to fight, free Merrill, or protect Kora. In the end, Kora had been the one to help herself and Merrill.

Pride had flooded Derek as he watched her before Miena had taken him away from her. Kora was a survivor. She had proven it many times. He had known she would find a way to keep going. She was the last thing he had thought about before Miena's magic slid into his mind and ventured to scrape away all that he was. She had nearly succeeded, too.

Yet Kora had saved him. She never gave up—even when others would have. Her determination restored what had been stolen from him. And in return, Miena had taken Kora. Not for long, though. Derek would find them. Just as Kora hadn't lost hope, he clung to his. She was the only thing that kept him going.

Derek stepped into the cavern as the screams rose to a fever pitch. His gaze took in the copious gouge marks in the rock where the dragons had desperately tried to escape, clawing at the sandstone to reach out for someone, anyone who might help. He should've heard their roars. He should've heard their calls for help.

He continued forward, looking about the cavern. His gaze lingered on the alcove where Gordon had rested. There were others he hadn't noticed when he was here last. Many with chains curled on the ground.

His steps took him to the table. Derek jerked back as a memory of Villette crushing horns, scales, and bone on the table filled his head. The table was also where she had attempted to create more like him and Bryok. Tried—and failed. She had forced him to watch, though he hadn't realized what she was doing then. He only knew she was hurting dragons, which had been torment enough. It was the first time he had tried to kill her.

Tried—and failed.

Derek hurled the table away from him, sickened at the memories and his failure to stop her. The table sailed through the air, hitting a wall. The wood shattered on impact. But it wasn't enough. Nothing could cleanse the cavern of the anguish and fear that seeped from the stone.

He dropped to his knees. The ghostlike dragons swirled lazily about the area, coming close but never too close. They were in all shapes and sizes and so numerous he didn't bother trying to count. They were silent now. He watched them anyway, waiting. They had drawn him here. They wanted to show him, make him remember all they had suffered. He couldn't shake the feeling that they wanted more.

Maybe to punish him?

He parted his lips to ask them to wait until after he'd freed

Kora, but he never got the chance. One of the ghost dragons dove at him from the right. Shock went through Derek when the force of the ghost knocked him to the left. He caught himself with his hand, only to have another hit him from behind. He barely got his other hand under him to keep from smacking his face against the stone.

Thin, white bands curled up from the ground and swiftly wound around his fingers and hands before he had a chance to jerk away. They held him down. Not even his magic could make them loosen their grip. As he struggled, more of them fastened themselves to his lower legs and feet.

Derek shifted. Somehow, they still held him. He thrashed his tail and head to no avail. The screaming started again, a chorus of anguished shrieks, tormented roars, panicked shouts, and frightened growls. The sounds reached a crescendo, his roar joining theirs.

The spirit dragons swirled above him, forming a single line before diving straight at him. Light blinded him. It came up from the ground and moved through him. The force of it threw his head back as light shot from his eyes. He roared, and the light filtered through his mouth and nose. It continued for what felt like an eternity.

Yet it was over in a millisecond.

The light evaporated. When Derek looked, he found he was in his human form, naked on his hands and knees. His head hung as he took in great gulps of air. There were no bindings on his limbs.

There was something else instead.

Derek slowly sat on his haunches and lifted his arms to find them covered in dragons in a red and black ink that seemed to defy comprehension. There were more on his torso. He stood and discovered more on the front and back of his legs, all the way to the top of his feet and over his toes. He knew without looking that they covered his back, as well.

He gazed about the cavern. The ghost dragons were gone. As were their screams. He looked down at himself again. Nay. They weren't gone. They were on him.

They had lured him here, but not to kill or punish him as he had assumed. They had wanted to mark him. There was no answer for why, but he had a feeling he would find out soon enough. He dropped his arms to his sides and called his clothes as his thoughts turned to Kora.

Derek walked to the right. As he approached the wall, something told him to keep going. He steeled himself for pain, but instead, he walked through magic. Once on the other side, he looked back to see that it had been made to appear like a wall. Villette had lied. There was a way from the cavern to Stonemore.

He peeled his lips over his teeth and started running toward the palace.

CHAPTER 33

Miena stood on the balcony of what had once been Villette's rooms. Her body was flush with a recent meal of magic. Aksel had brought her a young boy, but his magic was weak. It wouldn't satiate her hunger, but it was more than she'd had before. Even now, Aksel was searching for her next meal.

She listened to the distant sounds of roars and smiled. The next wave of dragons was attacking. More of her dragon soldiers had gone into the tunnels to find the Kings.

The air shifted around her. She was no longer alone. Miena turned to find her three siblings. She had known they would come but had hoped to be fully refueled first. The fact that Aksel hadn't brought her another child yet made her think Daelya might have grown a spine.

"I was wondering when you three would show up," Miena said.

"Where is Kora?" Lotti asked.

Miena shrugged. "She's cooling off."

"This can end now," Eurielle offered. "Give us Kora and walk away. We won't come after you."

Miena grinned as she eyed Villette. "There is no walking away. All of this was supposed to be mine. I'm merely taking back what was stolen."

"We're not meant to act as gods," Lotti stated.

Miena gave her a dry look. "You've been listening to the Kings. Of course, we are. Why else would we have such power?"

Eurielle took a step forward. "There's no running from us. Not if you choose to remain on this path."

"Nothing to say, Villette?" Miena asked.

Villette glanced toward Lotti and Eurielle. "The facts are plain. Three against one. It doesn't matter how powerful you are. You won't win."

Miena had spent too long locked away and dreaming of this moment to lose. Even without consuming the children's magic, she was stronger than Villette and Lotti. Eurielle was the one she needed to worry about. If only there had been time to find other kids. Villette had diligently cleared the city of those with magic. Most likely on the off chance that Miena got free. There was no time to go elsewhere now. They would all die, but she had a special plan for Villette.

"You look tired. Feeling drained?" Villette asked, a cunning smile tilting up the corners of her lips.

"I'm never too tired to put you in your place."

Miena struck before the others could.

"Merrill!"

Con's shout from behind him was the only warning he got before dragons came at them from both ends of the tunnel. They shifted immediately and moved back-to-back. It was difficult to move, and there wasn't room to open their wings.

The smaller dragons got past the larger ones to attack en masse. There were so many Pinks. Merrill had been overjoyed to find that the Pinks hadn't gone extinct as the Kings had believed. But right now, he would be thrilled never to see another. They covered him, clinging like jellyfish as their talons slid between his scales and sliced deep. He scraped them off, but they returned with a vengeance.

Merrill heard a grunt and looked over to find a Pink attempting to claw Con's eye out while he grappled with a Bronze. Merrill felt a Pink moving toward his eyes. He rubbed his arm over his face to knock the small dragons off before grabbing the one near Con's eye and ripping it in half.

Derek burst into a room from the tunnel. He stalked to the door and yanked it open so hard that it ripped from its hinges. Two soldiers turned at the sound and rushed him. Magic boiled up within him. He threw out his hands to release it and watched the men drop to the ground, unmoving.

He didn't stop to check if they were alive as he stepped over them and ran out into one of the many passages beneath the palace. Soldiers spilled out of rooms. He didn't break stride as he lifted his hand. Magic flew from his palm again and again, the guards falling instantly. A few were smart enough to run away.

His steps faltered when he heard the faraway sound of roars.

No doubt Miena had sent more of her dragon army after his friends. He paused, debating whether to help them or find Kora. His mate won.

Derek found a set of stairs and ascended them. At the top, he stopped and inhaled, hoping to catch Miena's scent. She had been in the palace, which made it hard. He got a whiff of her, but it was faint and too old.

He stalked down the next tunnel. Anyone who attempted to stop him felt his wrath. Word had spread, though, because more soldiers ran instead of taking a stand. Derek climbed the next stairs he found. It took him too long to get from the bowls of the mountain to the palace.

When he drew in a breath, he caught Kora's scent. It was strong, but then it vanished. Derek raced through the halls, trying to find it again. Each time he had it, it rapidly moved away. He stopped on the main stairs and waited. It wasn't long before he heard footsteps below him, moving lower. Derek peered over the railing and saw the shadow of someone descending the stairs.

He leaped over the side, falling until he dropped before the person. There was a gasp as a female servant fell backward.

Derek recognized the material of the sleeves the human carried. He leaned over the woman and demanded, "Where is she?"

"W-w-who?" the woman stuttered.

"Kora."

She shook her head and tried to shrug. "I-I don't know who that is."

"Where did you get those?" he challenged as he jerked his chin to the sleeves.

The woman was shaking so badly she could barely talk.

"Miena told me to carry them and run up and down the stairs until she said to stop."

"Give them to me."

The woman quickly did as he demanded.

"If I were you, I'd get as far from Stonemore as possible," Derek warned.

She wavered, but when he stepped back, she scrambled to her feet and raced away.

He tightened his fist around Kora's sleeves. This wouldn't be the last thing he held of hers.

"Wait for me," he murmured and took the stairs three at a time.

Rhi used her sword to chop off yet another dragon's head after it fell from the sky. Brandr, Hector, and Alasdair were bruised and bloodied, and each time a wound healed, another took its place. The dragon soldiers were relentless, a never-ending sea of scales.

She tried not to think about the fact that she was killing dragons. She consoled herself with knowing they were already dead. At least she hoped that was the case. The three Kings had tried to get through to them, but not a single dragon responded.

Rhi teleported to a white and blue dragon that had just fallen and let her blade slice into its neck. It wasn't a clean cut. The dragon was too big, and her sword was too small for decapitation, but she got the job done.

She kept waiting to hear one of the others call for her. There wasn't time to worry about them, not when she was dodging dragons plunging from the sky, and others coming at her. She saw movement out of the corner of her eye and teleported just as a dragon twice the size of an elephant charged her.

Rhi jumped onto its back and sank her blade into its neck, using a blast of Fae magic to ensure her sword reached the spinal cord. The dragon tried to call out as its body went slack and slumped to the ground. Rhi jumped onto another dragon in midair, slicing its spine before doing a front flip onto another and cutting its spine, as well.

There was a blur of movement, and something hard slapped her face. She realized it was a wing as her sword flew from her hand. Rhi teleported to the ground and formed a large bubble of magic between her hands. She threw it at the dragon who dove from the sky toward her.

Rhi.

The sound of her name on Con's lips made her stomach drop. It took her attention from the dragon, and a talon sank into her shoulder, yanking her from the ground. She dangled in the air as pain ripped through her. She formed a bubble of magic and threw it at the dragon.

In the next moment, she spotted moonlight glinting off gold and beige scales. Brandr was three times the size of the dragon who had her, and her son easily ripped her attacker in half. Its talon was still lodged in her shoulder, and when that part of the dragon dropped, it took her with it. Rhi didn't have time to do anything but prepare as she hit the ground.

"Mum!" Brandr was there, his long, black hair in disarray.

She gave him a smile. "I'm a little hung up."

He chuckled and removed the talon. Rhi glanced at her bloodied shoulder. Fae healed, just not as quickly as dragons.

"Your father called for me," she said.

He nodded. "Go to him. We're nearly done here."

"More could come."

"We'll handle it," Brandr said. He jumped into the air, shifting as he did before she could say more.

Rhi knew her mate's exact location by his call and teleported to him. She found him and Merrill in a tunnel and outnumbered. They were stuck with the dead reanimating as others continued to attack. In order for them to make any headway, they needed to move.

Her gaze briefly met Con's as she touched two dead dragons and teleported them back to her son. Rhi found her sword and cut off their heads before returning to her mate. By the time she got back with the next two dragons, Brandr was waiting. He removed the heads while she went back for the others.

She didn't know how many trips she made before she noticed that Hector and Alasdair were helping behead the dragons. With their foes dealt with, she brought Brandr into the tunnel. He joined Merrill and Con in battle while she removed more dragons. She didn't stop, didn't rest until someone took hold of her arms.

Rhi looked up into a face she knew well. She threw her arms around Con's neck and held him.

"I'm all right," he whispered. "But you're bleeding."

She pulled back and smiled up at him. "It's healing."

"Where's Derek?" Brandr asked.

Rhi jerked back. She hadn't noticed that Derek wasn't there.

"He had his own path," Con explained. "One we couldn't join him on."

Merrill leaned his back against the wall as he rested. "We're to meet him at Stonemore."

They were all exhausted, but there was no time to rest. "I'll get Hector and Alasdair," Rhi said.

Pain shot through Kora. She screamed as blood welled from her neck and gushed over her front, soaking her shirt. The warmth of it was momentarily disorienting. She couldn't hold her head up. It hung listlessly as prickles like hundreds of tiny needles ran down her arm and into her fingers.

She tried to lift her head, but her body wouldn't obey her. Miena wasn't there to inflict pain, which meant Villette had been injured. That meant they were battling. Who was winning? She hated not being there, hated more that she didn't know if Derek was okay.

There was a loud snap, and her right arm bent awkwardly at the elbow as a fresh wave of agony engulfed her. Kora welcomed the darkness when it came.

Miena was tiring much too quickly. But she had gotten several good strikes in on Villette. It was too bad she wasn't there to see how badly Kora suffered.

Lotti was a vicious warrior. Miena was impressed by the way she fought. Lotti might not have finesse, but she made up for it with heart. It was Lotti who sent the thunderous shot of magic. Miena tried to dodge it but was too slow. She attempted to block it instead. Miena knew it was a mistake the moment she did it. She was weakened and sluggish. What little strength she had gotten from the boy had long since been depleted.

Miena's entire body locked up, her muscles spasming when Lotti's magic hit her. She fell to the side and rolled to her feet, barely getting her arms up to block Villette's strike. It was why she never saw Eurielle come in behind her until it was too late.

Her flesh stung from the cut, but Miena hadn't come this far to give up. She peeled back her lips and bellowed as she slashed out her arm, letting magic spray Villette and Lotti. It had been a quick move, and they were too close to get away. It struck them both, sending them into a sprawl on the floor.

Miena spun to face Eurielle and dragged up the last vestiges of her power. If she was going to die, she would do it fabulously. She splayed her fingers toward Eurielle, but she was again too slow. Eurielle's magic struck from her face to her hips, knocking her into the railing.

"My queen!"

The sound of Aksel's voice spun her around. Miena spotted the infant in his arms and was at his side in the next breath. She laid her hands on the child. Miena gasped at the magic she found there. There was no time to do it gently. She called it to her, hastily pulling it from the child into herself until she had it all. The babe wailed from the pain. Miena was once more nourished.

"Bring me more," she ordered the priest.

"Miena!" Lotti shouted.

She turned to her enemies, Aksel and the wailing child forgotten. Lotti's face was a mask of rage as Eurielle stood aghast beside her. Villette pulled herself to her feet as the three of them stood against her once more.

Miena smiled as she motioned for them to attack. But she was ready when they came at her. Her body was flush with power, and it allowed her to be quick and agile, dodging attacks effortlessly. She tried to be careful so as not to use too much too quickly. The last thing she wanted was to be drained again.

She screamed when blood spurted from a cut on her forearm. Lotti smiled as she danced away, a dagger in her hand. Eurielle and Villette rushed her together. Miena had battled both too many times not to expect such a move. She evaded Eurielle and delivered a hard punch to Villette's kidney.

Miena then teleported behind Lotti and shoved her at Eurielle, who had to catch her instead of delivering another blow to Miena.

CHAPTER 34

Derek scoured one level of the palace after another, tearing through hallways in search of Kora's scent. Desperation and the icy hand of fear spurred him on and urged him to go faster. At one point, he heard the distinct sounds of battle but wouldn't stop looking for Kora.

He busted through a door, startling the servants within. Derek scanned their faces for Kora. He was about to turn away to go to the next room when he caught sight of sandstone dust. He whirled back around.

Derek pinned a middle-aged male with his gaze and motioned to the dust. "What caused that."

"R-repairs," the man answered.

"Where?"

"Top left part of the palace," a female replied. "The chamber that exploded a month ago."

Derek knew exactly where that was. He shot from the doorway, running faster than before. Why hadn't he thought to look for Kora where Miena had been imprisoned? It sounded exactly like something she would do.

His surroundings were a blur as he raced to the stairs, only to jump from landing to landing. And still, he wasn't moving fast enough. He debated whether to shift and fly to Kora, but he didn't want to cause the palace to crumble and kill innocent people or Kora if she was in a different location. So, he ran like the wind.

By the time he reached the top and slid to a stop at the long corridor, his heart was thudding like a drum against his ribs. Her scent was strong. He only paused for a second before racing down the hall and through the doorway, immediately coming to a halt. The debris had been cleaned, and the cracks in the floor and walls were in various stages of repair.

He turned, his gaze locking on the metal door. The new silver entrance had no handle or hinges, but that wouldn't stop him from getting inside. Derek put his hands on the door, the metal cool to the touch. Had Miena put Kora in the middle of the room as she had been?

Derek dropped his arms and studied the entry. The fact that there wasn't an easy way in meant that Miena expected someone to bust the door down. And if that was the case, it meant Kora could be near it. Kora would heal. If she died, she would still return to him.

Unless Miena had booby-trapped the area.

He let out a string of curses. The longer he waited to do something, the more Kora would be tortured. But he didn't want to cause her more harm. Her deaths and rebirths were excruciating.

He scanned the walls on either side of the door, trying to deter-mine if there was a better entry point. There were no answers since he couldn't know for sure where his beloved was.

Derek walked to the door once more, then leaned close and called out, "Kora? Can you hear me?"

He listened, but there was no answer.

"Fuck!" he shouted as he stepped away.

There was no other option. He had to break down the door.

Brandr was the first to spill out into an antechamber. Numerous smaller tunnels led out of it.

"I recognize these types of tunnels," Alasdair said as he came up beside him. "We're below Stonemore."

Hector looked at the different exits. "Do we split up again?"

"No' this time," Con said.

Merrill walked to one of the passageways and looked inside. Then he went to a second. "I navigated some of these, but no' nearly enough. There are hundreds."

"Thousands," Alasdair corrected. "And some doona go anywhere but to another room."

Rhi shrugged. "I could get us to Derek if he would only call to me."

"He could be anywhere," Con said.

Merrill's face tightened. "He's going after Kora."

"Who could also be anywhere," Hector pointed out.

Lotti spun as magic slammed into her side. She was struggling to stay in the fight. Villette and Eurielle were picking up the slack, but it was obvious she was the weakest of them. She gritted her teeth and dug deep inside for the power she had spent decades hiding because she hadn't known who or what she was. Alasdair had helped her find her way. He had shown her the power she wielded. Lotti hadn't overcome all of that to be the reason they lost.

Villette screamed and fell back, her head bouncing off the floor. Eurielle moved between Miena and Villette, and Lotti joined her. Miena was as bloodied and wounded as the rest of them, but nothing slowed her.

"Together," Eurielle whispered.

Lotti reached for more magic. It rose in her stomach and moved through her chest to roll down her arms and burst from her palms. Eurielle hurled her own and they smashed into Miena, somersaulting her backward over the balcony.

Eurielle helped Villette to her feet, but Lotti didn't take her eyes off the horizon. It was a good thing, too, because Miena returned, firing short bursts of magic at each of them. Lotti yelled at the others to duck. Villette dove for cover, but Eurielle took a hit in the back and dropped to one knee.

Then it was Lotti and Villette who stood shielding Eurielle.

Derek placed his palms on the door and closed his eyes, sending up a silent prayer to the universe. His lids lifted as he stared at the metal and pushed against it with his strength alone. The door groaned. The metal bent beneath his hands but held.

He stepped back for a moment before replacing his hands. The next time he added magic, moving it through him a little at a time. Yet there was no more movement from the door. And that left him no other option. He had never liked being backed into a corner, and he liked this instance even less because there was the potential that Kora could get hurt.

Derek drew in a deep breath. Just as he was releasing it, he heard a sharp cry of pain from within the room. That was all it took to get him moving. He shouted Kora's name as talons shot from his fingers to carve into the door. The screech of metal mingled with his bellow as he yanked back with all his might and magic.

The door gave some but remained in place. Too many people had stood in the way of him getting to Kora. He had been manipulated and fooled, his every thought and action controlled by others. But no longer. He was his own dragon.

And his mate needed him.

His skin sizzled, a reminder of the markings that covered him. Magic surged and burst from him like a tidal wave. He ripped the door away and tossed it to the side, tearing a hole in the newly repaired wall as he rushed into the room.

"KORA!"

Impatience needled Brandr. The first and second tunnels hadn't led anywhere. They were on their third attempt. The passage had led up, then down, and they were once more on an incline. Everyone in his group was anxious to reach the others.

"This better fucking be it," Hector muttered the words each of them was thinking.

Merrill stilled. "Listen," he bade softly.

They stopped. It was faint, but Brandr heard the unmistakable sound of armor.

"Soldiers," Alasdair muttered in disgust.

Rhi teleported from beside Con to the front of the group. "Let's show them they chose the wrong side."

"It's a diversion," Con stated.

Rhi turned her head to look back at Con and smiled. "Of course it is, my love. I'll take care of them while the rest of you make your way out."

Brandr grinned as his father muttered a curse when Rhi raced down the tunnel. They all followed and came out to find her fighting a squadron of Stonemore soldiers who had been waiting for them.

There was no time to respond as the Kings worked their way through the soldiers, moving toward the next tunnel. Alasdair reached it first, with Hector and Merrill right behind him. Brandr was last and looked back to see his parents fighting side by side.

"Go!" Con bellowed at them.

Merrill grabbed Brandr and yanked him along. They ran through passage after passage, zigzagging their way through the mountain. Soldiers poured out of every crevice in a bid to stop them. But the mortals were no match for four Kings on a mission.

"Here!" Merrill shouted when he found the stairs.

Brandr took the sword from the soldier he fought and sliced his throat before running to join the others already making their way up. Multiple tunnels branched off from the stairs, but they continued up the spiral staircase.

One moment, they were on the stairs. The next, they were running through the palace halls. Until a bellow stopped them cold.

"Derek," Brandr said.

Merrill's jaw locked as he leaped onto the balcony on the floor above. By the time Brandr followed, Merrill had already disappeared around the corner.

The sight before Derek was one of horror. The lava was gone, replaced by thick ice. Kora was bound in the middle of the room, her arms chained and stretched taut. She hung limply, her arms at odd angles and her head bowed. Dark red droplets splattered the ice below her head while more soaked her side to puddle on the ice at her knee.

He stopped at the edge of the frozen water. Reaching her wasn't the problem. It was getting her free. He scanned the ice, looking for any surprises. Just like the lava, it was thinner near the edges and thickened at the center where Kora stood.

Derek tested it to see if it would hold him. He thought about cracking it on purpose but decided to reach Kora first. When the ice held, he hurriedly made his way to her. He tried to lift her but couldn't budge her from the ice. If he couldn't take her out, then he would break her free.

"Hold on, Kora," he said. "I'm coming."

She gave no indication that she'd heard him. Derek raced back to the shore and reared back his fist, slamming it down with all his might. A thick crack formed from the impact and spread like a web beneath the surface. He struck the ice again, expecting it to split open. All he got were more fractures.

Derek hit the same impact point twice more in rapid succession. On the second blow, the ice finally tore apart. He jumped to his feet, ready to run to her and haul her out when she jerked and began screaming. Derek saw the reason when the ice that had opened near her leg shot out like small needles and sank into her skin, encasing her limb in ice. The crack he had worked so hard at producing had also healed itself.

"Nay!" he said in frustration.

He couldn't take her out. He couldn't break her out. What was he supposed to do?

"Need some help?"

Derek turned to find Merrill standing in the doorway. He had never been so happy to see anyone before. As Derek quickly explained what he had already attempted, Brandr and Hector arrived.

"Fire," Con said as he and Rhi entered the room.

Derek looked at the ice that now ran up Kora's legs. "The fire can't get close to her. There's also a chance the ice will attack her again."

"We willna know until we try. Besides, with all of us dousing it, there should be time for you to get her out," Merrill said.

Hector rubbed his hands together and eyed the ice. "Aye. It willna stay frozen for long."

"I'll get her out," Rhi said.

Derek shook his head as he walked back onto the ice to stand beside Kora. "I'll start working on it from here."

"Spread out," Con urged the other Kings.

Derek waited until they had taken their places around the shoreline before he warned, "Don't let the flames touch Kora."

"Soldiers are coming," Rhi said as she peered out the door. "I'll handle them."

Con grimaced at his mate's retreating back. Derek understood exactly how he felt. He had never attempted to breathe fire without being in dragon form, but if there was a way, then he would do it. One by one, the Kings released fire upon the ice. Derek watched it melt. He drew in a deep breath and touched Kora's cold fingers, then blew out, fire exploding from his mouth.

CHAPTER 35

She was conquering her rivals. It wasn't the grand confrontation Miena had coveted, but she was still getting the upper hand against her sisters. Unfortunately, that wouldn't hold true for long. She was burning through her magic too quickly, and Aksel had yet to return with another child. But there were other ways to win.

Miena teleported to Eurielle, her arms out. Magic exploded from her hands, wrapping around Eurielle's face. Her sister cried out, half in surprise and half in pain. Once Miena had a hold of her, there was no way Eurielle could break free. Villette and Lotti tried to stop her, but they couldn't throw their magic too close lest they strike Eurielle.

Miena dragged her sister to the edge of the balcony. She smiled as she leaned back and tumbled over the railing, taking Eurielle with her. Eurielle's gray eyes narrowed in confusion. She waited until Eurielle attempted to teleport back up. The instant Miena felt her sister's magic, she homed in on it. She knew from experience that she couldn't siphon any, but that wasn't what she wanted. All she needed was to keep Eurielle distracted long enough. The ground rose up quickly. Miena waited until she knew there was no escape for her sister. Then she released her, watching Eurielle collide with the mountainside.

Derek gradually moved around Kora, melting the ice, careful that his flames didn't get close. The Kings remained at the shoreline, their fire stretching toward him and Kora as they kept the ice from reforming. Derek began sinking as the thick glacial mass around Kora started to liquefy. But it was taking far longer than he had foreseen.

Rhi kept the soldiers at bay by herself. The clang of swords, dings of armor, and shouts could be heard over the rumble of flames. Everyone in the chamber was acutely aware of Rhi facing an unknown number of foes on her own. Con's gaze kept sliding to the door, waiting for his mate. He was concerned but not fearful. Because Con knew Rhi could handle it. Derek knew that same feeling. He glanced at Kora. He wanted to protect her and keep all harm from coming near her. But she was more than capable of taking care of herself—and taking on others.

Look what she had done for him.

His heart squeezed as a thread of fear spiked through him. How many more obstacles would they have to overcome before they could be together? He would never stop fighting for her. No matter who tried to come between them, they would find their way back to each other. Just as they had done several times already.

He silently begged her to lift her head. Derek needed to look into her eyes. He wanted her to know that he was there. But she remained unconscious, her blood continuing to drip dark red against the ice.

A mound took shape beneath Kora's feet as the ice liquefied. Fury ripped through Derek when he saw additional restraints tightly wound around her ankles. He carefully directed his fire away from his mate as he reached for the chains at her feet. The sight of blood churning in the water sent a dagger straight to his heart. He channeled that violence and his magic into the shackles. They fell apart in his hands. Almost too easily. But he'd worry about that later.

He unwound the chains from her ankles. When he stood, Merrill walked to where her restraints were attached to the wall. Derek stopped his fire and lifted Kora into his arms, cradling her against him. Merrill broke the shackles. Her right arm fell heavily. Derek looked the other way and watched Brandr sever the links holding her left arm. Once she was free, Derek didn't waste any time moving through the icy water to the shore.

The moment his feet touched the ground, the Kings ceased their fire. The water cracked and groaned as it refroze. Con, Merrill, and Brandr ran out ahead of them to aid Rhi. Derek carried Kora's shivering form out of the chamber as Hector brought the chains. Derek gently laid Kora down. There was so much blood. It coated her face and dripped into her hair. It soaked her side and her front. He had even felt it on her back when he carried her.

"She'll heal," Derek said, more to himself than the others. He looked Kora over, taking in the other injuries he hadn't seen. He touched her face. "Open your eyes, Kora. I need you to wake up."

Her body jerked, and a moan fell from her lips. It soon turned into a scream of agony.

"Derek!" Hector shouted before flames erupted from him.

Derek looked over in horror as ice from Kora's legs melded with more that had reached out from the room like a long finger. Hector severed it as Derek gathered Kora to him once more and moved her farther away from the chamber. If he hadn't tossed the door out, they would have had something to lock in the ice. Rhi, Brandr, and Merrill blocked the way out, fighting a sea of soldiers. Con extricated himself from the battle and strode to them. He put his hand on Kora. Derek waited, but her wounds didn't heal.

"What's wrong? Why isn't it working?" Derek asked.

Con shook his head, a deep frown forming. "I doona know."

They both looked at the chains dangling from her wrists and saw more ice crawling up them. Con and Hector each grabbed the thick metal and broke it apart. The next time Con tried to heal her, Derek observed her injuries heal before his eyes. But she still didn't wake.

"Time to go!" Rhi shouted over her shoulder.

Derek reached for his cuff, muttered a curse, and followed Con and Hector. Rhi, Brandr, and Merrill were suddenly there. Someone grabbed his arm. The sounds of battle were replaced by the peace of nature. Derek gazed at the tall trees and night sky beyond them. He would know Ferdon Woods anywhere.

"Now what?" Hector asked.

The King of Kings slid his gaze to Brandr. "It's your decision, son. You rule here."

To Derek's surprise, Brandr turned to him and asked, "What do you think?"

Derek looked at the faces around him before laying Kora on

the ground and calling up a blanket to cover her. Then he stood and faced the group. "We should work on the thing we all want. Miena dead."

Lotti kept looking for Eurielle, but she hadn't returned since she'd gone over the side with Miena. Lotti tried to get to the railing to look over, but Miena kept her and Villette away. And while she might be slowing, Villette and Miena didn't seem to be. The hatred between the two was evident in their strikes. Lotti saw the damage Villette took and couldn't imagine how Kora was faring.

She had hoped Alasdair and the other Kings would have arrived by now. Where were they?

Footsteps sounded behind her. She spun to see the same, red-robed priest as before yanking a screaming girl behind him. Lotti glanced at Miena and saw anticipation flare in her eyes. After what Villette had shared about Miena stealing magic, and what Lotti had witnessed with the infant, there was no way Lotti would allow her anywhere near the child.

Lotti stepped between the priest and Miena. "Leave. Now."

"I don't answer to you," he said, contempt dripping from his words.

She leveled her gaze at him. "I wasn't asking."

The priest looked from the girl, trying to pull out of his bruising hold, tears coursing down her face, to Miena, who was shouting for him. Lotti knew the moment he decided to chance it.

She closed the short distance between them and grabbed the girl, turning the child away as Lotti shoved magic into his chest, stopping his heart. Miena's screamed her displeasure. Villette shouted something to Lotti, but she couldn't make it out. She moved the girl so she couldn't see around her as magic seared her lower back.

Lotti smiled through the pain. "I won't let anything happen to you. Right now, I need you to get at least three floors down. Can you do that?"

The girl stared at her with wide, blue eyes, her dark lashes spiked from her tears. She nodded before attempting to look around Lotti when the floor shook.

Lotti moved with her. The child was already traumatized. She didn't need to see any more. "Go now. I'll come for you soon."

She turned the girl around and gave her a soft shove. Lotti didn't budge until the child was out of sight. Then she whirled around and rejoined the battle with renewed fury.

Kora opened her eyes to see stars blinking between thick tree limbs. Voices reached her then. The moment she heard Derek's, something inside her loosened. The ice prison felt like a distant nightmare, but it wasn't. Tremors still racked her body.

Her clothes were sticky. She moved the blanket, and pain exploded on her right thigh. She likely would've been brought to the ground had she been standing. She must have made a sound because Derek was suddenly leaning over her. It was too dark to see his face clearly, but she didn't need to. She knew every curve and contour by heart.

"You found me," she said.

There was a smile in his voice as he replied, "Always."

"Welcome back," Rhi told her as she stood on Kora's other side.

Derek ran a hand down her face. "Can you stand?"

"I don't know," Kora admitted. Her leg throbbed.

Someone touched her shoulder. She tilted her head back and saw their outline. Her pain suddenly diminished and then left altogether.

"That should do it," Con said.

Kora smiled in gratitude. "Thank you."

Derek took her hand and helped her to her feet. "We're planning our attack on Miena."

"First, let's get you cleaned up." Rhi snapped her fingers.

Kora's clothes were replaced. She touched her hair and face to find both free of blood. "That feels better."

"I always go into battle looking my best," the Fae stated with a grin.

Merrill cleared his throat. "Miena will expect us to come from the sky. She'll see us, but I still think that's our best advantage."

"Some of us should come from the palace," Hector said.

Alasdair shifted from one foot to the other, his body taut. "Whatever we're doing, we need to do it now."

"All right. Let's split up," Brandr said.

"Nay." Kora's voice rang out in the forest, halting everyone. They turned to look at her, but she focused on Derek. "She can be hurt, but we want to do more than injure her. My fire will kill her."

Derek's brow furrowed. "You aren't going after her alone."

"I realized something when I was in the ice. She's alone. Completely. And she's scared."

Con motioned to her. "What do you propose?"

"Something none of you will like." Kora took a deep breath. "Merrill's right. There needs to be an attack from the air, but one she won't see coming."

Rhi grinned. "You."

Kora nodded and met the Fae's eyes. "I'm going to need you, though." Then she looked at Derek. "And you."

"You shouldna be in the skies alone," Con said.

Kora looked at the faces around her. "I won't be."

CHAPTER 36

The idea had come to Kora when she was drowning in pain. Then, it had seemed so simple and perfect. Now, as her friends took up their positions, she began doubting everything. Who was she to decide on a plan? She didn't have the battle experience they had.

"It's a good plan," Rhi said as she came to stand beside her.

Kora looked up at the mountain. She could just make out the palace at the top. "Something could go wrong."

"Something always goes wrong. Don't worry about us. We'll do what we need to do." She looked past Kora's shoulder and walked away.

Kora turned to find Derek. He pulled her close and skimmed the backs of his knuckles across her cheek. "We can do this."

"I know." At least, she hoped—she hoped with everything she had.

"There isn't time to say everything I've wanted to tell you, or all

I should have said. So let me just say this. You are my everything. My past, my present, and my future."

Kora pulled his head down to hers for a soft kiss. "And you're mine."

His gaze became intense. "When you're facing her, don't hesitate. And don't allow her to make you think you aren't capable. You are. You brought me back."

"I did, didn't I?" she asked with a smile.

"She'll try to get into your head," Derek warned.

Kora drew in a breath and nodded. "I know."

"I love you."

"And I love you."

He touched her face once more. Then he released her and backed away before shifting. Kora would never get tired of seeing him change forms. She waited until he lay down before she climbed onto his back. His scales were hard. And slippery. Falling was a distinct possibility, but she couldn't allow herself to linger on that when she had bigger problems.

"He won't let you fall," Rhi said from behind her.

Kora looked over her shoulder at the Fae. She didn't get to answer as Derek climbed to his feet. A squeak escaped Kora as she pitched forward and tried to find something to grip as her heart beat wildly. If she was this clumsy when he was on the ground, how bad would it be when they were in the air?

Rhi moved closer and helped her sit up once more. "Don't worry about trying to hold on."

"Then how am I going to stay atop him?" Kora hated how high her voice was.

Derek turned his head to look at her. He hadn't moved again.

"*Feel* him," Rhi urged. "You'll be able to sense what he intends by focusing on his body and not the fact that he's in the air. Just like when you're in bed together."

That made sense. It was a little weird, but it made sense.

Rhi placed her hand on Derek's scales. "They're hard. A protective shell. But their warmth tells you they are more than just a covering." The Fae shot her a smile. "Most of all, feel the wind. There's nothing quite like flying."

Kora knew they were using precious time they didn't have, but she was glad she had it. Rhi's talk eased her fears enough for her not to change her mind about the plan. Kora placed her hand on Derek's scales and nodded. "I'm ready."

"I've got her," Rhi called out as she squatted behind Kora.

Kora had never had magic envy before, but the idea of being able to teleport and stop herself from falling was an ability she wished she had. All thought stopped when Derek unfurled his wings. She had seen them from the ground, but from this new vantage point, she comprehended just how huge they were.

A gust of wind hit Kora as Merrill, Alasdair, and Hector took to the skies. Con and Brandr were going through the palace to complete the double attack. Kora and Derek would be the third strike.

A sound rumbled through Derek. She felt the vibration in her thighs and heard Rhi chuckle. Kora's heart began to beat double. No matter how many times she repeated Rhi's words, she couldn't stop the nervousness that claimed her.

The only warning she got that Derek was about to take to the skies was the bunching of scales at his shoulders. He launched into the air, his large wings beating. Her stomach dropped as he angled upward. To her surprise, she didn't slide off. She looked down to see the ground becoming more distant. They soared over trees until they, too, grew small.

Kora shut her eyes, thinking that would help, but it only made it worse. Her fingers dug into Derek's scales when she felt his body level out. When she opened her eyes, Derek was flying straight, having reached the altitude he desired. The wind struck her eyes so hard it was difficult to keep them open. It whipped the end of her braid around and caressed her face with its cool hand.

The moons were so close she thought she might be able to reach out and touch them. Kora laughed as she settled more comfortably. Rhi had been right. Flying was incredible. Kora was definitely going to ask Derek for more rides in the future.

Her smile died when she saw the palace. The three Kings peeled off and headed straight for it as Derek once more angled himself to fly higher. Rhi had veiled them before they left the ground. The Fae had explained that they would be able to see everything, but no one could see them as long as Rhi kept the veil up. Kora experienced another twinge of magic envy at hearing that.

She could make out small dots moving on a balcony. They were Lotti, Eurielle, and Villette, battling Miena. They had been at it for hours. But...wait. Kora only counted three, not four. Someone had been hurt—or worse. She prayed it wasn't Lotti.

Kora bit back a cry as shooting pain went up her spine. Obviously, Villette wasn't the one missing. Experiencing Villette's injuries made things harder, but there was no way for Kora to get around it. Con might have healed her before, but he wouldn't be there in the midst of the battle. That meant she had to get to Miena quickly.

Kora breathed through the pain. She was so engrossed in not

letting Derek or Rhi know she was hurt that she missed when he leveled out once more. She glanced down as they circled the palace and saw flames cutting through the night. The sight of the three dragons attacking the balcony was mesmerizing. They dove and twisted, spun and rose, with unbelievable agility and grace. No matter how many times she watched the dragons, it always surprised her that they could move with such ease despite their size. Or maybe *because* of it.

She lost count of how many times Derek circled. They were too high up for her to see details, but Kora could spot Miena by herself, squaring off with the Kings and two of her sisters. Now, all Kora waited on was the arrival of Con and Brandr before her part began.

"There they are," Rhi said loudly so her voice would carry over the wind.

Derek had already spotted Con and Brandr and began their descent. Kora's heart raced, pounding in her chest while blood rushed in her ears. This was it. This was where one story ended—Miena's.

Suddenly, Derek tucked his wings and dove. The wind sucked the breath from Kora as it howled around her. She became weightless, and for a moment, she feared the wind might rip her from Derek's back. After the initial panic, Kora experienced a rush of freedom.

And just as unexpectedly, it ended with Derek spreading his wings and halting their dive. He soared between Alasdair and Hector, then dipped his wing and swung around to miss Merrill. Derek took her low enough that she could see blood splattered on the balcony floor.

On Derek's second pass, Kora smoothed her hand along his

scales and jumped. It was time. Miena was completely surrounded. Kora looked back at Rhi as she hung in the air before falling. The Fae gave her a nod of understanding.

Kora's touch was like a brand upon his scales. Derek spun around and headed for Miena. At the moment he dove toward the palace, he alerted the Kings to his location. Derek noticed Villette scanning the night sky as if she expected him to appear.

"*Now!*" Derek shouted to the Kings.

Merrill, Alasdair, and Hector maneuvered into position in the air while Con and Brandr left a large enough space for him on the balcony. Kora jumped at the same time Rhi lowered her veil and Derek landed with a roar. Miena whirled around at the impact. Kora delicately dropped to the ground. Sparks flew from the ends of her dark hair as her skin cracked to display the red-orange glow beneath. Flames swarmed Kora, devouring her clothes and swirling about her limbs as she started toward Miena. Kora's hair came free of its braid as the wind lifted the strands, sending the flaming tendrils into a wild dance as sparks filled the air.

Derek lowered his head, his gaze locked on Miena. His creator, the one who had given him life. She was surrounded by enemies—and facing the one who could end her for good.

But Miena didn't attack Kora. Instead, she threw magic that struck Villette. Villette stumbled back with no visible signs of injury. Kora jerked as her cheek split along the bone and blood spilled out.

Rage filled Derek. He would end Miena now if he could.

Kora cupped her hand as the flames doubled in her palm. They burned bright yellow, then nearly white at the center and red along the edges. She threw the fireball. Miena dodged it. Villette and Lotti moved back since neither wanted to be burned by Kora's flames. But the Kings moved in.

Kora threw another fireball. It traveled faster and nearly caught Miena when she didn't move quickly enough. The Star Person bellowed in rage and lashed out by sending a rapid-fire volley of magic toward Villette. Kora's leg buckled at the agony. Her flames sputtered, but she dug deep for her fire. It roared in answer. She climbed to her feet despite the debilitating pain and limped forward.

Miena's next attack went awry when Villette dodged the blast. Others might accept their end, but Miena wasn't going down quietly or easily. There was no crazed look in her eyes, no terror. Just a calculated stare. Kora understood in that second that she never would've beaten Villette had she faced her when she first came to Stonemore.

Something had changed in Kora, altered. She felt it in her flames, in her being. The hellhound she was now could take Villette. Miena would be trickier, but the flames told her she could do it.

Kora was ready for Miena's next strike on Villette. But Miena changed directions and lobbed her magic at Derek. He collapsed without a sound. Before Kora could get off a fireball, Miena struck Merrill, who tumbled from the sky. Kora threw flames, getting them close enough to encircle Miena, but somehow, she doused them before they landed.

The sight of Derek unmoving broke something within Kora. After all they had been through, he couldn't be gone. She lobbed fireballs that Miena managed to avoid again and again. Kora was fast, but Miena was quicker.

"Nay," Kora whispered.

Miena wasn't getting away. Derek wouldn't die. The battle belonged to her. She was the one who would decide Miena's fate. And her time was finished.

The flame within Kora's center heated until it burned a bright violet. Her limbs grew heavy with unbridled power. It pierced her, sliced her open as it sculpted something new and potent. It was persuasive and heady, compelling and violent.

And it had one target.

Derek clawed his way back to consciousness. Death had tried to take him, but he had fought against it. And won. When he opened his eyes, all he saw was chaos. Hector had tried to catch Merrill, and both had ended up hurt. Con had dove over the side of the balcony, and Derek had no idea if Merrill was alive or not.

His gaze sought Kora, who hovered in the air as purplish-blue flames covered her as a thick stream of flame connecting her to the ground, and another shot straight up to the heavens. Miena had shifted her focus and targeted Brandr and Alasdair. Lotti and Villette had renewed their attacks on Miena, which kept her from going after the other Kings.

Derek pushed up onto his forearm. He didn't remember shifting. The markings over his body sizzled as if to get his attention. He got to his feet. The Kings' voices bellowed in his head, but he tuned them out. His attention moved from Kora to Miena and back.

Miena was tiring. She was trying not to show it, but he saw it in the tightening of her mouth. She turned toward him, and he stilled, expecting her to see him. Her eyes moved over him as if he weren't there. Derek looked at his arms to see the markings pulsing red and black. He studied Miena, sensing when she was about to release a volley.

On a hunch, Derek drew magic into his palm. He smiled when Miena's attack on Lotti faltered. How had he not realized sooner that he had Star Person magic within him? He was Miena's creation, after all. She'd had to use her power to give him life.

He saw her raise her hand as if to snap. He knew without asking that she was about to kill the Kings—and possibly all dragons. Derek held out his hand, palm out. The force of his fury came from deep inside him and grew stronger as it rose and shot from his hand. Miena lifted her arm as if to shield her face, but there was no getting away. His magic knocked her onto her back, but she quickly jumped up and faced him.

Derek started toward her when flames surged from Kora, who stood on the balcony once more. They licked at Miena, coming at her from different directions. She tried to teleport, but the fire caught her foot. She spun instead, right into Lotti.

Miena's startled cry could barely be heard over the howl of the blaze. Kora moved her hands in an elegant dance, sending flames along the ground to Miena's left. It caused Miena to pivot to the right and come face-to-face with Villette. Miena hastily turned again, right into Derek's grasp.

His fingers wrapped around her neck as he looked into her green eyes that widened in shock.

"How are you alive?" she croaked

He looked past her to Kora, who stood waiting.

"Derek," Miena pleaded. "I'm your parent. I made you. You can't kill me."

He pushed her away. Miena whirled around, but Kora already had her ringed in fire.

"You need me!" Miena shouted to Derek.

Kora closed her hand into a fist. The flames smothered Miena, ending her life as her screams echoed around them. They stood in silence for a moment, looking at the ashes that had once been Miena.

Kora doused her flames, and as they vanished, her clothes reappeared. She sucked in a breath a moment later as white magic swirled up her arm. The vow with Villette had been fulfilled and would no longer bind them.

"She's gone," Kora said. "Villette's gone."

Derek didn't blame her. With Miena dead, what was to stop them from turning on her? Nothing. She had been right to leave.

His gaze sought Kora. Their eyes met, and they walked to each other as if an invisible string tugged them together. They fell into each other's arms. It was over. They had won.

"You did it," he said.

Kora leaned back to look at him with a smile. "*We* did it."

CHAPTER 37

Kora had to force herself to stop kissing Derek. She had grunted in disapproval when he clothed himself, especially before she got a look at the new markings on him. But she would take her time later, exploring his delicious body to her heart's content.

The nine of them stood on the balcony as the sun crested the horizon. They hadn't lost anyone. Merrill was a little worse for wear, but he was alive thanks to Con. Wounds were healing. There would be scars, though they weren't ones anyone could see. No one could enter a battle and not be scarred.

"There's no sign of Eurielle," Lotti said into the silence.

Alasdair rubbed her back. "We'll keep looking."

"Do you think Villette will return to Stonemore when we're gone?" Rhi asked.

Merrill nodded. "Without a doubt."

"I agree," Derek said.

Kora took his arm and shoved up his sleeve. "I'd like to know what these are."

"Tattoos," Hector said.

Con moved in for a closer look and lifted his black eyes to Derek. "How many do you have?"

"They cover him. At least his front," Kora said.

Derek made an indistinct sound. "And my back."

"Have they always been there?" Brandr asked.

Derek shook his head and shifted his jaw as if he would rather be talking about anything else. "It happened when I went into the tunnel. Mist shaped like dragons came out of everywhere...and then went into me."

"You saw something, too," Con stated.

Derek tipped his head forward. "A blinding light. When it was over, I was covered in these," he said, holding out his arms.

"And we didna think the magic was here," Hector said with a grin.

Kora frowned as she looked between them. "I don't understand."

"The magic on Earth chooses the Dragon Kings," Con explained. "Being a King allows us to shift forms, and each of us has a dragon tattoo."

"Just one?" Derek asked.

Merrill nodded. "Just one."

Kora looked at the different dragons on Derek's arm and how they were all interwoven. "Why so many on him?"

"Zora is different," Hector said.

Rhi twisted her lips. "Then why haven't any other Kings or Queens been crowned?"

"The dragons are no' in clans here," Brandr reminded them.

Derek shook his head. "These dragons are the spirits of those who were killed. They're the ones who called me to that place."

"To mark you," Merrill said.

Con smiled. "And name you King of the Dead."

Kora grinned up at him. "You are no longer an uncrowned King."

"And what of you?" Derek asked softly. "I saw the violet flames cutting through you, connecting you to the sky and the ground."

She glanced away, remembering what it had felt like to claim what had always been inside her and set it free. "I was reborn. All the gifts I had and shunned were awoken once more. Seeing you lying unconscious triggered it."

"Looks like both of you found what was missing," Rhi stated.

"I hate to break up the party, but we need to return to the others," Lotti said.

Kora tugged on Derek's hand. "Not until we find Daelya and Katla."

"The Druid is more than capable of handling herself," Brandr said.

"The priests took her," Kora argued.

Rhi turned toward the chamber doors. "She'd be in the tower, right?"

"Should be," Merrill said.

Rhi vanished but returned almost immediately. "The top of the tower is gone."

"Told you she could take care of herself," Brandr replied.

Derek took Kora's hand. "We can look for Daelya."

"Listen," Merrill said. They grew quiet, and the screams from the city reached them. "I doona think any of us should be walking the streets of Stonemore right now."

Kora shook her head. "I promised Daelya I would get her out. I don't want to make her wait."

"Rhi and I will look for her while veiled," Con said. "If we find her, we'll get her out."

It would have to be enough for Kora.

"Iron Hall it is then," Lotti said.

The moment they reached the underground city, Derek tugged on Kora's hand. She wanted some time alone just as much as he did. They slipped away from the others and hurried to her room.

They entered her chamber and closed the door. They were finally alone. She stared at the man she had almost lost so many times and sighed.

"Miena is out of our lives," Derek said.

Kora nodded. "I rectified my mistake." She had a feeling her family would be proud.

Derek took both of her hands in his. "We've not had a lot of time alone. I told you earlier there were things I needed to say."

"There are things I need to say, too."

He swallowed as he glanced away. "First, you should know that some of Miena's magic is in me."

Kora's eyes widened in shock. Then she thought about it. "She made you. It stands to reason that her magic would be a part of you."

"It's why she couldn't kill me. I discovered that if I used magic, it dimmed hers."

"Why didn't you tell the others?"

He jerked his chin to his arms. "I'm already different. Plus, I didn't want them to doubt me."

"They won't. You should tell them." She twisted her lips. "Since we're sharing secrets, you should know that the violet flames did more than awaken my abilities. There are other hellhounds out there in the universe. I can feel them."

"Then we'll find them. Together." He cupped his hand against the side of her head. "I don't want to be without you. You're my day and night. My sunrise and sunset. You give me hope that has eluded me for countless years. I didn't think I was worthy of love, yet you showed me differently. You've given me the family I never thought to have."

She smoothed her hands up his chest and around his neck. "I don't want to be without you, either. I found friendship with an enemy, and a love against all odds. You protected me when I needed it and opened a world of passion I didn't know was possible. You've given me the sky and freedom. You, my gorgeous King of the Dead, gave me a home."

"Spend forever with me."

"I wouldn't have it any other way."

EPILOGUE

A week later...

Derek reclined in the tub, lifted his hand, and let the water dribble from his fingers to drip onto Kora's spectacular chest as she leaned back against him. Her eyes were closed, but a smile curved her lips.

"We should be getting ready," she said.

He kissed her temple and rested his head against hers. "We have a little time until the ceremony. Are you sure?"

"You keep asking me if I'm going to change my mind. I'm beginning to wonder if you want me to."

"Never," he stated. "I just don't want to rush you into anything."

Kora sat up and turned to look at him, splashing water over the sides of the tub. "I love you. I know we're meant to be together. If you want to wait, we can. But I'm not going to change my mind. Are you?"

"I don't want to wait. And, nay, I'm not changing my mind."

"Then you'd better go," she told him as she stood.

Derek reluctantly rose, letting the water drip down his body. He and Kora had barely left the chamber since returning from Stonemore. He brushed his lips over hers and stepped out of the tub. As he walked to the door, he called clothes to him. He looked back at her before the door closed behind him. She blew him a kiss, which made him smile.

He sighed and headed toward the city's main area. Derek turned the corner and nearly collided with Rhi.

"Oh! Hi," she said. "Can't talk. Must get to Kora."

Derek chuckled as he watched her hurry down the corridor. He found Brandr and Hector by the pool.

"Cutting it close," Hector said with a grin.

Derek glanced down at himself. "I've never been to a ceremony. Is it formal?"

"As formal as you want it to be," Brandr replied.

Hector snorted. "Knowing Rhi, Kora will be dressed for the occasion."

"Which means I need to be." Derek shifted his weight from one foot to the other, embarrassed that he hadn't asked. "What should I wear?"

Brandr folded his arms over his chest. "Wear your colors."

"Aye. It's what Kora will likely be wearing," Hector added.

Derek looked at his clothes. "I'm already wearing black."

"More formal. And add silver," Brandr said.

It took a bit, but Derek was eventually outfitted in a black leather jerkin studded with silver, over a black tunic. Black trousers and boots rounded out the outfit. Derek ran his hands through his hair. He intended to grow it long again. For Kora.

"It's time to go," Brandr said.

Hector slapped Derek on the arm as the two walked away. Derek fell into step behind them as they left the city. Once outside, they crossed onto dragon land and shifted to fly to Cairnkeep. Despite his conversation with Kora earlier, Derek couldn't shake the worry that she wouldn't show.

By the time they arrived, he had convinced himself that Kora would change her mind. He was so lost in thought that he didn't notice the others until Hector nudged him. Derek looked in amazement at the new arrivals that consisted of Dragon Kings and their mates. Hector introduced him to each couple.

Before Derek knew it, Brandr motioned him over. It was time. Derek walked to the edge of the cliff, the same area where he had attacked Kora. He didn't want to think about that now. His gaze lifted to find dragons soaring above them to watch.

"Word about the newest King has spread to every corner of our land," Brandr said.

Derek twisted his lips. "Do the dragons know everything about me?"

"They doona need to know everything."

Derek met his gaze and dipped his chin in gratitude.

Brandr suddenly grinned. "You might want to turn around."

He did and found the group had split in two, leaving a large aisle. At the far end stood Kora. The sight of her sent a surge of happiness through him. Then Derek took in her sleeveless black gown. The black lace looked like the veins in his wings. It had a scooped neckline, the bodice contouring to her curves. The skirt flared from her hips down to the floor with a train. She wore gloves that went to her elbows with wings attached that mimicked dragon wings. As she drew nearer, he spotted the tail that curved along her train, complete with a barb at the end like his. All over the gown were small, silver accents.

Finally, she stood before him. Derek couldn't take his eyes off her. She was the most beautiful being he had ever seen.

"Told you I would be here," she said with a smile.

He grinned. "You are breathtaking."

Her head dipped, causing long, silver earrings to swing. They caught his attention, and he realized they were dragons with their wings spread.

"A gift from Con, welcoming me to the family," Kora told him.

"Welcome, all." Brandr's voice boomed around them. "Normally, my father, Con, leads the ceremony, but I asked to conduct Derek and Kora's. It isna everyday a new King is crowned."

The crowd cheered. Derek met Brandr's gaze and smiled.

"It's now time to welcome Kora as Derek's mate," Brandr said. "Derek, do you bind yourself to Kora? Do you vow to love her, cherish her, and protect her above all others?"

Derek grinned at Kora, his entire body bursting with joy. "Aye."

"Kora, do you bind yourself to Derek, the King of the Dead? Promise to love him, cherish him, and protect him above all others?"

Kora beamed as she declared, "Aye."

Derek knew what was next, both of them did. Still, Kora sucked in a breath as the dragon eye tattoo formed on her upper left arm.

"The proof of your vows and your love. Everyone who sees this will know Kora has been marked as Derek's mate for eternity!" Brandr shouted.

The cheers were even louder, but Derek didn't hear them.

There was only Kora as he pulled her into his arms. Sparks flew around him as the edges of the wings attached to her gloves erupted into flames. He'd had nothing for so long. Now, he had friends and a family. A home. But most importantly, he had his mate.

He lowered his head to Kora's and sealed their future with a kiss.

THE END

Thank you for reading THE UNCROWNED KING. I hope you enjoyed the end of Derek and Kora's story! These two have touched my heart deeply, and I hope they stay with you a long time.

There's a bonus short story featuring Derek and Kora. Grab it here: https://dgrant.co/bastard

If you want more Dragon King stories, don't worry. More are coming! Keep reading for a peek at DRAGON MARKED.

BUY DRAGON MARKED TODAY
at www.DonnaGrant.com

* * *

If you love the Dragon King series, you'll love the next Dark Universe book set in the Skye Druids series, BLOOD SKYE...

BUY BLOOD SKYE TODAY
at www.DonnaGrant.com

* * *

To find out when new books release
SIGN UP FOR MY NEWSLETTER today at
https://www.tinyurl.com/DonnaGrantNews

* * *

Join my Facebook group, Donna Grant Groupies, for exclusive giveaways and sneak peeks of future books.
https://bit.ly/DGGroupies

* * *

Keep reading for a peek of BLOOD SKYE and a glimpse at
DRAGON MARKED...

SNEAK PEEK AT THE NEXT DARK UNIVERSE BOOK

BLOOD SKYE, SKYE DRUIDS SERIES, BOOK 6

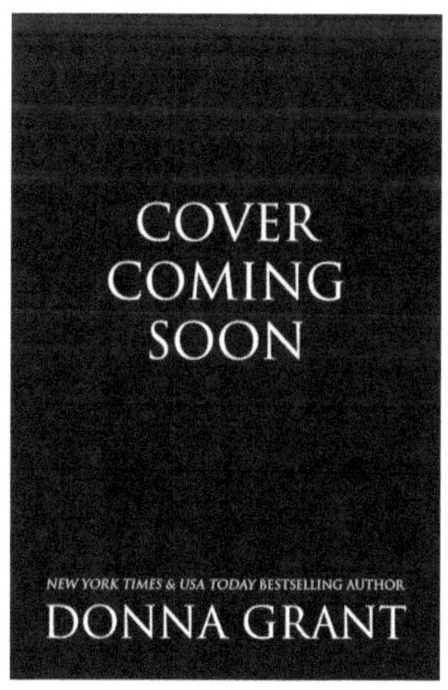

The only choice is surrender.

In my world, magic and danger go hand-in-hand. It has from my earliest memory. Magic was currency, and if you have it, you have power. I was shaped by some of the most influential Druids into a lethal weapon. Their weapon.

Until the night they betray me —and I wind up in the hands of my enemy.

He's nothing but a job for me. To him, I'm the key to finding his father. Too bad I know nothing.

But right now, he's the only thing keeping me alive, so I'll do whatever it takes. Yet, if we're going to survive, it means doing it together.

I've never allowed myself to care, to feel. To hope. He shows me a world that was always just out of reach, one I was never meant to be a part of—and a love that burns bright enough to scorch the earth.

Together, we will bring an empire to its knees.

Return to Scotland and *New York Times* and *USA Today* bestselling author Donna Grant's Skye Druids, where magic and danger intertwine and a tale of passion, revelations, and new beginnings unfolds.

Keep reading for an excerpt of BLOOD SKYE...

BLOOD SKYE EXCERPT

The night was gloomy and damp. Light rain pelted Carlyle's oilskin jacket as he watched the estate's side entrance from behind some bushes. His breath puffed from his lips as the dampness settled into his bones.

"Are you sure about this?"

Carlyle looked at the Irishman beside him. He and Finn had been through a lot together—all the Knights had in their quest to defend the Druids. But this was his mission. Not the Knights'. And not Finn's. "I told you to return to Skye."

"When do I ever do what you want?" Finn asked with a grin, his deep brown eyes sparking with amusement. He ran a hand through the wet strands of his short, dark brown hair and shrugged. "Besides, someone needs to watch your arse. You certainly aren't going to do it."

They'd had this argument a dozen times over the last twenty-four hours. Carlyle should've known Finn wouldn't leave. And he was glad. Even if he knew it would be safer for his friend to go. *Safe* and Finn didn't go together. Ever.

Carlyle's gaze returned to the structure. Something was dreadfully wrong at the estate. Not with just the manor but also with Mason. His longtime friend wasn't himself, as he'd proven during their last encounter. Mason had even cut off his sister after Ferne went to the Isle of Skye.

"We need a better plan," Finn said.

Carlyle shook his head. "The plan is fine."

"Hardly."

"I'm not waiting another second."

Finn blew out a breath. "Your father is smart and strong. Wherever he is, whoever has him will find him resilient."

Carlyle prayed that was the truth. His mother had died when he was very young, leaving him and his father alone. What had developed was a close relationship between father and son. It had never occurred to Carlyle that the London Druids would go after Thomas just to get to him. But they had made a mistake in doing so.

And he was about to show them why.

"There may be better ways of getting to Devon," Finn said.

Just thinking about her made Carlyle see red. She had been waiting for Finn and him at Thomas's townhome to let them know the elders were aware that Carlyle had been to the Isle of Skye. Per their rules, that was grounds for banishment. She also claimed not to know where his father was, but Carlyle knew she was behind his disappearance somehow. Add that Devon was embroiled in Mason's life, and it confirmed Carlyle's suspicions that the corrupt London Druids were pulling the strings once again.

Carlyle rubbed his hands together to warm them. "She's still here. That means we have an opportunity."

Headlights bounced across the ground as a 1970s Range Rover pulled into the drive of a cottage on the estate. A man exited the vehicle and made his way to the door before entering.

"Come on," Carlyle said as he bolted from the bushes, keeping low.

He moved around the side of the cottage and stood at the back door under the overhang. Water dripped from the awning, loudly striking the stones at Carlyle's feet. A light turned on inside the building, spilling its glow through the glass door and out into the night, illuminating him. Carlyle's gaze met the eyes of the man inside. Surprise flickered in the butler's dark depths a heartbeat before he hastily unlocked the door and swung it open.

"Quick. Inside," Billings ordered as he looked past them into the darkness.

Carlyle entered the kitchen with Finn. Water dripped onto the floor as Billings closed and locked the door behind them. Carlyle watched the servant, taking in his impeccable stature and dress to his neatly trimmed brown hair graying at the temples. Billings wasn't just the butler. He'd been more like a second father to Ferne and Mason after their parents died in a plane crash.

Billings faced them. "Did anyone see you?"

"No," Carlyle answered.

"Took you long enough to get here."

Finn looked between them. "Am I missing something?"

"After your last departure, I suspected Carlyle would want my help," Billings said.

Finn snorted. "I'm not sure we should accept it. You didn't let Ferne talk to her brother, after all."

"I know." The butler sighed, his shoulders drooping, making him look years older than he was. "It was on Lord Brannelly's orders. I tried to dissuade him, but he wouldn't listen to reason. He threatened to let me go if I went against him."

"Which wouldn't give us a way to get to him," Carlyle said.

Billings nodded. "Exactly. He kept a lot from Lady Ferne. She has no idea how deeply he's dug into their parents' deaths."

"She knows some of it," Carlyle said. "Both Mason and she believed they'd been murdered."

Billings motioned to the table. "Sit. I'll make some tea." He turned toward Finn. "And you are?"

"Finn," the Irishman answered. "Friend to both Carlyle and Ferne."

"It is a pleasure, then," Billings replied.

Finn wasted no time shedding his coat and sinking into a chair. Carlyle moved slower, his gaze skimming the kitchen area and Billings, looking for anything suspicious. He could trust so few now. He wanted Billings to be one of them, but the butler had to earn it.

"Lord Brannelly told his sister just enough to satisfy her. He was cautious while she was in the country, fearing repercussions." Billings put water in the kettle and set it on the stove.

"As he should have been," Carlyle stated.

Billings pulled three cups and saucers from the cupboard and put them on the table, along with some sugar and milk. As he did, he said, "Yes, well, be that as it may, things fell into place when the elders demanded that Lady Ferne leave the city. The moment she mentioned Skye, Lord Brannelly knew that was the answer."

"What right do the London Druids even have to tell someone whether they can live in the city or not?" Finn asked.

Carlyle ran a hand over his jaw. "That's the power they wield." He looked at Billings. "Ferne going to Skye went against everything she and Mason were brought up to believe. What we were all taught to think."

"But she was safe. As formidable as the London Druids might be, they don't hold a candle to those on Skye," Billings stated. "Yet."

Finn shook his head. "Bloody hell."

"The moment Lady Ferne departed, His Lordship went full throttle into the investigation," Billings said.

Carlyle sat up and put his forearms on the table. "I gather that took him back to London."

"Indeed, it did."

"And after?"

Billings' dark gaze dropped to the floor. "He returned as you've seen him. He's not the same man I watched grow up since birth. I've served the Crawfords for most of my life. They are my family. The plane crash devastated Mason and Ferne, but at least they had each other."

"And the woman? Devon?" Carlyle asked.

Billings went to the kettle when it whistled and poured the boiling water into a teapot. "She showed up alone before His Lordship returned from London. At first, I didn't think he knew her, but then she said something to him. They've been inseparable since."

"Are they sharing a bed?" Finn asked.

Billings shrugged as he brought the teapot to the table and filled their cups. "She has the room connected to his, but I assume they are."

Carlyle looked at Finn. "Why does that matter?"

"Just wondering," the Irishman said with a shrug.

Carlyle waited until Billings sat before he spoke. "Have there been any other visitors to the manor?"

"None."

Finn sipped his tea. "You said Mason went out. Does he do that often?"

"He's been back and forth to London more than usual," Billings answered. He met Carlyle's gaze. "I've not heard anything about your father. However, after your clash with His Lordship, I suspected you might seek me out for help."

"And why should we trust you? You could be as tainted as Mason," Carlyle replied.

Billings slowly lowered his teacup to the saucer. "I've given no one reason to look askance at me. I've done exactly as Lord Brannelly requested. And I've already explained how much this family means to me. You can believe me or not. One way or another, I will free His Lordship from whatever hold London has over him."

"That might be harder than you think," Finn replied.

Carlyle raked a hand through his wet hair and slumped back in his chair. Billings seemed trustworthy. Or maybe he just wanted him to be. It was difficult to sort through such things with his emotions getting in the way. It had been catastrophic the last time that happened. He needed to get himself under control. And he and Finn had to get into the manor. "Our first priority is getting Devon away from here. I believe her hold on Mason will break once she's gone."

"But he was acting differently *before* her arrival," Billings reminded them.

Finn added a sugar cube to his tea. "She was at the Olivers' townhouse, waiting for us."

Billings' face sagged with concern. "I don't suppose she mentioned anything about your father."

"She claimed not to know anything, but she's lying." Carlyle stood and moved around the chair to brace his hands on the back. "She's with London. I know they are involved in my father's disappearance. Devon connects my dad and Mason to the London Druids."

Billings nodded. "What do you need from me?"

"Entry into the manor," Finn said.

Carlyle shook his head. "I know a way in."

"Of course, you do," Finn quipped.

Billings grinned. "You and Lord Brannelly *did* have a habit of sneaking out."

"I can get us in, but I'm hoping we can get to Devon and Mason quietly. In case that doesn't happen, I need you there to keep the servants from interfering," Carlyle said.

The butler's brows snapped together. "You're taking His Lordship?"

"Just to have a chat," Finn said.

Billings swallowed, his throat bobbing. "What are you going to do with Devon?"

"Depends on if she tells me what I want to know," Carlyle answered.

Finn made a sound in the back of his throat. "It would be better if we could get to them at the same time."

"Mason won't go easily," Carlyle acknowledged.

Finn chuckled. "I don't expect Devon will either."

"What if you don't have to take them off the estate?" Billings asked.

Carlyle studied the butler as he straightened. "You mean keep them on the grounds? I don't think that's a good idea. One of the servants might stumble upon us."

"They could hear or see something, too," Finn added.

Billings' lips curved slightly. "Has it been so long since you and His Lordship had the run of the place that you've forgotten about the old mill in the northeast part of the estate? It hasn't been used in years."

It would keep London from speaking to Mason. But would it hold him for long enough? Carlyle rubbed the back of his neck and felt Finn's probing look. It was the same type Finn had worn when he argued that taking only Devon wouldn't do much but put more of a target on their backs.

"You know getting them at the same time is the answer," Finn said. "I've said it from the beginning. I'll handle Mason."

Carlyle blew out a breath. "It should be me. We have a history."

"And that's why it needs to be me."

Finn was right. Besides, with the right persuasion, it was possible Devon could lead him to his father. "All right."

"Wait," Billings said as he got to his feet. "Don't you need a place for Devon?"

Finn flashed the butler a wide smile. "We already have that."

Carlyle opened his mouth to speak when both his and Finn's mobiles buzzed. There was only one word on the screens:

DESTROY.

Neither wasted a single moment in obliterating their phones. Carlyle looked up and met Finn's gaze. The other members of the Knights—Sabryn and Elias—knew that he and Finn were in

England, but they didn't know where. Sabertooth, their white-hat hacker and all-around electronic guru, knew their exact location. But he had sent the message. And it was one they had never gotten before. It meant trouble. The Knights had been compromised. Which meant the rest of their friends on Skye could also be in trouble.

"You should return to Skye. They might need you," Carlyle urged Finn.

Finn rolled his eyes. "You might want to clean out your ears. You don't hear so well. I've already told you that I'm not leaving. Besides, this is a two-person job."

"I can help," Billings said.

Carlyle shook his head as he looked at the butler. "You've stayed out of the crosshairs so far. I want it to remain that way. London will come when they can't get ahold of Devon or Mason. If they think, even for a moment, that you're involved, they'll use whatever force necessary to get information out of you."

"I can handle it."

Carlyle glanced at Finn. He didn't need words to know they were both thinking it would be better if Billings had no memory of their conversation. Carlyle drank the last of his tea and carefully set the cup on the table. "Thank you for the tea, Billings."

"Of course."

Carlyle waited until Finn walked to the door before whispering, "I'm sorry, Billings."

The butler never saw the spell envelop him. Carlyle caught the man before he hit the floor, and together, he and Finn carried him to the sofa. When he woke in a few moments, he wouldn't remember anything.

Before they left, they cleaned up any evidence of their appearance and slipped out of the cottage. The storm had turned into a downpour. While annoying, it also made it more difficult for anyone to see them as they raced to the manor.

They reached it without incident. Carlyle scaled up the corner of the building to the second floor and scrambled over the edge of the balcony before climbing to the third level. He had to hold onto the wet stone ledge by only his fingertips as he shimmied to a small window. Water kept dripping into his eyes from his hair, and no matter how many times he shook his head to get the strands out of the way, they kept falling back.

He pushed at the window, but it held firmly—too firmly from what he remembered. His grip started to slip. Carlyle cautiously adjusted his hold and glanced down to see Finn plastered against the wall on the second-floor balcony, watching him.

Carlyle moved closer to the window. He pulled a small folding blade from his pocket and slipped it between the window and the latch. A smile tugged at his lips when it popped open.

BUY BLOOD SKYE TODAY
at www.DonnaGrant.com

GLIMPSE AT THE NEXT DRAGON KING BOOK

DRAGON MARKED, DRAGON KINGS SERIES, BOOK 10

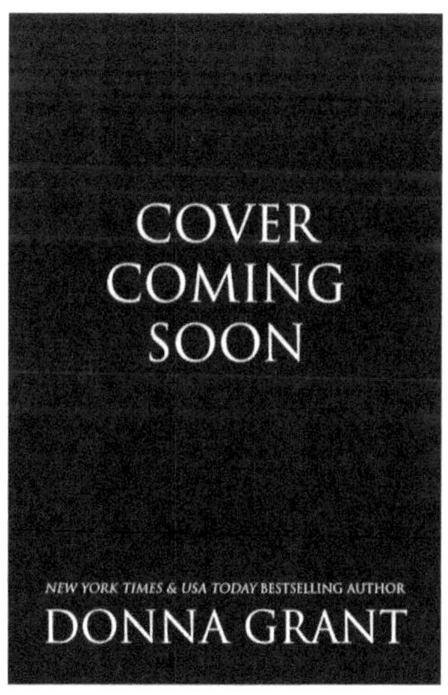

I would sell my dragon soul to possess her…

From the moment I saw her, she held me enthralled. It was more than her beauty. It was in the very way she looked at the world.

The way she looked at *me.*

She saw me as no one ever had. The scars I tried to bury, the wounds no one else knew about. She saw the worst parts of me—and she didn't look away.

Together we pursue a shared nemesis. While a terrifying foe stalks us at every turn.

Whatever enemy dares to get close, I will slay. Whatever path she walks, I will be beside her.

For I am hers. Utterly. Completely.

She's my greatest temptation. The other half of my soul.

My mate.

New York Times and _USA Today_ bestselling author Donna Grant delivers a powerful story of redemption, danger, and passion in the next chapter of the Dragon King series.

BUY DRAGON MARKED TODAY
at www.DonnaGrant.com

ABOUT THE AUTHOR

New York Times and *USA Today* bestselling author Donna Grant® has been praised for her "totally addictive" and "unique and sensual" stories.

She's written more than one hundred novels spanning multiple genres of romance including the bestselling Dragon Kings® series that features a thrilling combination of Druids, Fae, and immortal Highlanders who are dark, dangerous, and irresistible. She lives in Texas with her dog and a cat.

www.DonnaGrant.com

www.MotherofDragonsBooks.com

facebook.com/AuthorDonnaGrant

instagram.com/dgauthor

bookbub.com/authors/donna-grant

goodreads.com/donna_grant

pinterest.com/donnagrant1